The Pulse of Hopeful Life

Jeana Watters

Copyright © 2010 Jeana Watters
All rights reserved.

ISBN: 145637754X
ISBN-13: 9781456377540

Part One

❖ ❖ ❖

Some Nook Which Had No Memories

2003

Chapter One

I hate flowers. All of them. Daisies, roses, daffodils, lilies. I hate their bright yellows and reds and purples, their delicate petals, their overwhelming sweet odors. When I see flowers sprouting in a soil bed or sitting coyly in a vase, I have to suppress a desire to yank them by their slender green necks and snap them between my fingers. Scatter their petals. Discard them to wither and brown.

I haven't always hated flowers. It began the morning we buried my daughter as I peered down into the deep gloomy center of a long-stemmed white rose. I became lost behind the shadows of layered petals. My three-year-old daughter held one too, my husband prodded her to toss her rose on top of the little casket just before it was lowered into the ground.

A group of flower arrangements danced in the breeze, taunting me. Submitting to my disdain, the wind let up and they stood still, extending their necks, begging to be praised for their beauty.

Sympathy flowers, the florists call them. I call them apathy flowers.

I found myself at a cemetery again. But this time, it held no one I loved in its smothering mud. Just the idea of my baby suffocating in a buried box hundreds of miles away had brought me here. From the glow of the moon, I could see the overgrown wild flowers sprouting around the forgotten headstone of "Baby Girl Smith," and I clutched a group of black-eyed susans, sending their petals dripping to the ground. Dignity left me, and I cried. This cemetery was the only place where I let myself go, the one place I went and grieved openly and uncontrolled. I wished it were darker; the round eye of the full moon left me feeling exposed.

After the crying stopped, I pulled myself up from the weeds and grass, brushed off prickly stems from my face. I strolled through the labyrinth of random gravestones, haphazardly placed years before the city would have mandated orderly rows.

When I first moved to Hanover four years ago, I visited all the cemeteries. I walked through each one, pausing, stooping toward the markers, and reading farewells etched in stone. Figuring ages. Lingering a little longer at the headstones of children.

I happened upon this old cemetery by chance while jogging one morning. I was always taking different paths—new streets, through old neighborhoods, crunching along gravelly back roads. Running down a dirt path, past a trailer with a couple permanent rooms built on, I came to a dead end. Woods, I first thought, then saw several towering stones peeking through toddler maple and pine trees. I slowed to a walk, waited for my breath to catch up, and carved my way through the scrub.

This was indeed a cemetery and very old. Some of the visible headstones touted early-1800 death dates. Pulling back vines and weeds, I discovered broken headstone-shaped rocks, some of which had been mortared back together like puzzles. Broken spires were lying on the ground next to their bases. I stumbled over a large stone planted into the mud and realized it and the others nearby were makeshift markers pulled from the nearby quarry, probably by people who couldn't afford a headstone.

Nobody had been there in years. Did anyone remember it existed? Was it even an official cemetery? If it was, the city had abandoned it. Headstones went on and on, and I followed them until I came to the edge on top of the bluff and discovered seven identical headstones crowded into a corner, all shaped like pawns in a grassy chess game, each bearing the name McBeth.

At the edge of the cemetery grounds, I looked at the ravine below and assumed this was where the Mississippi River's course must have run many years ago, before it found a new path. A mound rose from the ground just before the drop-off. From its crown, I was able to see miles beyond the Mississippi into St. Louis. Wind whipped my hair and buffeted my face.

My foot bumped against another stone. I parted the weeds and found a pointed tip—perfectly smooth, not jagged like the quarry rock. Following the edges, I realized it continued on, slanting down like the pitch of a roofline. I hobbled down the mound onto a hillside step and turning around, looked straight into the yawning mouth of an old mausoleum.

It was built into the side of the bluff, and the marble was grayish, streaked with black, the result of uncounted harsh winters. Vandals had added to the natural deterioration, covering the marble with orange and green and blue graffiti. An angry swastika covered one of the four broken-scrolled ionic columns adorning the front. I walked through the arched entrance and found empty shelves with bubble-lettered swear words and mediocre high-school artwork. There were rows and rows of shelves. I counted and multiplied and found that there was space enough for 56 coffins. A morbid party. Backing out, I looked up at it again, some bushes poked through the masonry and vines covered the carved cherub faces. If you looked beyond its deterioration, you could see how beautiful it had once been.

This cemetery became my treasure.

Tonight, while standing on top of the mound, I watched a million little lights twinkle restlessly below. When gusts of wind slapped my face, I closed my eyes and hoped the night's tumult would settle. The wind in my face brought me back to the near end of my life, with a hovering helicopter about to touch ground. I heard the phantom sirens and the staticky voices and opened my eyes suddenly with fear. No, I couldn't let myself relive that moment.

As the wind dried my tears, I turned from my escape—the one place where I allowed myself to remember my baby—and walked back to the dark road through flashing fireflies. Claire never got to see a firefly. I wish she could have seen one, held it on her dimpled hand. When I was a child, I'd only heard of fireflies and thought they were mythical, like fairies. I nudged my index finger next to one, where it landed patiently, blinking and resting, then flew away. I envied fireflies their simple but fleeting courtships.

When I reached the road, I began to run and kept running down the hill toward town. This time of night, there were never many cars on Main Street. I ran faster, hoping my heart would pump out all my sadness. I ran harder and harder, my shoes pounding the asphalt like the hollow thumps of a boxer being beaten by his opponent. I tried to ignore the lone headlights of a black SUV as it traveled past me, but saw the driver's dark eyes following my sprint. I continued running for several more blocks, then slowed to walking a block from my house.

The moon reflected onto the tea-rose bushes hugging the century-old Victorian that housed my third-floor studio apartment. I pushed through the iron front gate and stepped up to the porch. On the front of my mailbox was my monthly note:

Andria,
Just a reminder that September's rent is due on the fifth.
Debbie

Debbie felt the need to give me a reminder about rent. It never seemed to be about money, more a protective, maternal instinct that just wouldn't give up. But I didn't need these reminders; I knew when rent was due and always paid on time. Crumpling the note, I pulled the rest of the envelopes from the box—some bills, but mostly junk mail. I stepped back down the stairs and around the corner to the backyard and trudged up the dizzying wrought iron spiral staircase two stories to my attic apartment. The first time I saw the stairs, I thought of a long helix strand of DNA. And vertigo. Debbie, the widowed owner of the house, finished the attic to rent in order to make ends meet. She recycled the original wood trims and light fixtures that had been stored in the basement when the house had been scaled down over the years. Debbie lived in the main house alone.

I turned the key into the door and slipped off my running shoes, shutting out the humid night. My cat Hero rubbed up against my leg. I flipped on the lamp and stepped lightly over the old wood floors, making sure to lift my feet instead of slide them—I'd received splinters from treading too heavily upon them before. The soft pine floor had been painted dark brown years ago and was chipping, its original light color peeking from the planks's edges.

I hung my car keys on one of the Christmas stocking hooks hanging under the lip of the fireplace mantel, one of the house's original pieces. I cringed when I first saw the hooks burrowed into the antique deep mahogany. But I always kept my keys there, figuring I might as well put the intrusive hooks to use.

This old house reminded me of those in Europe, rich and stately, infused with history. It was one of the reasons I managed to stay here so long—its antique appeal and authenticity, resilience to misuse. A house didn't have to be brand new and perfect to be beautiful, as I'd once believed.

I made my way over to my bed, and flipped on the ten o'clock news.

Hero hopped onto one of the Queen Anne chairs next to my bed, circled a couple times, then settled down for another catnap. I had found the pair of ratty old chairs at a garage sale I passed one Saturday-morning while walking through town. In an effort to escape my mind, I had delved into decorating this little apartment and had spent countless Saturday afternoons digging through garage-sale junk and secondhand store wares. I had to have those chairs, even though the fabric was a dirty orange and ripped. Ten bucks for the set. It took the next several months and a book, but I learned how to reupholster—stripping the fabric off the seats and replacing it with a brick-red damask. They turned out great, as long as you didn't look underneath to see the haphazard staples from my staple gun. I had placed the chairs perpendicular to my bed—which doubled as my couch—creating a conversation area. But who was I kidding? The only conversations that happened in this apartment were when Debbie was lonely and came up to talk, while I dutifully listened.

I relished the idea that I was in control of this space. For the first time in years, I had complete control over something. I didn't have to worry about what anyone else thought or liked. This was about what I wanted. And in my space, everything was in its place, just as I liked things to be. I thought back to the small gray house I'd kept years before in Oregon, the floors littered with toys and blocks and stuffed bears. From dawn to dusk, I watched the mess gather and would straighten up after the girls were in bed, the covers tucked under their pointy little chins. I'd loved that house, loved kissing those chins and noses and lips and foreheads goodnight, and wondered if Lizzie still lived there with her father and if her things—not bears and toys anymore but backpacks and flip flops—littered the same floor.

Banishing the thought, I looked around my apartment and felt an overwhelming emptiness. I listened to the weather report—the next couple days would be mid 80's, slight chance of rain—and flipped off the TV, climbed off my bed, went into the bathroom to ready myself for bed.

Sitting at the antique butter-yellow vanity in my bathroom, I slowly combed through my hair while looking hard at my reflection in the mirror. I stared at my oval face, my wide blue eyes. Those eyes that used to be the blue of ice. Eyes so expressive they always cheated me by giving away my thoughts. My one beauty that garnered attention when I was a kid. Even strangers commented on them, complimented my mother. Those eyes were hard to hide behind. But I'd lost the glimmer in them some time ago. They seemed dead now, the blue turned a cloudy gray. No one mentioned them.

I took a wet washcloth, wiped my face, and looked again. The laugh lines appeared more prominently around my mouth, which seemed ironic since I laughed so little. I didn't have the youthful fresh face I'd had before, but I could still sense men's lingering eyes when I walked past them on the street.

Meeting the scar above my left eyebrow, I gently glided my fingertips over it and pushed on the tiny sliver of glass the doctors overlooked when they were pulling shards from my skin. I'd applied scar cream for months, trying to bring the color back so it would blend with the rest of my skin. Even though the scar was barely visible now, I wore bangs that I'd once abhorred because they kept falling into my eyes. I continually brushed them back with my hand—just so no one would ask any questions. Sometimes I forgot the scar was there.

I stood up and opened the creaky old window to let some air in, turned on the portable radio I kept in the bathroom. The oldies station where I kept the dial was playing "Let It Be." I turned down the volume a bit, to ensure it wouldn't bother Debbie. Ah, the Beatles. I had to listen to something that kept me happy. Most music from the '50s and '60s seemed cheerful. Even if they were singing about something sad, the music just sounded happier. Maybe it was the beat.

I began listening to oldies after my dad left; they reminded me of driving around with him when I was a kid. Those songs brought him back for me, at least for a little while. That was a happier time for me, nothing but school dances and algebra quizzes.

The window exhaled a cool breath of wind on my face. In the summer, it got so hot up here that the air conditioner could never quite keep up. Hero had followed me and had curled herself into a ball inside the bowl of the bathroom sink. I stroked her striped fur and scratched behind her ear as I passed. She lifted her paw and curled it around my hand, so I wouldn't stop scratching. This crazy cat was all I had. It was her furry mug that made its way into my only photo frames. I left her in the sink, returned to my desk and applied moisturizer in front of the mirror.

After releasing my dark hair from its ponytail, I went to the dresser, undressed, and pulled on a pair of boxer shorts and tank top. I clicked the radio off and turned out the bathroom light. The room was still and everything was put away. I checked to make sure the front door was locked, turned out the light, and lay in my bed.

It always felt like something was missing when I went to bed. No recap of my day, unless I was feeling particularly chatty and Hero attentive. No good-night. Only a cat breathing next to me. I lay there listening to the silence disturbed every now and then by the swishing of a passing car outside. This was a noise that I'd gotten used to after the first months I lived here. It even helped me to fall asleep, the way the steady breathing of my husband used to.

I awoke at six the next morning to "Runaround Sue" playing on my alarm clock. Oh, to sleep five more minutes. I hit the snooze button and reached down by my feet where Hero usually was and patted around for her warm spot but couldn't find it. I made my way to the shower. Before undressing, I was putting a clean towel on the rack and noticed the window was still open from last night. Oh shit! Hero! Along the side of the house was a branch reaching out from the old Ginkgo tree only a foot away from the window opening. Even though Hero never responded to her name, I ran through my apartment calling her. I couldn't find her—not on the bed, the arm chair, by her food and water bowls. I checked the litter box in the corner behind the armoire.

While I slid on my flip flops, my mind was racing. Hero'd never been outside before. Why would a lazy cat—a cat who couldn't bother to eat the stray pieces of cat food that fell to the floor from her dish—venture out of the safety of the apartment? I imagined her torn to bits by a neighbor's dog, lying on the road after being hit by a car on the street, or just plain scared and hungry and lost.

It was ridiculous, I know, but I felt like my world was closing in on me. Most people would say it's just a cat, a cat's replaceable—you could get a new one out of a cardboard box in the grocery store parking lot on any given Saturday. But Hero was the only one who would even notice if I were gone. She would be hungry.

I ran out into the yard, yelling out her name. "Hero! Hero!" I was frantic, checking behind trees, under parked cars, in the window wells of neighboring houses. I knew how this looked—a tear-streaked grown woman, staggering along Main Street at 6:30 am, in boxer shorts and a tank top looking—not for a lost child, no, for a cat. I didn't care. I kept hollering and kept searching amidst thorny bushes and inside random open garages, under a lot more cars.

A man was jogging toward me on his morning run, so I turned and ducked into the next side street in an attempt to avoid looking into his face. I waited until he passed and then headed back toward Main Street.

This was useless. I should have looked more closely at the Ginkgo tree. Maybe Hero was stuck there, perched amidst the Chinese-fan leaves just waiting for me to rescue her. Yes, I needed to turn around and go back there. I walked quickly, but couldn't justify running. After all, I was wearing a tank top and hadn't bothered (or considered the option) of putting on a bra.

Shit, the same jogger was coming toward me again. I focused straight ahead and across the street, searching, trying to avoid eye contact. He was several feet in front of me when I noticed he was pulling the headphones out of his ears. He had dark hair kind of gelled up and was wearing a red Hanover High baseball t-shirt. He looked young, probably a couple years removed from high school.

"You lose something?" he asked and stopped, breathing hard. His forehead was shiny with sweat and his t-shirt was damp around his neck and armpits.

"Uh yeah, I'm sure it'll show up," I said as I kept walking, but did slow down as a courtesy.

"Hey, hold up," he said and turned to walk along with me. "I'll help you. What's lost?"

I smiled a little smile, thinking how I could startle him if I began to describe all the many things I had lost. This cat was just the least of them. I simply said, "My cat."

"What's he look like?"

"She's a short-haired tabby; big yellow eyes; a white chin, tummy, and a little arrow of white on the tip of her tail. Blue collar," I said and paused. "You know, don't worry about it. She's sure to turn up." It'd be best just to get this guy off my tail so I could focus on finding Hero.

"No, no, I have some time. What's her name?"

"She won't respond to it."

"Okay, what's your name?" he said.

I gave him an are-you-kidding look. This guy was hitting on me?

"You know, I think I'm just going to head home. Go finish your run."

"No, seriously, I want to help," he said.

"No, seriously, I don't need any help. Thanks but no," I spat and covered my mouth with my hand, perhaps trying a little too late to stop the angry words from flying out. This wasn't me. I didn't want to be rude, but I didn't want a partner in this—it was my mistake and I had to fix it myself. But with my hand cupped over my mouth, it reminded me that I hadn't yet brushed my teeth this morning.

He lifted his hands in a mock don't-shoot-me gesture and said, "All right. Good luck finding your cat." He wasn't mean about it, just plugged his headphones back into his ears and turned around and jogged off. I didn't look back at him.

When I returned to my house, I made my way along the side and scanned every branch I could see of that overgrown Ginkgo tree. Debbie had said the tree was over 150 years old. Its roots had cracked the sidewalk in front of the house; the earth couldn't contain it.

I don't know why I bothered looking around to see if someone was watching me before I started climbing the trunk, grasping onto branches, pulling myself up and up some more. I felt suddenly like I was a kid again, scaling the tree in the backyard, and I felt the freedom that disappearing into the branches and leaves used to afford, knowing that my mom wouldn't be able to find me— or reach me. I'd spent hours with a book up in that tree when I was younger. Hiding from my mom and dad, especially when they were fighting. They never thought to look up there. They were probably not looking at all, glad to have me out of their hair.

All the cars whizzing by on their morning commute, they'd never know I was here. Never think to look up. I would have been leaving for work about now. Right, I needed to get back on task and focus on the reason why I was up in a tree.

I continued climbing branches. A robin darted through the sky, thought about landing until it noticed me hanging around, and flew on. My bathroom window was several feet from where I was perched but no Hero. I settled onto a large curved branch near the trunk, like the arm of a friend around me, to rest for a moment. My eyes followed as many skyward branches as possible. I wasn't shouting anymore—this clearly would hinder my attempt at being inconspicuous—but I did whisper, "Here kitty, kitty, kitty" every so often.

As a child I would have been thrilled to get so close to a bird's nest with cracked egg shells and leftover feathers still clinging to the straw or be within arm's reach of a startled gray squirrel, but today my eyes only grazed them as I continued searching for a flicking cat's tail or Hero's moon eyes. After a while, this began to feel useless. Hero wasn't in the tree anymore. She had wandered off, and I would probably never find her. And I'd have nothing breathing next to me in bed tonight. The idea of a completely cold bed brought tears to my eyes. I'd have nothing to care for, nothing to feed. I pressed my hands over my face to disappear for a moment and Lizzie's three-year-old face appeared out of the darkness—baby fat plumping her cheeks, her eyes green with a blue outer ring, imploring, asking why, her face tilted up at me. That was the image that always came—and her look was always the same, her stance, her questioning eyes, imprinted in my mind as clearly as a photograph on paper.

I re-opened my eyes to send Lizzie away and saw movement down below on the sidewalk. It looked to be the jogger from before. I tried to stay as still as possible. It wasn't until he was nearly past the house that I realized he was carrying something. Hero!

I didn't know what else to do. I had to yell out to get him to stop; he didn't know where I lived. I wished I had asked his name earlier so I wouldn't feel so ridiculous shouting out "Hey!" from my perch entrenched in the tree branches.

He stopped and looked around, across the street. I yelled again, "I'm up here."

He looked up at the house, at the top windows.

"I'm coming down." It wasn't until I was wrestling the branches to descend from the tree that he saw me and was watching with an amused grin on his face. At the bottom branch, I jumped down the several feet and landed on the grass. I slipped on the flip flops I had abandoned at the base of the tree before I started climbing.

"How did you find her?" I asked as I slid through the iron front gate onto the sidewalk where he waited and pulled Hero from his arms. I buried my face into her fuzzy neck and several tears trickled into her fur.

"I saw a cat prancing across one of the side streets while I was jogging home and noticed the blue collar. I was sure it was yours. I hoped I'd run into you again by coming back this direction. Hey—" he stopped speaking and looked square into my face, noticing the tears that hadn't stopped flowing from my eyes. "Are you okay?"

"Yes," I said and shook my head no. He brought his hand up to my cheek and wiped away at the tears. Startled at his touch, I stood rigid, and he jerked his hand away. We stood there awkwardly, unsure what to say. Maybe he was embarrassed at the intimacy of touching a stranger's face, or just my reaction to it. Still, I couldn't help how vulnerable I felt before him. I hugged Hero a little closer now and she was squirming to be let loose. "I've got to get her back inside."

"Okay." He stood there.

I began walking toward the house, turned back to him, and said, "I didn't thank you. Thanks, of course. I don't know what I would do without her." I should have just shut up then. Maybe it was the residual awkwardness from the face touch. But it had been so gentle and concerned. "I wish there were something I could do for you. If you lose your dog, if you have a dog or—"

"I'm glad to help," he said. "You could do something for me."

Hero was starting to struggle in my arms. "Sure," I said and shrugged.

"Your name. You didn't tell me your name."

"Andria. And this is Hero," I said as I lifted Hero up just a bit. I turned back and walked through the gate. As an afterthought, I shouted, "Thanks again," and turned around the side of the house toward the back. This time, I watched him as he jogged back along the sidewalk. I was cloaked behind another tree, a pecan. I watched until he was out of sight.

I was already a half an hour late for work, so I walked up to my apartment and took a quick shower.

As I stepped dripping from the shower, I wrapped a towel around me and cinched the edge underneath my arm. I stepped toward the same window from where Hero had escaped and pressed my fingers to the glass. The colors outside seemed so alive—my world turned from sepia to color at that moment. I stared into the vibrant green leaves of the Ginkgo branch that was reaching over, the very one that had lured Hero out. Beyond that, another tree was prematurely turning gold in anticipation of autumn. I peered between the trees down to the sidewalk below and thought about the jogger. The way it felt when he touched my face, like something awakening in me, a butterfly from a chrysalis. The way his forehead furrowed with concern and his dark eyes sincere when he tried to wipe away my tears. He hadn't scoffed about my crying over a lost cat or laughed that he had caught me hanging around in a tree.

I turned away from the window and sat down at my vanity to comb out my hair. As I looked into the mirror, I imagined how he had seen me this morning. I pulled the comb through my hair slowly and found myself trying to pull down a frail smile. My eyes were reflecting some of the blue from the sky that was coming in through the window, making them seem bluer than they had in years. Like my old photographs.

When I stepped out of my apartment and down the stairs, I felt the tiniest hop in my step as I headed along the side of the house to my car. That's when I noticed the pink and yellow roses bobbing their heads in the breeze, like laughter, which absolved my smile. As if a solemn blanket had been wrapped around my shoulders, bringing me back.

He pressed his way into my thoughts all day. I spent seven hours—I was an hour late to work that morning—staring at my computer screen and speculating about him: who he was, where he ran in the mornings, where he lived, what his name was. I hadn't even asked him his name. I didn't want it to seem like I wanted to know. And I hadn't. Then.

I still didn't. This was an area that was off-limits to me, albeit self-prescribed. I didn't date. But I couldn't stop him from running back and forth through the sidewalks of my head.

He'd seemed so young but looking back, I thought that maybe he was one of those guys who just looked young. When I replayed the moment he was standing before me, he wasn't much taller than I was. That always made someone seem younger.

Why had he kept asking about my name? I knew I was playing it up too much. Perhaps he was just being polite or liked to know the name of the person for whom he was offering to spend half his morning.

I needed to stop obsessing over this. I tried to focus my attention back to the user guide I was writing, but I couldn't think about tracking software right now. I thought about Hero asleep on my bed. With her full tummy and a warm patch of sun streaming through the window and warming her bristling fur. And perhaps she still had the lingering smell of sweat on her, from him.

That's it. I had to lock this up once and for all. Put these ridiculous thoughts away, just as I had locked away every photograph I had brought here imprisoning my girls' faces—sealed in an unlabeled envelope and locked in my old wooden chest.

I drove home from work that night with my attention back where it belonged, on the mundane—what I was going to eat for dinner. Although at times I noticed my mind shifting back toward the mystery of who he was, I jerked myself back and realigned my thoughts. By the end of the week, my memory of him sat still and neglected where it belonged—out of reach.

It was just another night, another dark run through the lonely streets of Hanover. The cold wind of autumn had flown in several days before, requiring a jacket that night. When I reached the house in a brisk walk, spent and out of breath, someone was sitting on the steps on the front porch. From the lamplight on the street, he was only a silhouette—crouched, arms resting on knees. He stood as I walked through the front gate and up the sidewalk. A layer of sweat covered my body and I swept at my dripping forehead with the back of my hand as I climbed the several steps to my mailbox. He was holding something out to me.

"It's for Hero," he said. I looked down at a can of soft cat food and took it, then looked back up at him. "I don't know how it ended up in my grocery bag." He grinned, clearly lying. His smile was nice, lopsided, and his hair was gelled up in the same messy hairdo he had when he was running, but he was wearing bold, black glasses. They made him look artistic.

"You shouldn't have," I said. "Hero will get spoiled and expect this soft stuff every day."

"Debbie said I could wait for you here. I hope you don't mind."

"No. It's nice to see you again," I said and hesitated a moment. "I never got your name."

"Quentin," he said.

We were both just standing there, I was twirling the cat-food can around and around in my hands, standing at the base of the steps while he was looming over me two steps up. It felt a bit awkward. It wouldn't hurt anything to sit on the wicker chairs on the porch so I invited him. He sat while I pulled my mail out of the box, then I made my way to the chair next to him, flicking through a grocery-market ad.

"I hate this time of year, when all the fresh berries get more expensive," I said and turned to the next page of the ad. There were so many questions I could have asked, all things I'd wanted to know about him before but wasn't sure I wanted him to know that I wanted to know. But here I was, safe in the produce department of conversations.

He was going on about how apples are underrated and that a good Granny Smith is enough to keep him going. An apple a day. I responded by asking him his preferences about raspberries, strawberries, melon. We sat on the porch discussing our favorite fruits, while I stared down into the meat department but stutter-stepping away from it toward the exit in my mind.

I noticed movement in the front window and saw Debbie's fingers pulling back the curtains from inside. She peered out onto the porch and simply waved when she saw me. Maybe she could hear us. Or this was her motherly way of warning me that it was probably time for me to head up to my apartment.

When we had exhausted all avenues of fruit and as a lull came, before things could head down a more serious street, I veered away. "I guess it's time for me to head up. If I'm not home by 10:30, Hero starts to worry."

I began to get up, and Quentin stood up too. "Wait, Andria. I'm not really here about cat food."

"No?"

"No. I wanted to see if you'd want to do something sometime." His words couldn't have been more vague, but I knew exactly what he meant.

"You mean like a date?" My voice was skeptical, and I stood quickly, my feet planted firmly on the ground in my resolve.

"I guess kind of like a date."

I shook my head no and said, "I don't date. I have nothing to offer." I was bowing out for his sake, being a martyr.

He didn't buy it either. He stood up. "I don't need anything. I like talking to you. After all, where else can I find out about which fruits have the best prices?"

"Your local grocery ad," I said and smiled. Yes, he made me smile again. "Sorry. I just can't."

"Okay. How about a non-date?" he said. "Just friends." He offered his hand to shake.

I hesitated, eyeing his outstretched hand suspiciously and replied, "Well, that depends. Do you mean a friend who is your friend until you talk her into dating you or a real friend?" I knew I sounded shrill and cold, but I just couldn't have him imposing too many expectations on me now.

"Come on. What if I were your jogging friend—or walking friend? It's not safe to be out here alone so late."

I stooped over, pulled out a small pocketknife like a boot knife from my running shoe, flashed it, then returned it safely back. "I'm covered. I don't need a bodyguard."

"Okay." He shook his head slowly, like I was being difficult, which I was. "I like to walk, and I won't feel safe unless you can protect me with your dagger. Will you do that for me?"

I laughed, but settled back to serious. "I'm sorry. I can't. You seem great but I'm not what you think. If you could see inside me—" I thought of the difference from my reflection in the mirror to the rotting filth under my skin. And although he couldn't see it, I knew it was there, dead and waiting to give me away with its stench. "Look, I gotta go." I left him there alone, watching me walk away. I turned back and he waved with just a slight raising of his hand.

Hero must have been asleep when I unlocked my door, stepped inside, and exhaled. The cat stood and arched her back in a sleepy stretch, then settled back down to sleeping again.

I watched her for a minute and felt a pit in my stomach. It wasn't just that it had been a man. It didn't matter, man or woman. I didn't allow myself relationships or friends or anything closer than an acquaintance. I had to be alone. I had to be. That was a decision I had made long ago, rather a punishment, and I had to work off my penance. The avenues of lighthearted talk, about nothing really, that we had taken tonight weren't allowed. At work, I stuck to work. At home, I stuck to Hero or whatever book I happened to be reading. On my walks, I stuck to myself. My only friend was Debbie downstairs, and that relationship was detached and one-sided. In ways, she reminded me of my mother who I hadn't spoken to in years. My own mother didn't even know where I was.

But I hadn't wanted to stop tonight, couldn't have just stood up and walked away. I wanted to be there discussing the differences between the golden raspberry and a red one.

Thinking back on it, I felt tired. I changed clothes and filled a glass of water. While drinking, my eyes drifted to a single red apple resting in a silver latticed bowl on the counter. Tomorrow's breakfast. My mind shifted to Quentin again, and I thought about all the useless words we wasted on fruit tonight, how he would have preferred a green apple to this red one. No, I didn't want to be done with him. Why was that ripe apple of hope still clinging to the tree? It was overripe and should have fallen long ago, but here it was, still hanging on.

Chapter Two

Lizzie was too little to get up onto the swing by herself. I grasped her around her little waist, plucked her from the ground and set her on the chipped blue seat of the swing ride. We were at the carnival. Music-box melodies fought each other and against the voices of spent parents, crying children, noise horns, the mechanical whirring of rides. I clasped the hook of the loose chain around her, checked it again, making sure it was sturdy. Then walked back and waited at the periphery, beyond the marked chains, amongst other parents while the ride began cranking circles. She sat suspended only by a hook and several chains holding the swings together, each chair facing outward, and kicked her legs back and forth. On the first slow circle, she smiled and waved to me, exhilarated; the second time, a high-pitched squeal escaped her mouth; on the next circle, her smile was gone and her eyes were nervous; the next went faster and her eyes were closed, her hands clutching at the chains on each side and her head leaning back like she was just feeling the wind on her face. And with the swing spinning at full velocity, I lost her. I searched as the ride kept circling, faster and faster. I saw child after child—the red face of a white-blonde kid, two boys trying to kick at each other from their seats, a girl with long black ponytails swaying—but my golden-haired girl was gone. I couldn't find her striped blue and green sundress, her dangling feet with white sandals. I searched and searched and the ride kept going, but Lizzie was gone.

I bolted upright in my bed, my heart beating furiously. She was gone. Again. This recurring dream, having replayed itself so many times in my sleep, always socked me awake. Socked at my heart, my head. A sliver of sun lit the edges of the curtains, pushing through. The tip of daybreak. I pulled myself out of bed and yanked out a sweater, stuffed my shoes onto my feet, and made my rapid course to the cemetery. Several cars passed on the street as I walked, headlights blazing. Most of the town was still sleeping; only a handful of light-painted windows gave away life within the houses along Main Street. The distant cry of birds were my only company.

When I reached the cemetery, I crept to the uppermost tip—where the pitched roof of the mausoleum grew—and fell to the ground and sobbed. This time for Lizzie—Lizzie who trusted me, Lizzie who had needed so very much from me, Lizzie who I'd thrown away, Lizzie who I also lost. I held my arms around my head and cried face down into the earth, my tears mixing into the dew on the grass. I cried until my eyes grew dry, then pulled myself up and wiped from my face the remaining moisture and mud.

I saw movement toward the path into the cemetery—expecting to see a deer or a rabbit or birds—and through my blurry tear-choked vision, saw Quentin's familiar face and eyes burrowing right into me. Like I was caught at something I didn't realize I was hiding. I stared back, unmoving, until he turned and jogged off. I wiped at my eyes with both fists, but when I looked back, he was gone. What was he doing up here? He was a morning jogger, I knew that much, but why had he come here and how long had he been here?

Long enough, I thought, as I made my way through the weed-thick trail past the tired stares of broken headstones. I kicked at some overgrown wish flowers, which sent their unused wishes flying, and stomped and twisted my foot on some orange lilies, their color bleeding onto the soles of my shoes.

I still wanted to know why he had come here. Quickening my pace, I made my way out of the wooded cemetery and looked but didn't see him along the steep decline back to town. I couldn't have been imagining him there, standing at the edge of the cemetery. Right? But I shook my head as I walked. I saw him; he saw me; that was clear. I marched straight into town and into my apartment and into the shower, all the while reflecting on seeing him watching me in my private grief, the only grief I allowed myself. There wasn't room for anyone else. As the water slapped against my body, I became angry. Had he followed me? How dare he think he knew me enough to invade this part of me?

Over the next several days, my anger waned. Still, I needed to know why he had been there. I didn't know why this consumed me. Why did I even care about what he had seen? I felt like I needed to explain to him, but why? And I knew I wouldn't really explain anything to him anyway. Why did it matter?

I thought back on the dream that had catapulted this whole chain of events—the anxiety I felt over losing Lizzie, which manifested itself over and over in my unconscious, uncontrolled sleep. And because I didn't allow myself to grieve at home, I turned to the only respite I knew, where my grieving was open and welcome and I grieved not only the physical death of Claire but the death of my entire family. This cemetery was a place where I was always alone. Until this morning. Why would my solitary grief open this type of door for me, a door that would allow things to enter my life—those things I'd tried for so long to keep out? And if this door let Quentin in, then what? He falls in love with me maybe, maybe I fall in love with him. We have sex, sex makes babies, babies require so much love and puts me in the vulnerable position that I swore I'd never find myself drowning in again.

But despite all my logical reasoning and I knew the sensible thing to do was let it go, but my mind was spinning circles around him and what he saw of my grief and I could not let it go.

He was a morning jogger—what if I followed him, see how he liked being followed. That night, I skipped my run and pulled myself out of bed early the next morning, pulled on my sweats and running shoes, and began running. I ran faster than usual, but didn't find him. I detoured my way through town, taking random backstreets and then wondered if I should stick to Main Street. I wound up jogging past my house, but no, I wasn't finished yet. I turned back and headed to the outskirts to the gravelly path up to the cemetery. Maybe he was there, looking for me. This was a ridiculous game of blindman's tag, child's play, I knew it as I thumped through the streets of Hanover, but I couldn't let it go. I had to find him.

I slowed to a walk when I came to the gravel, not wanting to slip under the rocks's shifty surface so I could take slow control of my steps so as to not give myself away. But when I reached the cemetery, it was empty and abandoned as I had come to expect it to be. As hollow as the inside of the mausoleum. I glanced over into the shady corners but nothing was there but the flitting bodies of the cardinals and robins who were used to me as if I were a statue.

Disappointed but also relieved, I ran back down into town. My house loomed a block away on the left. I pumped my arms, got my legs going although I felt worn and my legs were rubber. There he was, running ahead of me quite a ways. After a while of sprinting, I pulled closer to him—it was Quentin, I could tell by the same Hanover High t-shirt he'd been wearing the first time I saw him—and ran behind him for a block. I could see the wires that held headphones into his ears and felt an odd comfort following behind him unaware. I noticed his head turn and his eyes follow the house as he ran, looking up into the tower that was part of my apartment, where Hero usually watched the cars below. I could see her there now, a dark silhouette in the window. My anger melted off like the sweat dripping down my back. This person looked for me, I realized as I ran pace by pace behind him, my footsteps matching his. I sped up and fell into stride beside him and he looked over, his eyes recognized me and he exhaled "Andria." We fell into a fast walk, while he yanked his headphones from his ears.

"What were you doing there?" It wasn't exactly a greeting, but I needed this out of the way.

He stopped mid-step and turned to me. "At the cemetery?"

I nodded.

"I was jogging, I saw you up ahead, I—"

"Followed me?" I finished his sentence with a question of my own.

"I wanted to talk to you, is all," he said.

We were both taking the heavy breaths from jogging and our breathing was still in unison, as were our steps just minutes before. I held my breath a moment longer, to get off his rhythm.

"You still want to?" I asked with sarcasm. After what he'd seen up there, it wouldn't shock me if he wanted to run far, far away. I guess I was there to explain but wasn't ready to do that. And I wanted to see how easily he scared off and prove to myself that no one would ever want what I had left over, just in case I'd had any doubts.

"Yes," he said and looked boldly into my eyes. "I do."

I exhaled again, not realizing I had been holding my breath again, long and steady and it left me with nothing. I took another deep breath in. "Look, Quentin, I'm gonna give you a get-out-of-jail-free card here. I'm messed up and I'm not going to explain it to you and I know you thought I may have seemed interesting or something, but it's not worth it. Take my card and go."

"You don't have to explain anything to me," he said. "I don't need your card. I'll walk by here tonight at 9. If you want to join me, you can. If not, you can use the card yourself."

"I'll see you," I said and turned to go but I wasn't finished. "I don't know if I'll—" as I turned back, but he had already plugged his ears and had stepped back into a jog, his back to me. He didn't hear me.

I decided I wasn't going to think about it all day; my mind was made up. I swatted his face away every time it appeared and made a clearer focus on work. I made it through the day but found myself at home, sitting next to Hero on the window seat looking down below, watching the several cars roll past. They weren't in any hurry. Small town USA seemed to have a pace of its own. People strolled by on the sidewalk below, stopping and gabbing with others who were gardening their front beds or sweeping their porches. I looked down at my watch. It was 8:30. In a half hour, Quentin would be walking past, and I didn't want to be peering out from these windows then. He would look up here when I wasn't on the sidewalk, to see if I was there as he had done this morning. But I wouldn't be, and I wouldn't be waiting for him down below.

Being an observer, just as I had been for years now, allowed me to watch everything below me from my attic and remain detached. I liked being unnoticed and yet noticing everything going on around me. I knew that the old man who sold the fresh peaches at the Farmer's Market on Saturday came by after packing up his things to bring a peach to our widowed next-door neighbor, Grace. She waited on the porch for him, pretending to tidy up and what not, but she was always waiting for him. I liked seeing it unfold below; I just wanted no part of it. From up here, I was safe, exempt from the emotion of involving myself in other people's lives. No risk in observing.

That morning, I had started to tell him that I wouldn't be there, not to bother coming this direction if it was just on account of me, but he hadn't waited and now I felt like it was all open, anything could happen, and that was why my chest felt tight, my palms had an oily film of sweat. I didn't want to hurt him, see his solitary figure walking down along the sidewalk and then turn back alone to leave, but I didn't want to hurt me either.

Looking down in my lap, I realized that I hadn't changed clothes. I was wearing a pair of old jeans and a peasant top I'd worn to work. Perfectly presentable, I thought, and imagined myself climbing down the stairs to meet him. Becoming a part of the world below I was so comfortable watching. Why couldn't I?

I knew perfectly well why it wasn't possible. I struggled back and forth, why I could go just this once, why I couldn't. But Quentin was a person—a rare one, it seemed—who was willing to take a chance on me. Someone he'd seen face down in the side of a hill, smeared with mud, damaged and alone and unworthy. I glanced at the clock. 8:55. Before I could stop myself, I patted Hero on the head and made my disorienting, circling way down the spiral staircase and flew around the corner of the house. He was there, in the evening light, just a dark form leaning against the lamppost in front of the house. He didn't see me, was staring out at something across the way, and I took a deep breath and peered up into the sky to compose myself. A yellow hook moon was poised in the sky.

Taking light footsteps, I made my way toward him. Light, I reminded myself. This can be something light; it doesn't mean anything. He heard my footsteps and turned. He was wearing a Cardinals baseball cap. "Go Cards," I said, lightly.

"I think they're going to make it to the play-offs this year," he said. "Both Houston and the Chicago Cubs look good."

"I see." I nodded indifferently. "I guess you could say I'm a little detached from sports." Or not interested at all.

"I won't bore you with my worries about Chicago's pitching rotation then." He pulled himself away from leaning and we eased into step, heading toward the heart of Hanover, which to be frank was a pretty pitiful heart. Hanover was thriving with over 4,000 residents.

"You can talk about it all you want," I said. "I just can't guarantee that I'll listen." I suddenly felt at ease with him, like I'd known him for years, like he was a friend from high school. We could have sat together and sliced a formaldehyde-soaked frog with a scalpel at a high school biology lab, breathing through our mouths and squirming.

Quentin looked back up into my lit window and said, "Your roommate is watching us."

"Hero," I replied, looking up at the framed cat, sitting motionless, her round yellow eyes fixed on us, small as mice from where she sat.

"So, where'd she get such a distinguished name?"

"You might think it came from the sandwich, but no, although I do enjoy a hero sandwich from time to time. Actually, I got into Greek mythology a bit in college. Her name is from a Greek story, Hero and Leander. Hero was also a character in *Much Ado About Nothing*." I stopped talking suddenly. Although I found Greek mythology and Shakespeare interesting, most guys didn't. "Do you know the story of Hero and Leander? I could tell you."

"You could tell the story," he said and a smirk played on his lips, "but I can't guarantee that I'll listen." He paused for effect and I rolled my eyes and smiled. "No, seriously. I'm listening."

I shot him a sideways, suspicious look. He was waiting so I told him about beautiful Hero and Leander who fell in love with her and how Leander swam across a strait each night, using the lamp in Hero's tower to guide him. They spent their nights together, then he swam back at the first sign of the sun rising. One night, Hero lit her lamp and Leander began to swim across, but it was particularly windy and cold and Hero's lamp died. Leander struggled in the waves, lost his direction, and drowned. His body washed onto shore. When Hero saw Leander lying dead the next morning, she flung herself from the tower and died. Their bodies laid side by side on the edge of the water.

We walked in silence for several minutes after I finished, listening only to the sound of our footfalls and the swish of cars zipping past, before Quentin said, "You were inspired by that tragedy to name your cat Hero?"

"It's tragic, yes, but it's beautiful."

"I would have gone with the sandwich explanation," he said. "A guy can always be inspired by food."

There was Quentin, being all light and breezy, while I was telling stories about suicide. What was the matter with me? My life was draped with tragedy and I couldn't go on a well-meaning walk with a stranger without plunging into it; I was like a moth to light.

"You're making me hungry," I said, gesturing toward the deli shop on the right with the CLOSED sign lit up. "It's a tragedy we can't get a sandwich now."

"It is getting late," he said.

We stopped and headed back the direction from which we came.

Moments later, Quentin detoured back by saying. "I actually like tragedies. In plays. *Romeo and Juliet. Othello.* Shakespeare's. He's one of my heroes, you know."

"No, I didn't know," my voice doubtful. "You're into Shakespeare?"

"I guess you could say it's one of my hobbies. Theater, in particular. I played Shylock in college. That's when I became famous." He was waiting with shining eyes for me to respond, like a boy with a secret. I could glimpse back 20 years and see the little boy who turned into this man, just by looking into his eyes.

"I would have never guessed."

"I don't tell just anyone I meet," he said.

"You just met me."

"You're not just anyone."

I didn't look at him or respond, just adjusted my eyes down to the dark sidewalk. Not so light now.

"Okay, so you got me. I wasn't famous, but I was pretty good. I still feel it sometimes, that urge to be up there, in front of everyone."

"I like the theater too. Not being in it, of course. But I like to go and watch."

"We should go to Forest Park. See the Shakespeare Festival next summer."

I remembered how I had waited alone, on my grandmother's quilt, at Forest Park, for *The Tempest* to begin last June. It would have been nice to have someone there next to me. "I'd like that," I said. I realized as I said it that he had hooked me, the image of me scooting over on that patchwork quilt for him didn't seem wrong. It was a big enough quilt if I made room.

It hadn't been so bad; it was harmless really. I told him we could do it again. And we did, we walked every night. With the onset of fall and the cold, my jogs receded and I got to the cemetery less and less. I missed those nights when I could let loose and sob out my grief. Lizzie didn't come to me as often, not in my dreams or into the blackness of my head. And Claire faded too, her emerald eyes not quite so bright, her image not so omnipresent in my mind. I tried to make time for her by revisiting the cemetery on lonely Sunday afternoons. But as with sorrow in the sunlight, my grief had dimmed. I tried to hold on to it, but it faded as I had never wanted it to, for then Claire was gone forever.

Quentin waited for me by the same lamppost every night. And each night, I'd wait at the window seat until I saw him approach and then would head down. One night a week later, I went down to meet him and noticed a misshapen nearly full moon, just one side flat, like a dropped Play-Doh ball, hanging in the sky. The stars lightly glittered above. Diamonds in the sky, I thought sadly, realizing that the old overdone children's song really did have a morsel of truth in it.

Quentin motioned up toward the lit window and said, "You always leave the lights on?"

"I don't like to come home to darkness," I said. "And Hero likes it on."

"She does, huh?"

"Yep. Hey, is it all right if we swing by the bookstore tonight?"

"Sure."

"I just need to pick up a book. I'm making my way through the complete works of Thomas Hardy."

"What book do you need?" he asked.

"*Far From the Madding Crowd*. I fell in love with *Tess* in college. There's something about the tragedy in Hardy's work that I like." I had been through *Tess of the D'Ubervilles* so much I was officially on a first-name base with her. I continued, "It's all very tragic."

"You love your tragedy," he said. And it was true. I did. I devoured tragedy because that's what life was—tragedy. It was normal and I wasn't so different from everyone else when I was engrossed in it; it was the movies and stories about people who got their happy endings that left me angry and saddened. I wanted to be surrounded by those who understood sadness, even if they were fictional characters. Tess and I would have seen eye-to-eye.

"I don't choose books for inspiration."

We hiked across the street to Maggie's Corner Book Store where a teenage girl with black wavy hair, an Indian scarf, and a nose ring was standing inside, next to the glass-paned front door staring out. She was watching the clock.

When she saw us coming toward the store, she pushed the doors open and said, "We close in five minutes."

"It'll just take a second." The bookstore was both floors of an historic brick building and still had metal stars adhered to the front. Inside, the exposed red-brick walls were outlined with backless, thin-boned book shelves and filled with new and secondhand books. Maggie's smelled of musty printed pages—no doubt from the antique section—and coffee, as it housed a small café in the back corner of the store. I knew my way around this place like the house where I grew up. We walked past my favorite reading chair and to the back wall, the fiction section. I grazed my hand over the rows of books, found Hardy, and plucked out a second-hand paperback copy, worn with wrinkles. I paid, and we went back outside.

I stuck my hand through the handle of the bookstore's paper bag and let it slide onto my wrist, swishing as I walked. We walked in silence, in a comfortable palpable silence that didn't send me grappling for another route of conversation, just looking out onto the street and watching the cars go by—sometimes in clusters, sometimes a car didn't pass by for ten minutes. I didn't speak, and I didn't want to have to try to come up with witty, clever things to say.

A car came tearing down Main Street honking and brimming with teenage boys. The boy in the passenger seat leaned halfway out the window, waving his arms wildly about his head at us. A soda can clunked to the street as they passed. Quentin nodded to them in that cocky way high-school boys do. I shook my head and thought of a time when I was young and naïve and thought the entire world was at my disposal.

"You know them?" I asked.

"Yeah, he's just one of the punks living on my street. He's a good kid."

I nodded skeptically. "He probably thinks you're his age. How old are you anyway?"

"Twenty-nine. What about you?"

"You look younger than that," I spoke indifferently, not exactly a compliment. Of course, I was trying to throw him off. What thirty-something woman wants to tell her age? Men don't care; age makes them more distinguished. Women just get wrinkles and cellulite.

"And you?" he repeated.

I waited several moments. "Thirty-four." He didn't respond, it was fine.

"What do you do?" he asked.

"I'm a technical writer," I said. "I write the stuff most people laboriously plow through to install software or hardware. I always thought I'd write something interesting, like a memoir or a novel. Technically, I've written books. They're just not the type of books anyone wants to read. People are forced to read them if they want their software installed properly. I fear most of my books are sitting in a dusty pile in a dark, looming IT closet." I sighed. "No, in all honestly, I like my job. I write what needs to be written. And it's very much to the point."

"You know, I've always wondered about the brilliant minds behind all those dry words. I've had to install my share of computer software."

"Really? Do you do something with computers? I guessed you were more the artistic type."

"Hmmm. So, I had you speculating about me? That's interesting." He was mocking a pensive pose, his forefinger resting on his chin. I wasn't sure if he thought it was interesting that I was thinking about him, speculating about him, or that I thought he was artistic, but didn't want to pursue it enough to ask.

Quentin broke our silence several minutes later, "Did you see that falling star?" He pointed to the sky.

"No. You know, I've only seen one in my life." The falling star had been cartoonish in its beauty, like someone from props in a movie set would have thought it up, so dramatic and—Disney. But it was amazing that it was there, in my sky. I remembered lying on my back in the large green field behind my apartment in college. My boyfriend and I had lain on our backs in the dewy grass and stared up into the sky to find constellations and planets and just watch. That's when I saw the shooting star, only that one time.

I looked up into the sky, hoping to glimpse another one, but instead stumbled into a rock border along the sidewalk. Quentin grabbed my arm lightly, protectively, and said, "For safety reasons, I don't stare up into the sky when I walk."

Chapter Three

I had just been thinking about him always being there—reliable Quentin, waiting by the rusty lamppost as if he needed to catch the nine o'clock bus every night—as I slipped on my shoes, then my beanie, then my coat. I circled down the stairs and edged around the side of the house to find the lamppost solitary, glowing uselessly. A little shocked he wasn't there, I shook my head and settled against the lamppost in his usual pose. We'd walked for months now. I depended on him being down there, always waiting. I expected him there as much as I expected to see my car parked along the street every morning.

It had been so long since I had spent so much time with a man—even if only for these simple walks. Months of walks filled with mild conversation and banter. We knew each other on the surface: food, movies, books, sports teams. We didn't go any deeper, didn't need to. This friendship without questions wasn't so bad after all. Even so, he made me feel I knew him intimately. His familiar footsteps were home to me. Outside in the chilly dark nights, I felt more sheltered and safe than dead-bolted in my apartment.

After several minutes, I noticed Quentin's black SUV parked several spaces up the street. I strolled up and looked in through the passenger-side window, flitted my fingertips in a single wave when he saw me. He was talking on his cell phone and gestured "just a moment" with a raised index finger. I went back to the lamppost and waited his moment. I dug the heel of my shoe, behind me, into the lamppost.

Tonight was cold. I felt the cold creep through me until I shuddered. I dug into my pockets and pulled out my crushed mittens. Our walks became so ingrained in my winding-down-from-the-day ritual that on the rare occasion we missed—one of us had to work late or had something come up—I had a hard time falling asleep, so I wasn't about to bow out because of a frozen nose.

I wondered who he was talking to on the phone. Maybe a girlfriend. But I doubted he would have time; he was with me every night. He had never mentioned wanting to date me again after that first night on the porch. Perhaps he had truly wanted a friend. Great, then we were happily planted on the same page.

But my mind raced and I wondered where he went after our walks. I didn't know much about him really, where he lived. I realized with a shock that I didn't even know where he was while I sat at work. I'd never asked. With a sick ache in my stomach, I wondered how very little I had wanted to know about him, how little I asked, how little (it must have seemed) I cared. But that was what I'd wanted, right? I didn't want to care about him. And I didn't want him to think I cared about him. My convoluted reasoning wore me down, so I stared up into the blank sky of night and waited until I heard his door slam shut.

Meeting him halfway, I turned to walk along, stepping into his pace. I sighed with dramatic effect and said, "I couldn't expect you to stay single forever."

"You couldn't be farther from the truth. I was talking to my mother."

"A mama's boy." I nodded, hiding a smile, looking down.

"Guilty as charged." He looked ahead and then said, "Andria, I have something for you. It's not a big deal." He dug a hand into his coat pocket and pulled out an envelope, handed it to me. The envelope was blank and sealed. I felt it, bent it a little, trying to figure out what was in it. Like a child on Christmas morning. But I felt a dread that never came along with the printed Santa paper and bows of my childhood.

Sliding my index finger across the envelope to open it, I pulled out two tickets and read aloud, "*Aida, A Musical.* Saturday, November 15, 7 pm." I looked over, wary, and he looked down to his feet, then back up as if forcing himself. His eyes vulnerable.

"Quentin, you know I—" I paused, trying to choose my words carefully—can't, already told you no, don't date–squeezing and testing them like I would with an avocado I was considering at the market, until I found the softest one. "Shouldn't."

"Why not?"

"I just can't."

"Why?"

"You wouldn't understand," I said, shaking my head.

"Try me." He wasn't giving up.

"You should take someone who can appreciate it more."

"You told me you liked musicals," he said.

"I do."

"Have you seen Aida?"

"No. It's not that. I just can't date."

"Andria," he said, throwing his arms into the air around them, tinged with exasperation. "What has all this been? Our walks. You're telling me that this has been nothing but walking."

"Yes." Simply, yes. He wasn't angry, I could tell by the softness of his eyes, the vulnerability that still lurked at the corners.

"If that had been a girl on the phone with me just now, if I were taking her to the theatre and not you, you wouldn't care?"

"No," I said with a shrug. "Of course not."

"Okay," he said and held out his palm.

I hesitated, holding onto the tickets, unsure whether I should just drop them into his waiting hand and wash my hands of him. But in all honesty, I didn't want to be rid of him. He added something to my life I hadn't felt in years, a softness that rounded off my rough edges, the anticipation of what our walks would hold each night. I liked knowing that someone was waiting for me. My hand held the envelope, teetering between giving it back and continuing to live a solitary life and holding on it and stepping into a vulnerable place that I hadn't dared go. Even if it was with someone I had grown to trust. I grasped onto the envelope, my decision made, and shoved it into my coat pocket.

Pressing my lips together to keep them from quivering, I bumped myself into his side in a playful push to keep walking. "I won't be able to make our walk on Saturday. I just got two tickets to see a musical, and I need to find a date."

Quentin offered to cook dinner before the show on Saturday and that was it, this was officially date-like with dinner and a show. But I had made my decision. He gave me his hastily scribbled address on the back of a gas receipt I dug out of my coat pocket.

When I returned to my apartment, I tacked the tickets and address to the bulletin board next to the front door. I thought about him as I slipped on my pajama pants and t-shirt and lay in bed, anxiety about Saturday night creeping deeper and deeper inside me. "It's not the end of the world," I reminded myself, trying to settle down but I had betrayed myself, second-guessed the choice I'd made five years ago to live a lifeless existence, and it ate at me. I felt raw.

But it wasn't the beginning of the world either, I thought as a memory crowded into my troubled head. It was almost ten years ago, in college, when something so trivial as a simple invitation to a play turned into the beginning of my world. I was a sophomore then. The invitation was from a guy in my film and theatre class. He didn't know I existed; he had invited the entire class.

Our film lab started at one on Thursdays, so I'd wait around in the lobby of the arts building reading an assignment or studying, and eating lunch, which was usually a small package of peanut butter crackers I'd picked up from the university bookstore for thirty-five cents. I was putting myself through school; my mother didn't have the money to help and I wouldn't give my father the pleasure of asking him for anything. I understood and accepted my lot.

This guy was always waiting for class there too. I didn't wave or acknowledge him. He would usually be reading something, and I'd look up from time to time, just to make sure he was still there.

He wore t-shirts that usually said something interesting or bold and he was your typical college guy, except for one thing: his shoes. He always wore some odd or different shoes, like these blue suede clogs or funky leather oxford rock-climbing shoes or stringy Jesus sandals. Stuff no one else could pull off. When I mentioned him to my roommates, I called him Shoe Boy. I knew his name, but chose to keep that as just mine.

His hair was a trimmed short mass of black waves. His eyes were slits, mysterious, green-gray. If you walked close enough by him, you could see a spray of light freckles across the bridge of his nose. And he had an innocent dimple on his chin, which gave him a sexy-but-he-didn't-know-it look. He wasn't a stand-out. In fact, he was rather plain. Unless you were really looking. And I was.

Because I fell in love with his voice. Not actually the sound of it, but his inflections and his pauses when he spoke in class. He'd say these things—so smart—about how the proxemic patterns in

Like Water for Chocolate made him understand just how intimate the two lovers were. Or how the cinematographer's dizzying crane shots and low lighting did such and such for *Citizen Kane*. And he wasn't afraid to say it, out loud to the class, while I was cowering in my seat, afraid to raise my hand or say something wrong.

But more than anything else, it was the words he used, as if they came from years of voraciously scouring poetry and important literature. I'd write his words into my notebook, then run home to leaf through the dictionary until I found them and read them over enough that they were concreted into my vocabulary. The words brewed in my head until the right moment came to use them and were sweet on my tongue when I finally did. He intimidated me, but I guess it wasn't such a bad thing—I picked up some new words along the way.

On the day in question, as Shoe Boy sat one aisle over, the professor turned down the lights and played a black-and-white film. It was silent, no dialogue—just sad guitar music. It was a love story, about a boy and a girl—I think they were Latino—who wrote an ongoing correspondence to each other as graffiti on a tall stone wall or bridge in the middle of a hard, dirty city. I watched and doodled in my notebook next to my notes on camera angles. When I looked over, I noticed Shoe Boy was scribbling on a sheet of paper. He could have been writing a note to his girlfriend, for all I knew. But at that moment, we were the characters in love from the movie.

The lights flicked on, stinging my eyes back to reality. I shut my notebook and bent over, hiding it in my chocolate-brown corduroy backpack. Shoe Boy stood next to the teacher up front and cleared his throat and said loudly, above the eager murmur of class dismissing, "I'm directing a small play for my Theatre 311 class. Blithe Spirit by Noel Coward. It's tomorrow night at Wilcox Hall in Room 212. And free. Please come if you can."

The lab teacher added, "You could use this as one of your required plays for the semester. Just write up a short one-page review, and it'll count." They stood in front of class talking to each other as I scribbled the details in ink on my palm and shuffled out the door, careful not to fist up and lose the words from sweating.

I was as excited as if I'd had a date with him. Just to have a connection. Something. I wished I knew someone in my lab better, someone to walk in with, to sit by. But I figured I'd take an innocuous seat in the back, slip in and out without being seen.

When I arrived, it was hard to hide. Room 212 was a small auditorium classroom, and the lights were as bright as the middle of day—no dark pathway to a dark seat and then out to a dark night afterward. I lugged my backpack in, as if I were there for a class, and pulled out a book to read until the lights dimmed. I looked around and saw people standing together mingling, other students, maybe friends of people in the play, maybe friends of Shoe Boy. I saw him scurry in just before the lights dimmed and then disappear again.

The play made me laugh, which I tried to muffle with my hand. But I felt gloomy as the curtain finally fell, that what I'd been laughing at hadn't been funny. The main character, Charles—played by a quirky but serious-browed, lanky guy with brown hair gelled down flat on his head—conjured up his first wife from the afterlife while his current, very-much-alive wife stood by. Shoe Boy stood on the stage afterward and thanked everyone for coming. He was talking to a group of people as I walked out undetected, I thought.

I felt the light touch of a hand on my arm from behind me in the hallway. I turned abruptly, embarrassed I was there and there alone. Shoe Boy said, "Hey, thanks for coming. Did you like it?"

"It was great."

"I'm glad you came."

"Me too." He turned away and went back inside. I strolled back to my apartment obsessing about the tingling pressure on my arm where his hand had touched.

Quentin said five o'clock on Saturday. I smoothed on light make-up, enough so that it was noticeable I was wearing some—even eye shadow, which I hadn't used in years, although I still couldn't go less neutral than brown. Using a silver-blue eyeliner, I sketched around my eyes and brushed mascara on my lashes. The mascara tube was so neglected that when I pulled the brush from its tube, black flakes drifted down, gently, secretively, like snow falling. I lined my lips with a golden brown liner and added lip color. And I never used blush. I'd heard once that blush and lipstick were created to give a woman the flushed appearance of just having had sex, associating her with sex.

I combed my hair into a tight, sleek ponytail, my bangs swooped down over my left eyebrow. I contemplated my reflection. Perhaps I overdid it. I leaned over, grabbed a tissue, wiped the color from my lips. The true pale color of my lips was bland underneath the lipstick veneer. That did, however, take me down a notch.

As I had fingered through the clothes in my armoire, I pulled out a traditional black A-line skirt and stepped into it and buttoned up a traditional white shirt.

I looked again in the mirror, this time noticing for the first time in years, my eyes gleamed ice blue again. Must be the brown eye shadow, the contrast. I looked harder and saw something deep and hopeful in the darkest black of my pupil. Something I barely recognized, from years before. Was it hope, potential, something unknown? I didn't know exactly what I wanted from this, perhaps just a little more substance in my life—to play a part, even a small part, in the world I observed. I worried tonight would lead me through a door—grown over with ivy and thick dust from neglect. A door I hadn't even known was there. Like the secret garden door, I remembered my mother reading to me as a child. But I couldn't have what was on the other side of it. I knew this and I wished I didn't have to keep batting the idea away. Nothing's changed, I told myself. I wondered how I had come to this. Why had I accepted? I'd sample life, get a glimpse of the world that would never be mine again. But I had told him I'd be there, and I would.

Quentin lived in a neighborhood in Hanover that I'd jogged through. I parked my car in front of his brick rambler on Willow Drive. The house and yard both looked well kept. I walked up the neatly swept sidewalk to the front door and rang the doorbell. The door swung open, and Quentin held it open. I clicked onto the tiled entry.

"Wow. The mysterious quarters of Quentin Adams," I said as I sat on a bench in the entry and nudged off my thin strappy sandals, leaving them in a heap near the door.

"You look great." He stood still for a moment. He was wearing a black sweater over a striped button-down shirt, the top button left undone. I noticed immediately the absence of his glasses, remembering the first time I saw him jogging by, he hadn't worn them then either. He looked great tonight. His hair was slicked back, more sophisticated than his normal gelled-up style. I wanted to tell him he looked good too. Why was it easier for men to say such things—as if in passing—and it was no big deal, like it's just expected? But I couldn't choke it out. Instead I remarked, stating the obvious but stating it awkwardly, "You look different without your glasses." So I had a hard time doling out compliments.

"I've still got a little work to do in the kitchen, come on in." He gestured toward the kitchen, and I followed him around the corner. The house smelled of cilantro and hot peppers and chicken, and my stomach ached. I hadn't eaten much today, just a bowl of cereal around eleven. He stood at the counter and began tearing lettuce, so I climbed onto a barstool nearby. I looked around me. An open family room adjoined the kitchen—the walls a conservative taupe, the carpet was a darker shade of the same taupe, with several orange and red modern paintings scattered on the walls. Worn, brown-leather couches faced a flat-screen television on the back wall, with orange throw pillows tucked neatly into each armrest.

This kitchen was definitely not the original kitchen in the house, too much stainless steel. Quentin's house was nice and clean and well-kept. However, I suspected I might find a mound of dirty clothes on his bed, if I were able to get a glimpse into his bedroom.

A mission-style dining table was set ready with black stoneware dinner plates, silverware in the right places, cloth napkins folded neatly on the plates. Quentin was chopping celery directly on the countertop, his knife clinking against the granite rhythmically. "You throw many dinner parties?" I asked.

"Not really, although I like to cook."

"Can I help you with something? I'm an expert at chopping," I said.

"No, I'm finishing now. But you could take the salad bowls to the table." He finished crumbling feta cheese atop the mounds of romaine lettuce in each bowl. I clutched them and set them on top of the two dinner plates. He carried over a small dish with candied almonds and a bottle of dressing and set them in the center of the table.

Quentin pulled out my chair as I was about to sit. I wasn't expecting him behind me, and I stumbled backward into him, he steadied me and directed me into the waiting chair.

"Oh, a gentleman," I said. I sat down and unfolded my napkin, laying it over my lap.

"It was my mother. She always made sure I knew how to set a proper table. Told me women expected to be treated a certain way. I've found that most women now are more startled by a sliding chair than impressed." He held the bowl of sugar-coated almonds toward me, "Try these." I took the bowl and sprinkled an abundant spoonful over my salad.

He brought over the chicken enchiladas after the salads.

"It's good," I said after swallowing my first bite of enchilada.

"There's this Mexican restaurant I used to go to a lot, still do when I visit my parents. I always ordered these there, the sour-cream chicken enchiladas. So I just tried to make them, by taste. I think I got the recipe pretty close," he said, having a bite.

"You're a much better cook than I am. But I guess it's hard to be good at something you never do. I feel like it's not worth the effort to spend time cooking something just for me." I thought miserably of the stack of tasteless frozen meals in my small freezer.

After dinner, we drove downtown and parked a couple streets away from the theater. We both agreed we were up for walking, of course we were. We walked quickly, blowing small puffs of air as we breathed in the chilled air, our shoes rhythmically tapping music against the sidewalk.

Our seats were in the front row of the mezzanine. I glanced around at the beautiful gilded scrolls, the mural of cherubs on the ceiling, and settled into my chair. We both leafed through the program.

Quentin asked, "Do you know the story of Aida?"

"No."

"I've not seen this before, but it came recommended by my mother. Couple of Tony Awards, I think."

I looked down at my lap and said, lowly, to myself, "I always thought that someday I'd have season tickets to the theater."

Quentin said, "When I was in high school—when I would rather lock myself in my room than go anywhere with my parents—they bought season tickets. We went to a musical every month as a family—required family entertainment."

"So you've seen a lot of them. Which is your favorite?"

"This is going to sound so passé, but my all-time favorite is Les Miserables. I love the storyline, the music. Never gets old for me. I've probably seen it ten times, will probably see it thirty more before I die. You've seen it?"

"Yeah, years ago, after I read the book—well, mostly. I tried to read the unabridged version—my pretentious English-major friends told me I just had to read the unabridged version. I got about 1100 pages into it and just couldn't stay with it anymore. I liked it, but I got to the point where I had to move on, read something else. I always meant to go back and finish it." The image of my baby's soft dimpled hands carelessly yanking the bookmark from its holding place swarmed my mind. Then I remembered how she was always pulling books from the bookshelves and leaving them opened and scattered on the carpet. I tried to shake that image away, of books strewn about. I looked at Quentin, shrugged. "I lost my place."

The overhead lights blinked a two-minute warning. I sank into my chair. As Quentin sat back in his seat, his leg grazed mine. The overhead lights dimmed, the curtain lifted, and the orchestra began to play. I relaxed and let my mind wander to a world where people broke into song and dance through their hardest times. In the dark, I was always aware of his leg against mine, his warmth penetrating through my skirt to my skin. Enraptured by the story, I felt complacent and warm and whole.

I fell in love with *Aida* that night. I sympathized with Aida, being thrown into a world and circumstances that she could not control. But I envied her one thing—that she got to die with the one she loved in a tear-stained embrace, that she didn't have to go on and try to live without him.

With a jolt, as the music ceased and the lights flicked on, I realized that I'd been letting myself slip into love with Quentin. His leg against mine, his touch, even if inadvertent, was incandescent. Everything suddenly clear. And inside this play world, I believed I was safe beside him. With the light, I felt exposed and shrank back, embarrassed and scared he could read me.

We were stuck behind a crowd of stagnant people, everyone trying to inch closer to the door. We were *Far From the Madding Crowd's* Gabriel and Bathsheba amongst a tight flock of sheep. Quentin grabbed my hand, to keep together, and I shuffled behind him, veering through sheep. When we walked out of the building into the night, his hand attached to mine felt good, and comfortable.

Quentin hummed, surprisingly on key, one of the recurring melodies from *Aida* as we walked to the car, along the gray downtown streets past other people scurrying to their cars. Our hands were still clasped, just an innocent "buddy system." I breathed in through my nose and exhaled, blowing smoky frost into the air.

Quentin flung one arm around my neck and flippantly sang out, more loudly than I was comfortable with, "Is it written in the stars? Are we paying for some crime?" He sang loudly, and several groups of people ahead turned around to get a good look. I shrank back and laughed nervously. He knew I was embarrassed and, like an annoying little brother, saw an opportunity. I braced myself. He stopped mid-step, thrust his other arm into the air dramatically, stood with his legs apart, his head thrown back, and sang emphatically in melody, "Is this God's experiment in which we have no say? In which we're given paradise, but only for a day?"

I yanked on his arm to keep moving and we laughed and stumbled up the sidewalk to the car, like children playing tag. I felt a giddy happiness and couldn't will the smile from my face.

Chapter Four

I awoke the next morning trying to shake last night's feelings. I tried to dismiss them as a mere continuation of the emotions from the characters on stage. I smiled thinking of Quentin—his childishness, singing loudly, freely, uninhibited—and was anxious to see him again. But in a way, I hoped we could go back to being just two friends walking at night.

The feelings didn't leave, just hung around clinging on like a shy child behind her mama's legs. When I saw him the next night, I was glad the night was dark and the half-moon didn't glow on me. It was mostly hidden behind charcoal clouds, but would make appearances every now and then.

His shape moved toward me and we headed our usual direction. We walked self-conscious steps, our shoes speaking, *thwap thwap-ing* on the sidewalk, because we didn't. I adjusted my crocheted beanie for the second time since I left my apartment and buried my hands into my coat pockets. After a while, I blurted out, "So, why are you still single?" Yes, something in me had most definitely changed. Was it as obvious to him as it was to me? I always cringed when I made this kind of transparent comment.

Quentin eyed me sideways and added a smirk, saying, "It is the question of the century: How I, Quentin Adams, local high-school biology teacher and expert chess player—yes, I'm the chess-club founder at Hanover High—could still be single."

"It seems to be a little clearer now," I said with a laugh. He seemed to be laying it all out on the line now and answering the questions I had been afraid to ask.

"Oh, there was a time when the girls were flocking. I didn't have time for them. No, there'd be plenty of time for that. In college, I didn't bother, couldn't be bothered with dating or relationships. I just plowed through school. Then plowed right on through medical school. And by the time I was a resident, and moved here, I was helplessly alone. Not a soul to care for me in the world—but my family hours away."

"You went to medical school? You are a doctor?" I tugged again on my beanie to cover the bottom of my earlobes.

"It doesn't really feel like that was ever me. Really, I went through everything so fast, like a dream. I didn't actually wake up until a couple years ago, while I was still a resident at St. Paul's Methodist Hospital, up to my nose in student loans, and I realized I didn't want to be a doctor. Funny, isn't it?"

"I guess you weren't exactly laughing," I said and leaned my head against his arm in a much-too-intimate way.

"No, I wasn't, and neither were my parents. You'd think I had shot someone the way my mother reacted, as if I were ruining my life. All that work, and school, for nothing."

"Your mom didn't think it was a great career move, huh?"

"I've been trying to climb back onto her pedestal ever since. I'm the same person."

He walked, looking pensively at the moon before the clouds moved back over it. Too pensively. "So to answer your question from at least five blocks back, I'm afraid being a high-school teacher doesn't exactly put me at the top of the most eligible bachelor list." He let out a sigh. "It's ironic that when I had a job that would have impressed the ladies, I had no time for them."

"Ahhh, life's little ironies. So, if you had it to do all over again, would you still have become a teacher? Is it what you thought it would be?"

He shrugged. "I don't know. I don't think I make the difference in the kids' lives I had hoped for."

"I guess, as opposed to saving people's lives."

"I guess. But I do like it, and I'm not sorry I became a teacher. I just wish I hadn't gone all the way through medical school and halfway through residency to figure it out."

I pulled my beanie down over my ears again. I needed a new hat, a larger one.

"I'm surprised you're not spearheading the drama club—you know, in addition to the chess club." I coughed, stifling a laugh.

"Yeah, yeah, laugh all you want. Give me a chess board, and I could take you down in five moves."

I raised my eyebrows. "You're on."

"Do you know how to play?"

"Of course."

"You have a board?"

"No, I don't play much anymore. It's been a while. Certainly you've got a board."

"Yes, you're welcome to come get beaten."

I laughed. We walked the several blocks to his house. Upon arriving there, he opened the front door and we discarded coats and gloves and hats at the entrance. He swiped a cloth off the side table—which exposed light- and dark-stained chess squares on the veneer—and maneuvered it around, so it sat diagonally between the couch and an overstuffed chair.

"Throw me that blanket," I nodded toward a blanket he was about to discard onto the floor from where it had been resting on the back of the couch.

He tossed it to me, and I wrapped it around my shoulders. Then he began placing the chess pieces on the table.

"So, you asked about the drama club earlier. I wanted to do it, but I'm waiting for Mrs. Cross to retire. They've been performing 'Our Town' every year for twenty years straight. She's bound to retire soon."

"Then you'll take over and introduce Hanover's high-school drama enthusiasts to Samuel Beckett and Tom Stoppard. Maybe a little Wendy Wasserstein."

"Yeah, we'll see. Are you ready?" he said as he placed the last piece on the board.

"Yes."

Quentin moved his pawn first.

As I studied my pieces, eyeing him suspiciously, I said, "What about you though? Have you ever thought about going back to the stage? Doing it for you? You know, I think there's a lot to be said for re-inventing yourself. Or, I guess in your case, re-emerging." I moved my pawn.

"Not seriously." He grinned. While he moved his knight, he grinned, like just thinking about being up on stage made him happy. Wait, now I wasn't so sure he was smiling about the stage, rather than his plot to take me down on the chess board. "It's just not practical. Should I pick up and move to New York?"

"People have done stranger things." I paused, moving my knight, then continued, "You know, you wouldn't have to do it completely. What about doing it on the side? Doesn't the Muny downtown use locals?"

"Yeah, I think, although I never seriously considered it." He sat thinking, unwilling his hand to make the next move.

"Teachers have summers off, right?"

He was silent. After several moments, he picked up another knight and moved it, setting it down with a thoughtful clink, then said, "That might bring my mom closer."

"Really? Why is that?" I said, carelessly moving my pawn.

"I didn't tell you about my mother, *the drama professor*?" He enunciated drama professor cynically, maybe this title had worn him down over the years. He picked up his bishop and placed it.

"No." I moved my knight again.

"Our family lived in Champaign so my mom could be close to the university where she taught. They still live there, in the same house where I grew up. A brown Tudor. She always encouraged us in the performing arts."

"Right, you said you were in some plays in college."

"Yeah, but it started when I was younger. She was always putting us into drama camps and classes. She used us sometimes too. Every once in a while, when my mom needed kids as extras in some of the plays and musicals the university was putting on, especially if she was in a bind, we'd get to do it. I was a lost boy in Peter Pan more than once." Quentin picked up his bishop, slowly made his move, then set it down, with a flourish.

"So, you sing too? And dance?" I asked, as I moved my pawn.

"Well, I could, but I don't do it much anymore. With stuff like singing, you have to continue training your voice or you lose range. Check mate." I eyed all our queens and kings and rooks stranded helplessly in their square prisons.

The game was over. I didn't care all that much, as I hadn't expected to win. I used to play with my father when I was young, but hadn't played for ten years.

In a way, I was relieved. And comforted to know that life was a puzzle for Quentin too, although he did seem to know his way around a chess board. Maybe life was one to everyone, deep down, despite how they appear. I guess we don't have it all figured out. We get pieces along the way and try to fit them in, but it doesn't always work so perfectly. It's not like we're getting the piece that fits in at just the right place, at just the right time—not usually.

I had a huge pile of jumbled puzzle pieces in my pile, and it seemed less unusual when I had glimpsed his. A little comforting. I had time. No rush. I wasn't ready to show him my pieces anyway.

"Yeah, that's it. That's what you should really do: go back and pursue the stage. Be the high school teacher who moonlights in musicals."

"Maybe." Yeah, we had lots of time, I considered thoughtfully as we walked back to my apartment, where his car was waiting.

As I lay in bed later that night, staring up at the lights and moving shadows reflected on the ceiling from the street, I thought about the way I'd reinvented myself—just picking up and starting over. Not exactly something I considered ever doing. Maybe I'd write a collection of short stories, or take violin lessons, study interior design—that's how I imagined I'd reinvent myself. I never believed someone really could do a complete overhaul. Just wash everything away. A chalkboard so black you couldn't tell it had ever been used.

Everyone has a dream tucked neatly away in a pocket or old trunk. I remembered learning about all the little files of dreams Shoe Boy had filed away. Almost until they didn't exist anymore. Dark and hidden and lost. After I knew him more intimately and used his real name, Brett, then his shoes didn't quite seem so extraordinary anymore, just fit who he was.

I thought going to the play Brett directed would be a turning point. Maybe he would see me now and—I don't know—care I was there. But the semester ended with nothing more than a couple of wistful glances.

Summer passed. And fall semester, until I was several weeks from the end of spring semester. I hadn't notice how the early flowers of spring were startled that morning by the frost, I was so intent on finishing the final pages of *Orlando*. I was close and already five minutes late to class, so I walked to my ten o'clock British Lit class, my hands wrapped around the book, reading when I heard that voice, saying my name. Very even toned and matter-of-fact. My eyes already downcast, I saw a pair of dark red Doc Martens planted on the sidewalk and lifted my eyes into his and closed my book.

He was standing so close to me that his face—the face I had ingrained in my head for so long—wasn't quite his. In the morning chill, I could feel his warm breath on my cheek. "Hi," he said.

"Hi." Several people were trying to get by on the sidewalk, so we stepped off onto the frosty, crunchy grass.

"How's your semester going?" he asked.

"Good," I replied. Wow. I couldn't say anything more than monosyllabic words with him. Of course I was a fairly intelligent person. Still, here I was mustering up the few words in my head I could find to use.

"How'd you do in Film and Theater?"

"Okay." I couldn't remember what grade I'd got in the class. Probably a B. I usually got a B. I had a theory on grades that helped me get through college, that the amount of work that it takes to go from a perfectly satisfactory B to an A was so much greater than the joy you got out of it, that it wasn't worth it to me to put in the extra time studying. I was a well-adjusted B student.

I looked nervously around, but Brett wasn't trying to get away. Just stood there like he was in charge of class times and me; I let him be. I shifted my weight onto one leg and tapped my other foot onto the pavement.

He shook off his backpack and left it hanging from his hand. "I'm done with this semester. I'm ready to take off."

"Where will you go?"

"London, to do study abroad."

"I signed up for that," I said. I imagined our names leaning on each other's on the list, giving us a connection I didn't know of. Of course he would be going. I had signed up but withdrew shortly after. I simply couldn't afford it and couldn't bear to ask my mother to help.

"You're kidding."

"I can't go though. Gotta work this summer."

"That's too bad."

My British Lit class was gnawing at my mind, a clock's long arm moving with every pause. I was at least fifteen minutes late now, I had to say something. "I've got to go. I'm late for class." I was anxious but unable to will my legs to walk away. Chances were I wouldn't see him again. Especially since he'd be leaving soon for London, where I should have been going.

"My bike is parked right here. Do you want a ride?" he asked. He gestured toward a motorcycle, an old rusty bike, dirty orange, shaped like a banana with big outstretched handlebars. I knew it would take longer for him to start it up, get on it, and drive the several yards to the front doors of the Humanities building than it would take me to walk, but the thought of being so close to him overpowered my desire to make it to class faster. "Okay," I said. It was worth being another five minutes late.

I followed him to his bike. He climbed onto the bike and started the engine and stood, holding it steady while I climbed onto the seat. He sat. I hesitated, then put my arms lightly around him, on his waist. My face was so close to him I could see small hairs sprouting on his neck. I blushed—glad he couldn't see me behind him—and actually thought I wished I could lick his neck.

Moments later, he stopped the bike and I hopped off and skipped toward the front of the building. Several steps off, he shouted to me, "Hey, do you want to come with me to an art exhibit tonight?" Several people walking past turned to see—dare I thought—a date-in-the-making.

I smiled, stopped, and turned. "Yes."

"Meet me here at seven," he said and pointed to the art building, the same one where we used to wait for our film class to begin. I turned and smiled so big it hurt and went into the building.

That night, I borrowed clothes from my roommate and wore my hair down, long and straight over my shoulders. I knew little about him—aside from his vocabulary and his favorite movies.

The atrium in the arts building was dizzyingly busy, like the chaotic scurry of ants after a disruption to their nest. I couldn't see him. People were crowding both directions, stopping at the maze of art displays. The room echoed with chatter. Amidst all the people, my feet took me to the bench where he had always waited for class, and he was there, waiting. For me. He looked up and waved. I sat down next to him. "Have you been to one of these before?" he asked.

"No."

"They announced the winners about a half hour ago. That's why it's so packed. It should settle down in the next little while. I hate crowds."

"Yeah."

"Were you late to class today?"

"Yeah."

"Miss anything important?"

"Nah."

We waited at that bench, until the place cleared out some, and he stood. He was so sure of himself, so confident, the way he slid his hand over and grasped mine. Just like he was putting on his backpack or getting a drink. But I couldn't ignore the feeling that ran through me, like sitting in The New Globe in London watching Hamlet or seeing my named printed in a byline for the university newspaper for the first time. Like this was something monumental.

We entered the opening to the maze closest to us. We paused at each piece of art. I wished for something intellectual to say. I hadn't studied art, didn't know exactly what to look for. Just admired the pictures, nodded, and kept quiet, while he did most of the talking—about the colors, the brush strokes, the symbolism.

We paused at a charcoal sketch of an empty street dotted with lampposts and buildings. Some solitary antique cars parked alongside. The hill behind this little village arching toward the horizon. Small trees stair-stepping up the hill. I looked at the sketch for several minutes before I noticed his name attached to it. I smiled warmly and looked up at him, "I didn't know you—" then I turned back to study the drawing more carefully.

"It's my major, art," he said.

"Really?" I kept my eyes fixed on his sketch, following the lines, the shading, minutely, until it erupted into a fascinating whole. "You're good."

"I guess. It had always come naturally for me. But I had no idea how brilliant everyone here would be. Now I'm nothing special. A pebble amongst diamonds." He was being modest, of course, but the person standing beside me was not suffering from self-esteem issues.

Nodding at the canvas, I said, "I think it's great. And the play, you know the one you directed last year, it was so—" I grasped for the right word and didn't seem to come up with it, my cheeks flushed from the delay—"professional." I felt awkward and looked away, pretending to see another painting I liked up ahead.

He smiled and shrugged. "Thanks." Then we walked to the painting, which was a modern monochrome piece, just a blue rectangle of color. It was a nice blue, like the sea on a still day.

"What's your major?"

"I spent my first two years in business, but just switched to English. I was so bogged down with finance, and marketing, and business law." Now I loved all my classes. I wouldn't spill to him that I eagerly anticipated the book lists when they came out. Sometimes I even snuck books from other classes I wasn't taking, just eager to read something good.

"And theater and film was—"

"Just a fun class." He smiled at me expectantly, waiting for me to continue. "I like having the freedom of taking classes I want, just because they sound interesting." I took all sorts of oddball classes just to fill my interest—not requirements—like bird-watching, sculpting, interior design, Greek studies.

He nodded.

We went through the entire exhibit, looking at the drawings and paintings first, then covered sculpture and glassworks. I wished we could get lost in the middle and stay there forever. I didn't want to walk in opposite directions when this was over—just wanted to stand next to him, looking at art I didn't quite understand and trying to understand him more.

I had finished reading Hemingway's *A Farewell to Arms* a couple weeks before for my American Lit class and could imagine myself turning into Catherine over this guy, the Catherine who was so intensely in love that she got the same short, crude haircut as her lover. Wanting to be so like him that she wanted to look like him.

Later, I held little pieces of his voiced thoughts and replayed them verbatim in my mind, for their uniqueness, because they belonged to him. I grasped onto any thought of his I could hold, keep. Sometimes I held onto them for so long I'd used them as my own ideas, an in-love fraud, I suppose.

As we stepped away from the last sculpture, he leaned into me, close, his arm grasping my shoulder, and said, "I know art isn't how I'm going to make my living. It's just something I like to do." His eyes locked mine as he spoke. He was serious, as if this were a declaration that there may somehow be an opening, a door, for me into his future life. This was crazy. This was the first night we had spent together. I wished I could snap out of it.

But I never had to.

Crumpled onto the window seat with Hero, overlooking the small town of Hanover, I couldn't erase from my mind the image of his charcoal sketch of three pigeons perched atop a skyscraper, that cheaply framed piece hung over the toilet in the bathroom of his college apartment I saw after the art exhibit that night. After we'd slept together. Way too soon, but it seemed right.

That night, I found those pigeons endearing and could even see a troubled expression in their eyes—was that remorse or grief?—as they stood watching over a great city.

I never asked him which city that was. I meant to, as we packed it into our car a year later, buried under mounds of clothes and books, to drive to Oregon together.

And several years after that, as I stowed another box of unused baby toys in the attic, I rediscovered the drawing stacked behind a mound of boxes filled with college textbooks and bags of dried-out art supplies. I pulled the picture out, brushed off the dust, and sat staring at it—remembering how perfectly I'd loved him then, how he'd just seemed to fit into my world. The right puzzle piece at the right time. His art and paintbrushes and chalk all sat stored in the attic, useless, just like our love had become.

Tonight I closed my eyes tight and finally drifted to sleep, at last seeing exactly what it was in those pigeons' eyes I couldn't get so long ago—that they saw the tragedy of life, happening below them, and stood there looking on, eyes like stone.

A week later, on another freezing night, Quentin and I tread on a sidewalk glazed with ice—the snow shoveled and brown and towering over the curb—and I began to lose my balance, grabbing onto his arm. We laughed. He patted my elbow, which was still laced through his arm, and said, "You might want to hold on. And I'll hold on. We'll keep each other up."

Our steps were slower tonight. I asked, "You said your family lives in Champaign. Do you see them often?"

"I should go visit more. Mostly on holidays or when my mom has a play showing. Something special. It's only about a three or four hour drive. One of my sisters lives there too. She usually hangs around a lot when I come home. But my brother lives in Chicago now, and my other sister is still in grad school, in Michigan."

"Big family?"

"I guess so. My brother is the oldest, and I'm the second child. Then my two sisters, they're twins. About three years younger than me. When we get together, even now, it's like the years melt away and we're all kids again, joking and playing, no pretenses. We even pull out the Scrabble, just like we did."

"I see." My thoughts veered to my own family, which I hadn't seen or spoken to for nearly five years. I desperately missed my sister Anna. The last time I saw her, she slept on my hard floor with old quilts and flat pillows. To hold my hand, stroke my hair.

"Is your family around here?" he asked.

"My sister and mom live on the west coast. I grew up in a Washington, in Mount Vernon, outside of Seattle."

"I assumed you were always here. I've never been to Seattle, but I've heard it's beautiful."

"It is," I said.

"Your dad?"

"My dad left when I was fourteen. We saw my dad sometimes—not often. He remarried. Started a new family. I guess it was one he preferred. It's okay. I dealt with this a long time ago."

I pushed a stray hair back into my ponytail. "But my mom was always there. She was a teacher. We didn't have a lot of money, but it was okay. I always felt like we were real characters in *Little Women*. A bunch of girls alone in our house, without much else. I had to look at it that way, thinking of ourselves as bookworthy."

"Are you close with your mom and sisters still?"

I hesitated and felt a hollow in my stomach. "No. I haven't talked to them in years. It wasn't a fight or misunderstanding or anything like that. But I miss them."

We walked along for a while, silent, just our unsure footsteps, and the distant sound of a couple of dogs barking back and forth.

He tugged onto my elbow and stopped walking, then looked hard into my eyes, cocked his head as if trying to see into my past, then said, "Well, you could do it now. You should call them. You might feel better." He didn't know what it would mean for me to open myself back up like that. They didn't even know where I was.

My mind wandered to my mom and sister. I pictured my mom settled on the couch in the small white clapboard house we grew up in, rustling through the local paper, shaking her head at the news as she'd always done. She still lived there the last I knew.

Living hours away made it easier for me to distance myself. Especially when I first moved here. To just cut the tie. That way, I didn't have to explain what I was doing, why I left. Perhaps I was afraid they'd call me on the fact that my move wasn't right. But

I didn't want to hear it. I didn't want to reason. I knew it wasn't right. It just seemed easier to leave them in the past too.

And my mom, so efficient, clearing away what she thought was a mess, trying to help. But I needed something, something left in the nursery or in my house that proved my baby had existed—not a bunch of storage boxes up in the attic I could hardly get to. My mom packed everything away. I never told her how angry it made me to see my house so tidy, when what I wanted to see was a high chair in the middle of the kitchen with some sprawled, discarded Cheerios and maybe a smear of food on the tray. Proof. But my mom swooped in with her wet rags, cleaning everything away, keeping busy. Helping.

When I returned to my apartment that night, I felt jittery as I discarded my snow-packed shoes by the front door and stripped off the layers of clothing. I jumped under my down comforter, and Hero settled in the crook of my arm. I pictured the room my sister Anna and I shared, our white spindled bunk beds, the pink wallpaper with butterflies. There was a strip of wallpaper that had been on the verge of falling off the wall. I used to stare at to avoid doing my homework; it had hung there precariously for years. I clicked off the lamp on the table next to my bed and my thoughts swarmed to the past.

I remembered trying to fall asleep as a child, worrying about things only kids would. That after I had said a bad word on the bus, Shelley Dougherty was going to tell her mom who would call my mom.

Late into the night, when sleep wouldn't come, my mom would quietly open the door to our bedroom. I would lay motionless with my eyes closed, trying to breathe at a regular interval, feigning sleep. She'd lean over and kiss me on the forehead. She did it every night. Some nights I was still awake, some nights asleep. But I knew she loved me, still would, even if Shelley's mom did call her.

That kiss told me everything I needed to know—that I was safe, loved, accepted. I lay in bed for so long tonight, tossing, tossing, sleep so far away. I was waiting for something. I was waiting for the comfort and peace only a mother's kiss could give.

Chapter Five

I had the January blues in December and couldn't get into the Christmas cheer that gripped everyone around me, but this was nothing new. For years I had ignored the optimistically hung wreaths and lit-up holly leaves on the lampposts across Main Street. Just a little extra light invading my place through the curtains. But this year, I had a nagging feeling, like an annoying puppy just wouldn't let go of my ankle. Holding on.

Perhaps I dreaded spending another Christmas alone. I knew Quentin was planning to spend it with his family, and I wasn't looking forward to the empty nights.

My morose mood didn't pass unnoticed. One night as we walked in mid-December, Quentin said, "You've been quiet. You all right?"

"Yeah." I stared ahead.

"Okay." On a normal night, I would have brought up something from work or a new movie I wanted to see. "I just hate this time of year."

"You hate Christmas?"

"Okay, maybe not hate. Just—I wish it would just never come. If it has to, why can't it leave me out of it?"

"I guess I won't expect a gift from you."

"Yeah, that's not really my thing."

"Do you—do you think you would hate it less if you had somewhere to go?"

I eyed him sideways. "You're not inviting me to spend Christmas with your family, are you?"

He laughed and said, "No, of course not."

I breathed an audible sigh of relief.

"Unless you wanted to."

I didn't hesitate. "No. Everyone would hate me because I hate Christmas. I'd just bring you all down. Then something would be amiss in your perfect family's perfect Christmas gathering." Yeah, it came out just as bitter as I'd thought it might.

Quentin didn't respond.

"I'm sorry. I don't mean to take it out on you. It's all this." I waved my arm past the row of annoyingly lit-up houses and bobbing blown-up lawn Santas and reindeer. "And I miss my family. Especially at Christmas. Just reminds me again how alone I am. I miss them. I miss the way I felt so warm and safe at home. I miss the freedom of being taken care of." Funny, I thought, how it seems like freedom now; for when I was younger, it had seemed dreadfully restricting.

I realized with a start that I was confessing much too much. He wouldn't understand why I couldn't just go home and spend the holidays with my family. I was relieved when he caught on to a different strand and said, "I think you miss being a kid."

"Right."

"I know what you mean, though. You're in such a hurry to grow up, to drive, leave for college. And so much depends on your childhood—the most impressionable years— in determining who you turn into, how screwed up you ultimately become." He was joking, of course, and laughed—this chuckle, always the same length and inflection, when he laughed at his own jokes. His own personal courtesy laugh.

"What was your childhood like?" I asked. "I mean, except for tromping around Neverland."

"Pretty normal. My parents helped me with my homework, we had family dinners together, I played a lot of video games with my brother, I teased my sisters. We were your typical American family, but we weren't perfect."

"Sorry." I watched the tips of my shoes appear and disappear with each step. I had learned along the way that most families, especially the ones that seemed perfect on the outside, were far from perfect behind closed doors. That's how I got by, telling myself that yeah, they have the perfect two-parent household, with their manicured lawns and their private schools, but they must be harboring some deep dark secret inside their walls, like their father's gambling problem or the fact that their mom's secretly a drunk.

"Most of my childhood memories are good ones," Quentin said. "Sometimes we see what we want to see. But there was one thing—" He hesitated and again kicked a rock he'd been kicking along with us for the last several feet.

"What?" I asked.

"It's nothing. Water under the bridge."

I didn't press it. I knew how it felt to need to keep something contained inside and needed the same courtesy from him.

"It's just something I can never forget. You wanna hear my traumatic childhood experience?" He wanted me to know. His eyes narrowed and shoulders slackened.

"If you want to tell."

He inhaled and let out a long deep breath, then began his story. "When I was about twelve, my sister Sarah came home from school late, didn't say anything, just ran up to her room. I didn't think anything of it, just a tough day for an eight-year-old at school. Still, it was unusual for her. She usually told us everything, good or bad. Sarah and Leah were always talking.

"Later that night, she came into my room all jittery while I was doing homework. I asked her what was wrong, and after a while, after I had to 'promise not to tell anyone,' she told me when she was walking home from school—Leah had gone over to a friend's house—a neighbor of ours who lived a couple houses up the street asked her to come help him with something. I think he said he couldn't find his dog. She went around to the back of the house and bent down to try to look underneath his house, through the crack, to see. She told me that he had tried to touch her, put his hands on her, held onto her arm tightly—she showed me the bruise—and wouldn't let her leave. I was livid, Andria. I wanted to kill him." Quentin's voice cracked, like he was regressing to the physicality of a 12-year-old boy. I looked over but he wouldn't look at me.

"Quentin," I said.

"I told her that we had to tell someone, Mom or Dad. But she was so scared, afraid of what would happen, to him even. She finally agreed, and we told our dad. He was calm, silent for a while. I suggested we go over there and do something. I didn't know what. I was just a kid. My father called the police, and they brought him in to talk. I just didn't think it was enough. I don't think he even had to spend any time in jail. I was so angry that he could just still live there. Like nothing ever happened."

He quickened the pace, and I quickened my pace to keep up.

"A couple weeks later, I went over there when it was dark, when I should have been asleep. I think it was ten-thirty or eleven. I took a rock, a pretty big one I'd found lying on the street, and I flung it into his front window.

"I ran. My house was about eight or nine houses down. As I ran home, I saw some lights come on, curtains moving in the windows. They'd heard it. I hid behind a tree in my next-door neighbor's yard. A large gumball tree, I remember, because I grabbed a bunch of gumballs, to use as ammunition in case anyone found me.

"I got caught. The police came to our front door that night, and I wasn't in my room. Eventually, I had to go home."

He still wouldn't look up.

"My parents made me pay for that window. Doing jobs around the house, mowing the lawn, helping my dad spread mulch in the yard. I didn't think I should have to. He was the one who should be punished, not me." Quentin's eyes were wild, and in them, I could see him as a scared boy with the pricks of gumballs denting his palms, trying to make justice in the world.

"You were a good brother. Of course you'd try to protect her. I'm sure your parents understood that."

"He moved a year or so later. Maybe it was my rock that made him leave. I always thought so as a kid. That it was because of me. I was young, I didn't think what I was doing was against the law."

"I understand you wanting to do something. I definitely wouldn't want him living in my neighborhood. Children should be protected from people like that."

"It makes me think twice sometimes, you know, about ever having children, being responsible for bringing them into a corrupt world. That you wouldn't be able to protect them. But I always thought I'd have a family."

Realizing, I was still holding on to his arm, I let go. I tried to shrug off the resurgent feeling of trying to protect my girls so long ago, hesitated, then said, "Yeah, I'd always wanted a family."

After dragging my heavy feet up the steps to my apartment, I flopped face down on the bed, startling Hero from her sleep. She padded in a circle and settled back nearby, her tail whipping my arm.

I felt something closing in on me, could hear the incessant ticking of some time bomb, or was that my heart? No, it was the beat of music coming from a passing car on the street.

I looked around my apartment. I'd meticulously chosen everything in this place, tried to make it resemble me. Antiques and dainty pieces scattered throughout. But everything I'd brought in from antique shops and flea markets were relics of someone else's life. Yes, it held history—even the house where I lived had its history—but the problem was that it wasn't my history. And it said very little about who I was. Where was the proof that I existed? Where was I in my home?

I plucked a book off the coffee table and stared at it, not even daring to open it, and my mind wandered back to years before and faces I'd known more intimately than my own.

Brett and I were married just a year when I got pregnant. I wanted to have a baby, his baby, all our cells, DNA, merged and entwined so close and tight that it could never separate—in our child, half him, half me.

I waited for him—the phone to ring or to hear the garage door hum at the end of each work day—with the same intensity that I'd anticipated our first date. That feeling never deadened the way I'd heard it would.

Each night, I'd do everything I could to be closer to him— read in the same room where he was, sit nearby as he heated up his dinner, ask about the insipid details of his workday but it wasn't boring to talk to him. He always made me feel so alive. But I feared something would inevitably push Brett away from me. It couldn't stay like this. I worried one of us would end up with a terminal illness, and our intense love affair would never get the chance to refine itself—end with us old, putting the toothpaste on each other's toothbrushes and leaving out each other's vitamins and prescription drugs each morning.

We found out I was pregnant with Lizzie the day we hosted a Super Bowl party. The Cowboys played that year, and the house smelled of beer and pizza and over-cooked queso. About eight or nine close friends came. A friend of Brett's from work brought his wife and baby. I watched the way she was holding the infant, so close, and had been avoiding the test for a week now. I'd bought it, just hadn't told Brett yet.

I took the pregnancy test during the third quarter—that messy, urine-splashed test—and there they were, the two blue lines. I waited until everyone filed out to tell him.

The ultrasound several months later proved my initial thoughts that this baby was a girl. I bought little pink and yellow outfits, filled the spare closet. We started moving things into other rooms in the house, to make a nursery. We bought a mahogany sleigh crib; bedding with butterflies and bluebirds on pink gingham; all the baby essentials—baby shampoo, diapers, rash ointment, baby Tylenol, everything. I ate all the things I was supposed to eat and none that I shouldn't. Listened to classical music—Bach, Mozart, Beethoven—in the car during my commute, for the baby's sake. I read the "What to Expect" pregnancy bible.

Yet, I still had those dreams. You know the ones you have when you're worried about being ready for something. I had them often in college—sitting in the exam room, taking a final exam for a class I hadn't attended all semester.

She came a week late, refusing to come naturally, clinging to my uterus until her heartbeat plummeted and the nurse shoved a form and pen in my lap to sign. Yes, it's okay to do a Cesarean. As they rushed me through the hall, I refused to think about why the heart rate dropped and, instead of crying, thought about Julius Caesar. Odd yes, but it was my way of coping. He had supposedly been delivered with a cut and lived on to do so many great, important things. But didn't his mother die? I thought as I felt the sharp stab of my flesh being sliced. I screamed. "Can you feel that?" an anesthesiologist asked.

"Yes," I cried. Brett gripped my hand.

I woke several hours later, moaning, begging for water, my tongue like sandpaper. Brett ran off and came back with a cup, then fed me ice chips with a spoon. "Is Lizzie here? Is she okay? How big is she?" Brett later told me that I'd asked those same questions over and over, probably five different times throughout the night, every time I woke.

I didn't meet her until the next morning. Brett pushed me in the wheelchair across the hall into the nursery. I gasped and cried. Not because she was beautiful, which she was, but because she had an IV intruding into her head and all I wanted to do was protect her. I held her in my arms and tried to nurse her. Tubes and cords tangled, intruding between us. "The operating room hadn't been sterile when they did the C-section because they had to act quickly," Brett said, sensing my frustration. "She needs the IV for antibiotics. She'll be fine."

Brett or I stayed up most nights the first several months because she preferred to sleep while the sun was up than in the quiet darkness of the sun's absence. I breastfed, made my own baby food out of fresh fruits and vegetables. I quit my editing job at the outdoors recreation magazine.

Lizzie grew—sat up, crawled, walked, everything in the right order. Started talking. Yanking all the Tupperware out of the drawer. Bursting into our room in the middle of the night, first thing in the morning, toddling around the house all day. I fell into bed each night, exhausted. I felt invisible next to the blonde-haired, green-eyed toddler, and I wondered if Brett saw me when he staggered home from work. Sex became just a memory in our current toddler-focused house.

We tried to do things—spend more time talking, notice each other more, perform little acts of kindness around the house. He'd clean up after dinner, change Lizzie's diapers.

One night, after Lizzie was tucked into bed sleeping, Brett suggested we play strip poker. "Ha," I laughed, "You're joking."

"Come on."

"Yeah, all right." I offered a shy smile. We forgot about diaper rashes and baby food and talked about us, about the craziest things we'd done in high school, our insecurities, our dreams. We saw each other illuminated by the dull lamp in the corner.

I laid on my side on one edge of the bed, while Brett laid on the other. The cards between us. He was so confident, he'd taken off his shirt before I dealt the first hand. Just stripped it off. I laughed and shuffled the deck, worried that the sharp snap of the cards would wake Lizzie.

I played poker the same way I lived—conservatively, folding when I knew I couldn't win, unable to even try bluffing. I never understood bluffing—if you have a good hand, you put your money in; if you don't, you fold. Simple. But after Brett nervously fidgeted his cards, wearing only his boxers—while I was still fully dressed—he said, "You're so predictable. Loosen up a little."

"You mean with my money?" I laughed, knowing that when he had a good hand, he'd adjust from lying to sitting, and when he had a poor hand, he'd tap the bottom of his cards casually on his palm. Likewise, I felt like he could see right through the backs of the cards just by looking into my face.

"Well, yeah, that and with your clothes." He nudged a little closer, and I acquiesced and pulled off my shirt. Several minutes later, I won his boxers with a flush, then threw both hands of cards onto the floor.

Claire was conceived that night.

When she was born and the doctor pulled her free—a much easier C-section than the first—he lifted her above the curtain hiding my opened flesh, her red face scrunched up and wailing. So different from Lizzie who had white-blonde hair, fair skin, and elfish features, Claire was black-haired, olive skinned, and her head as round as a saucer. I worried that I wouldn't love this child who was so unlike Lizzie. Lizzie, in all her glorious two-year-old self, seemed a giant in comparison to this tiny thing.

She was our Claire Bear, as Brett dubbed her the first time he held her. It didn't take but hours for me to realize I loved this one just as much.

I was now the mom of two small children. Their needs—eating, sleeping, playing—dictated my life. Lizzie taught herself to read shortly after Claire was born and was in a morning preschool class. All the while she was gone, Claire and I would cling to each other, our world, just the two of us. We'd read baby books or I'd sit down with her while she pulled each toy from the wicker basket behind the pink gingham curtain hanging over her closet. We sang songs—the wheels on the bus, twinkle twinkle little star, baby bumblebee. I know it sounds like some fairytale world of motherhood. And I suppose in my memory I've glamorized it a bit, but truly it's what I remember. Of course, I did laundry, cleaned the house, made beds, changed diapers. It was no eight-hour workday editing kayaking articles—just longer, and more wonderful and less wonderful, and oh so very tiring.

Claire groped onto me like she'd never see me again, crying every time I tried to pass her to someone. Brett was frustrated when he'd *help* me while I longed to do dishes, pick up in the family room, anything but hold the baby at the end of the day. She'd lean toward me, wherever I was in a room, until she was nearly falling out of his arms. Brett and I joked she had displaced abandonment issues. Her emerald eyes would plead for me, her arms outstretched—I could never turn down those eyes—so I'd lift my soapy hands and finish the dishes while she clung to me. Brett would shake his head, then move on and help Lizzie along with a puzzle or oversee her coloring or reading or whatever independent activity she'd chosen that night.

This memory of my arms overloaded and my head filled with children's songs and my shirt caked with baby food left me still, lying on my bed in my solitary apartment. Yearning for that feeling again of being needed and wanted, reached for. I tried to conjure up the scent of the lavender lotion I used to rub onto Claire's arms and legs and tummy after a bath, that clean-baby smell, but it wouldn't come. I couldn't remember how her skin felt against mine when I held her. My eyes and nose burned with the onset of tears as I realized I couldn't remember what it felt like to hold her.

I flung the book onto my bed and crept to the wooden chest, which I used as an ottoman and coffee table, but never opened. Everything I'd brought with me from my life before was contained inside its mahogany frame. I knelt on the rug and lifted the top slowly. I closed my eyes and inhaled, taking in the cedar scent, which transported me back to the northwest of my past. I slipped my hands around a soft, worn envelope underneath a stack of recreational magazines from my editing days. I hadn't brought much with me when I left. I'd had to grab what I could without making a sound. I left the chest's lid stretched open, then settled more comfortably on the floor.

Holding the envelope in my lap, I smoothed it over, caressing it, unsure. My personal Pandora's box. I hadn't looked at these since before I arrived. I hesitated, knowing I'd be releasing everything—the memories, the grief, the love, the anxiety, the anger, the helplessness. I spilled the stack of photographs from the envelope into my lap. I focused on the photograph on top. A dark-haired baby—my Claire—penetrated me with her emerald green, tear-shaped eyes. I picked up the picture and held it close to my face. My tears ran their course.

I wanted to thrust the photos back into the envelope, their dark home, but I was mesmerized by her face, as I had been when I was with her. I brought the picture to my chest. Trying to be closer. But all I had left was this unloving piece of paper, not the soft body I used to hold in my arms. That I used to rock to sleep. That I fed, and bathed, and rocked.

Turning the photo over, as if willing it away, I read my own smudged handwriting on the white photo paper, *Claire Porter, 14 months old.* I began sifting through the other photographs in the stack and lingered on the family photograph—my husband, three-year-old Lizzie, and me, holding Claire.

I struggled for breath, then unimaginable, loud, gasping sobs erupted from a place inside me. Trembling, I froze when I heard the steps outside. I wiped the tears from my face, waiting, silent, still. Hero's ears pricked to alert mode, her eyes wide. She flattened onto the floor, motionless, ready to pounce.

Several soft knocks tapped on my door.

Go away.

The knock sounded again, patient, unsure.

I pulled myself off the floor and shuffled to the door. I didn't want to have to explain to Debbie why I was crying, she must have heard through the walls. Unlocking the bolt, but leaving the chain latched, I peered through the slit into the darkness. Quentin stood there nervously, holding his baseball cap in front of him in both his hands. "Hey," I whispered out.

"Andria. Can I come in?"

"What is it with you? Why do you always find me like this?"

"I don't know. I don't know really why I'm here, just something didn't seem right tonight when we parted. I drove home but couldn't get out of my car. So I'm here."

I unlatched the chain and held the door open for him. "Come in." Quentin stepped carefully into my apartment. He walked over to where Hero sat on the bed and stroked her fur.

He turned back around toward me. "So, what's going on?"

"I'm not crying," I said, knowing my face was splotchy and red, a paper-thin white line just above the ball of my nose, a line that appeared each time I cried. It was my feeble attempt at a joke that neither would laugh at.

He tilted his head, his eyes soft. "I'll stay as long as you need me."

I nodded. I went over and sat down on the bed, pulled on his arm so he'd sit next to me. He settled onto my bed, arranged a throw pillow behind his back, and slouched against the headboard. I needed someone close tonight. I couldn't bear to be alone. No, not just someone. I wanted Quentin's arms around me. I nudged closer to him, leaned my head on his shoulder briefly for a moment, before I could squeeze words out.

"I don't think about my family much. I don't let myself. I didn't realize I'd feel so isolated just talking to you about my mom and sisters." I tried to explain but knew I'd have to start at the beginning. "It's not just them. It's—a long story."

"I've got time."

My eyes traveled to the pile of pictures scattered on my floor. I fought the impulse to jump down and pick them up, to keep hiding. I looked away, left them abandoned on the floor, and said, "I had a family."

Part Two

✤ ✤ ✤

To Escape the Past

1998

Chapter Six

Late-August morning. I kept my eyes closed, trying to keep out the morning sun slanting down through the blinds. It felt warm on my cheek, friendly, but also a warning. "I know, I know, it's six," I groaned. My body woke, paralleling the sun's intensity with the time to wake.

Brett was still breathing heavily. I climbed out from under his arm, shed my nightshirt, stepped into my jogging shorts and stretched my tank top over my head. Sitting on the tufted reading chair, I slipped on my socks and shoes and twisted an elastic band around and around a fistful of hair into a ponytail. Quietly, so as to not wake the girls, I opened the door and slipped out, adjusting my headphones while I stumbled into a reluctant jog.

The crisp morning air rushed against my face. Breathe in through my nose, out my mouth, I always had to remind myself at the beginning. After the first block, I felt especially invigorated—I'd forgo my usual path and head a new direction. I ran, keeping steps with the beat of the music on my headphones, adjusting my cadence to whichever song came next.

Up ahead, I saw a moving form—another jogger, perhaps, or someone out walking a dog. I focused on my feet and watched the cracks of the sidewalk—counting to see how many steps per sidewalk square, two steps and a couple inches. I knew the couple inches in every step would culminate to my having three steps on one square. I waited and waited, finally three steps. I laughed a futile gratification, just to keep going, I focused on something mundane so I didn't think about the heavy breaths, in and out, in and out.

Only several feet away from—yes, it was a jogger—I lifted my eyes. I was on the sidewalk; he was on the edge of the street running toward me. He didn't wear headphones. He was thirtyish and bald, shaved bald. Probably had thinning hair and refused to look into the mirror each morning and watch it go slowly, slowly, until he was the victim of baldness.

I eyed him as he jogged, waiting until the perfect moment when he was passing to widen my fingers in a simple stagnant wave: Hello. We're in the same club, morning joggers.

There was a precise moment, the perfect time to wave, like turning the page of music for a pianist. I'd heard there was a book written on that—the timing so important someone had actually settled down once and written a book on the science of page-turning. Right as we were passing, I smiled a fleeting, exhausted smile and lifted my arm, croaked a simple, "Morning" mixed with heavy exhalation. He waved back.

Several blocks later, the sweet, overpowering scent of fabric softener wafted out of a log house. Multi-colored poppies bursting out of window boxes upstairs. A little old lady, white-haired in curls, probably lived there. Loving her flowers and watering them tenderly and doting on them, like the children who had long since moved out of her still, quiet house. Up early and doing the laundry. I checked my watch, thirty minutes already. I chose this house as my marker to turn around and head back.

This morning, I had a strange limitless amount of energy. My steps felt strong. I formed a mental checklist of all the things I needed to do that day: start my laundry as I was almost out of onesies for Claire; take Lizzie to her first day of ballet lessons at ten; stop by the market and pick up milk, eggs, bread, and meat for tonight's tacos, oh, and a special little toy for Lizzie—just something to show her how proud I was for her being so brave at dance lessons; mop the kitchen floor; get a babysitter for Friday night.

When we moved to Oregon four years before, I'd had no idea how many hours and late nights Brett would spend starting his own software company. Most nights his side of the bed was cold until nearly dawn, with meetings and planning. This Friday, I was to accompany him—the ever supportive wife—to a casual dinner with a man from the venture capitalist company and his wife. I wasn't sure what I should wear, something professional but casual. Maybe I needed to add a quick trip to the mall to my to-do list as well.

I stopped running a block from my house and laced my hands behind my head while I continued a brisk walk toward my house. In the front window, Lizzie waited inside the curtains. Not rolling up in them and playing as I often asked her not to do, but just looking outward, toward the street, waiting for me. I waved and her eyes shone, and she began waving back. I hopped up the steps and hugged her in the doorframe. She didn't mind the sweat from my shoulders and neck, just held on while I flipped off my running shoes. She grasped my hand as we made our way back to my bedroom, from where I heard singing muppets from the television.

Brett was still sleeping, his arm flung over his eyes to keep out the morning light, while Claire sat upright on the bed, leaning against pillows, sucking on the remote control and watching Big Bird. I gave her a kiss. Lizzie brought me a diaper and the box of wipes—our morning ritual. I changed Claire's diaper, trying not to move the mattress too much—let Brett keep sleeping—then left both Claire and Lizzie on the bed to watch Sesame Street, while I stepped into the shower.

An hour later in the kitchen, as the blender whirred bananas and strawberries around for our breakfast smoothie, Brett rushed through, kissing Lizzie and Claire on the tops of their heads. "Sorry honey, no time for breakfast. I've got an eight-thirty conference call."

He opened the refrigerator and grabbed a yogurt. I went to him and yanked lightly on his navy tie. "Not so fast." I kissed him deep and full on the mouth and he clasped his arm around my waist, hidden behind the open refrigerator door—you had to take the little bit of privacy you could get—until the cold air raised goose bumps on my neck and shoulders.

"I gotta go," he said and shut the refrigerator door. "Lizzie, good luck at your dance lessons," he said as he made his way through the door.

"Bye daddy," Lizzie shouted and Claire waved from the high chair where she sat picking through a scattered pile of dry Cheerios.

Peeking back through the closing door, Brett said with a smile, "I love you guys." He let the door swing shut, and we listened for the automatic garage door to rumble shut.

After breakfast, it was time to get the girls dressed for the day. I pulled the tags off Lizzie's new pink leotard with its flowy gauze skirt, a little rosette at the top where the pink met her delicate neck. Lizzie had been eyeing the leotard with fervor for several weeks, while it hung like a prize in her closet. This morning she finally got to wear it. She stepped into it like a princess being dressed by her maidservant, then stretched the straps over her shoulders. She twirled around the house—seeing how far she could get the skirt to fling into the air—until she collapsed on the carpet. Then jumped right back up to circle around some more.

She grabbed Claire's pudgy fingers and twirled her around. "Careful," I warned Lizzie. "Claire's still kind of wobbly. You have to hold her up." Obedient Lizzie, always obedient, went in slow circles, Claire smiling. Claire was wearing the new shoes she'd picked out at the shoe store last week, after she took her first tentative steps. Baby pink tennis shoes with white butterflies at the ends of the shoelaces.

When Claire's new footing finally landed them on their bottoms—like the climax of ring-around-the-rosies—I helped them both up. "Okay, we've got a little time before we have to leave. Want to play outside?" Lizzie skipped toward the back door, while I held onto Claire's hand, walking her there.

I always had to be on time, always planning ahead for the worst scenario—a dirty diaper just before getting in the car—so I was usually five or ten minutes early for everything. I pulled weeds from the flowerbeds while Lizzie gathered dandelions, disrupting the search every so often by chasing a butterfly or grabbing a handful of roly polies, and Claire followed close behind Lizzie.

After wiping smeared dandelion yellow from Lizzie's hands with a wet wipe, we climbed into the car and drove through town, singing along to the Peter Pan musical soundtrack. *I Won't Grow Up*. Lizzie sang while Claire hollered along from her car seat, sometimes falling on key. I flicked on the left blinker and waited behind a red truck in the left-hand turn lane for the light to turn green.

I was nudged awake by the sound of staticky voices on a radio, ambulance sirens, and a man's voice asking, "Ma'am, are you okay?" A blurry paramedic in a navy-blue uniform spoke through a jagged hole in my side window. My forehead throbbed. My neck unable to hold my head. I lay my head back against the seat. How could I have fallen asleep? I was too weak to turn my head to see if Lizzie and Claire were still in the back seat, but it was silent so I knew they couldn't be.

"What happened?" I asked through the taste of blood.

"You've been in an accident," the paramedic said.

"Where are my girls? Are they all right?"

"They're being taken care of." That's when I spotted the back of Lizzie's car seat on the grass. Another navy uniform bending over her. I could see her tennis shoes bobbing up and down uncontrolled.

I didn't see Claire or her car seat. The man was talking into the radio: "Her legs are pinned and the right arm." Were they talking about me? I felt the dash of my car contoured around me. I tried to wiggle my toes, to make sure my legs were still attached. They moved.

In a panic, I wondered if they were talking about Claire, but soon lost consciousness again.

In and out of consciousness. I woke and mumbled, "Call my husband. 555-2435." My eyelids were heavy; I didn't have the energy to fight with them to keep them open.

"We can't get through," his voice was rushed but calm.

My eyes opened, and I realized where we were—the same intersection where I'd been waiting to turn. Several paramedics were wrenching my door off the hinges, the metal tearing and shrieking.

My memory didn't hold what had happened at the moment of impact—just blank, black, nothing. It seemed as if I had slept through it. The last thing I remembered, I was humming along with the music, waiting to turn left. Everything else was gone, a black hole.

Fifteen to twenty people were milling about on the grass outside a mini mall, the same mini mall I'd driven past hundreds of times, with a karate studio, hair salon, and an ice-cream shop.

My driver-side door was gone now. Just a hole, not obscuring anything, whatever it was that laid beyond was visible now, if I could just keep my eyes open.

Through the space, I recognized Alison from my neighborhood out on the grass near Lizzie's car seat, talking to her. She was kneeling by her, a nervous smile on her face, her hand raised toward Lizzie's face, maybe brushing disheveled hair out of Lizzie's eyes. She had a daughter Lizzie's age.

Fuzz again.

A voice woke me again, "Your legs are pinned. We have to break the windshield completely through to pull off the dash.

We'll lay this sheet over you so the glass won't cut you." At least they had been talking about me, not Claire. Where was she?

Too many words. I didn't have enough energy to speak. Someone draped a heavy cotton cloth over my face and shoulders. I heard the sharp crack of glass, and a familiar voice, loud, anguished, crying out, "Alex. No," then Brett's sobbing, convulsing, the weeping of a man. I imagined his body crumpling to the ground like broken glass. The crying stopped—hopefully one of the paramedics held him up, explained why the sheet was laid over me, not because I was dead but to get my body out of the car without glass ripping through more of my skin.

Then again, nothing.

I woke, being placed onto a stretcher. I heard the beating, rhythmic cutting of a chopper, felt its wind slapping my face, whipping hair into my eyes. The cool sharp metal of scissors trailed down my side, slicing my bra and shirt, my shorts, until I was lying completely naked under a thin cotton sheet. My flip flops were gone. I felt my body lifting upwards, into the helicopter.

I heard movement and felt Brett near me. "Alex, I think—"

"Stay with Lizzie and Claire. I'll be okay," I said in a voice I didn't recognize, so tired and low.

He squeezed my foot, and the door banged shut. The helicopter ascended into the sky while the rhythmic sound of the propeller lulled me back to unconsciousness.

I woke again in the helicopter. A man asked about pain. "Yes, my arm. My head. My knee." I felt a strong hand lift my arm slightly, turning it over, examining. Then set it back down on the hard surface of the stretcher.

When the beating rhythm of the helicopter crawled to a stop, I regained consciousness. My stretcher wheeled in through nervous, squealing doors, and the smell—the sterile hospital smell, the antiseptic, and the cold blast from the air conditioner—rushed over me.

"Do you know anything about my children? Are they okay?" I asked the person whose footsteps were all I knew of him, whoever's hand was attached to my stretcher as it sped through the corridors. I had hoped it was the same paramedic from the helicopter.

"I just spoke to someone at the accident scene," he said. "They're both en route to State Children's Hospital—your baby is being Life-Flighted there and your husband went with the older one in the ambulance. I don't know anything more. I'll try to call over and find out if they've arrived yet."

"Thanks." My voice was slurred. My stomach ached at the thought of Claire alone in that harsh loud helicopter. "What time is it?" I asked the same paramedic adjusting his portable transmitter, trying to call someone on the other end.

"Almost noon."

"Claire's diaper needs to be changed. Can you make sure they . . ." I was slipping again.

"Don't worry," he said. "They know what they're doing. They take care of babies all the time."

But I couldn't follow him. My body was being lifted and transitioned to a bed. I was still covered with the thin sheet and began shivering. The hairs were rising on my arms. An invisible hand laid heavy, heated blankets over me. Another invisible hand poked an IV into my arm. Then a sharp poke, a shot injected into my forehead. More invisible hands tugged slivers of glass from my forehead. I felt the pressure, the movement, but it was painless—I felt like the plastic guy in the Operation game I played as a child as we yanked bones and organs out of him, flat and inconsequential.

My eyes remained closed and my thoughts ran back to Claire. I recoiled at the thought of my baby being placed onto a steely, hard, unwelcoming stretcher as I had been. Was she frightened?

Although the pain was gone, I winced and shook while the doctors worked. I was nervous and jittery and couldn't hold my foot still, couldn't control or still its shooting movement. A man came over and gripped my hand. "Squeeze if it helps." A deep voice from the blackness. I latched onto his hand, as I used to with Brett when I'd get blood taken. The touch of another man—besides Brett—felt foreign to me. My mind ran through the memory of the first time Brett touched me, his hand on my arm after directing the Noel Coward play. I remembered the first boy who held my hand when I was in fifth grade, I thought I remembered his name was Bobby, and my thoughts swam back to the owner of this detached strong hand, who I reasoned was probably a student observer feeling idle, observing the bloody pile of glass growing on the operating table. I didn't care why he offered it; I needed to borrow his strength.

The doctor laced thread through my skin, as if I were some home-economics sewing project. I could feel my skin stretching upwards, the thread pulling. I was a voodoo doll being poked, the pain being deposited somewhere else, on someone else, or maybe stored away for later.

My body drifted from room to room. At one point, I felt myself shifting forward and back in a hollow tunnel. X-rays, CT scans, MRIs. I wasn't sure what they were doing. They probably told me, and maybe I nodded or blinked as the words streamed through my head. A hot fluid entered my body through the IV, lava flowing through my arm up into my throat then down, down, all the way to my groin. I dismissed the feeling that I'd wet myself. Not enough energy to care. A deep monotone computerized voice told me, "Take a breath. Release it. Take another breath. Then hold." I attempted to follow the voice's instructions but was overwhelmed, distracted, weak.

I was moved to a hospital room. A large male nurse guided my gurney through the hospital corridors. He left me lying on the gurney, while he fidgeted with his watch, in the room. He finished with his watch and pulled the sheet down to the foot of the bed. He rolled the gurney until it was flush with the bed, then lifted, rolled me. I heard the sound of tiny chips of glass drizzling onto the bed before he laid me on it. The glass bore into my naked back. He whistled as he pushed the gurney toward the door, then waltzed to the sink and washed his hands, lathering, taking his time. I was cold and leaned toward the sheet. He turned back, saw me struggling, then continued rubbing his hands. I finally pinched the edge of the sheet with my fingers and drew the flimsy sheet over me. I let myself drift back to sleep—a real sleep this time, longer than the minute intervals from earlier.

The rest of the day and the night I saw and felt bits and pieces—my best friend Sammy's anxious face, the warmth of a familiar strong hand on my face and neck as I slept, nurses checking my vitals, some familiar faces—relatives of Brett's, people Brett worked with, a couple friends from the neighborhood. Did I speak to them at all? Or did they sidle in and watch me sleeping, deposit things on the table, and leave?

Late the next morning, the door opened and Sammy walked in and slumped into the bedside chair. Her chin-length hair coiffed perfectly in place, make-up on, she crossed her legs and fiddled with some beads on her flip-flops. "I've been waiting out there to see you for a couple hours."

"How did you know?" My voice was scratchy and weak. I licked my chapped lips and looked around for some water.

Sammy jumped up, fled into the bathroom where I could hear cabinets slamming, then water running. She walked out with a glass of water and a wet white hand towel. She sat down next to me, tipping the glass toward my mouth, like a mother helping a small child. Setting down the glass, she leaned toward me, held my left arm, and began wiping it. I looked down and saw my arm freckled with blood.

"I saw the twelve o'clock news yesterday," Sammy said. "I didn't recognize your car and they wouldn't say any names, but my phone rang off the hook. News travels fast. I got a sitter and drove right over. Do you remember seeing me? You weren't much there." She paused, not making eye contact, and stopped trying to scrub the blood. She placed the damp towel on the table in defeat. It wasn't just surface blood on my arm; each speck was a tiny cut. I buried my arm under the sheet so I wouldn't have to see it.

Her voice slowly punctuated each word as she said, "I went by State Children's first. They wouldn't let me see Claire, but I saw Lizzie."

"What's going on there?" I asked. "Nobody will tell me anything. You have to tell me what's going on. Please." No one would give me straight answers. I had received the generic answer: "They're doing everything they can," from the doctors and nurses who were treating me.

"I saw Brett, but he couldn't tell me anything."

"Sammy, could you do me a favor? I can still feel glass digging into my back. You've got to get it." My body ached as I yanked on the bed rail to pull myself forward. She rinsed the same white towel under the sink and stroked down my back. I'd never understood why these hospital gowns never cover your back, just that flimsy string holding everything together. One slip of the knot and you're completely exposed.

As Sammy wiped my back, a woman walked in—maybe a nurse supervisor or social worker. Either way, she announced, "You're being released. We'd like to keep you here for another night, but you need to be at State Children's with your daughter." She was holding a clipboard and handed me several pages of prescriptions. Muscle relaxers, pain killers, sleeping pills—I flipped through them casually, as if I were reading a useless *People* magazine waiting for check-out at a grocery store.

"Can I call my husband? I haven't talked to him yet." I don't know why I was asking permission from this stranger to call my husband. She motioned toward a mustard-yellow telephone—like the one I had at my house as a child, from the '70s—on the table next to me.

"Just dial nine to get out." She looked up from her chart and turned to leave.

I picked up the receiver of the phone, then quickly placed it back. "Excuse me. I don't have any clothes. The paramedics cut them off."

"Oh," she said as if she hadn't realized.

"I've got a sweatshirt in my car, if that helps," Sammy offered.

The nurse said, "I'll see what I can do about getting you some pants." Then walked out the door.

Picking up the receiver, I dialed Brett's cell phone number. It rang several times before the voice mail picked up. "I wonder if there's a phone book here, to get the number to State Children's," I said, placing the bulky phone back on the receiver.

Sammy pulled a phone book from a drawer, read out loud the number. I called, stumbled through a conversation with an efficient-sounding woman who sent my call through. The phone rang once, then Brett's hollow voice, "Hello." Sammy gestured just-a-minute with her finger as she slipped out of my hospital room.

"Brett. It's me."

"Alex, you're awake."

"What's going on over there? How's Lizzie? How's Claire? Have you been able to see her? Is Lizzie scared? Is everyone okay?" I rambled the questions off like a machine gun, shooting one question after the next, afraid to stop talking, afraid to hear the answers.

"Alex, listen. Lizzie is fine. I'm with her. All she has is a couple of stitches on the top of her head and some scrapes on her arms and legs." He laughed here, "And she's got My Little Pony Band-aids all over herself. It's not as bad as it looks though." I smiled, thinking of Lizzie, picturing her with Band-aids trailing up and down her body, then sighed, thinking about Band-aids and their magical healing quality in a child's eyes. We went through box after box of Band-aids, putting them on her when there was no cut. Their ability to make her stop crying was indeed magical.

Brett hesitated and then his voice was hushed, like a whisper, "But Claire. She's in intensive care. It's her brain. It's swollen. They're worried. The social worker here has been working to get you released so that you can come over here and spend time with Claire. Are you coming?"

That should have been a red flag—I should have known. But I was naïve and thought that things would be all right, they had to be. Normal people don't lose their children. That's only something you hear about happening to someone else. It never happens to you.

The woman came back with a pair of light-blue scrub bottoms with a faded hospital logo. "It's the best I can do."

They looked comfortable; I nodded. Sammy returned several minutes later, holding out a Duke sweatshirt for me.

I inched out of the hospital bed, my body aching as the drugs wore off. I shuffled into the bathroom and glimpsed myself walking past the mirror. "Sammy!" I yelled. Her shoes padding toward the bathroom. "How can you just talk to me like everything is normal when my face looks like this?" My forehead was completely covered with blue-threaded stitches and dried blood. My left eye was surrounded by a puffy blue and purple ring.

Sammy came in and put her arm around me, "You mean that little scratch?"

Sammy drove me to State Children's Hospital, while I reclined my seat and closed my eyes. No energy to speak after making the journey out to the parking lot.

My mind drifted to yesterday—when Lizzie, Claire, and I cut and colored, creating a playhouse out of a refrigerator cardboard box a neighbor was throwing out and offered us. We made a moving door, windows, even a sunroof. Their little fists clenched around fat magic markers—blue, red, orange, green, purple— the girls left their scribbled marks over the walls of the playhouse. Lizzie dragged a blanket inside, pink with white kittens, and spread it on the floor. Lizzie and Claire drifted in and out of the playhouse all day, carting dolls and stuffed animals into the house, lined them up in a row against the wall, picture books piled in the corner.

The house had been unusually quiet as I wiped the counter after lunch, the stillness that mothers innately know isn't good, isn't right. I ran through the house calling their names, checking the closets, the bathrooms. I checked the front-door, relieved it was still locked.

"Where are you?" I shouted and then heard them, whispering and giggling, "shhhh" from the cardboard box. Claire's tiny fingers gripped the window, her eyes peeking out, then she disappeared. I slunk to all fours and crawled to the front door, poking my head inside. "Gotcha," I laughed, as Claire leaned into me, arms stretched so I'd hold her. I squeezed inside the house— I hadn't exactly had adult entrance in mind when I'd sized the door—and sat Indian-style on the floor, Claire perched contentedly on my lap.

"Mommy, read me this, please." Lizzie pushed a book toward me. I shifted Claire to one leg while Lizzie settled onto the other, then read. The Very Hungry Caterpillar. They listened intently, as my voice pitched through the same rhythm I'd read hundreds of times. I felt a tingle in my shoulders, through my skin, that I was satisfied with my world. I was having one of those moments— a perfect moment—that only comes along every so often, especially when you're bogged down with diaper-changing and folding laundry. I knew it wouldn't last. As I snapped the book shut, I'd wished it were a longer story.

Sammy's car crawled to a complete stop; we were in the parking lot of the hospital. "Stay put," Sammy ordered, as if I could have easily gotten on my feet and walked in, just like that. She rolled a wheelchair to the side of the car. I heaved my body from the passenger seat into the wheelchair. Sammy guided me to the hospital's side entrance, then up the elevator to the third floor. We found Lizzie's room empty, but the nurses directed us to a waiting room where Brett and his friends and coworkers, even some of his relatives who lived around Portland, were seated around the table. As soon as Sammy wheeled me into the room, Brett turned and jumped up, darting toward me. He burrowed his head into my neck, whimpering. I grasped him on his neck as everyone in the room turned away, giving us the little privacy they could.

"Mommy," Lizzie shouted, looking up from coloring in an oversized coloring book. Several of Brett's cousins' children surrounded her, busily coloring their own pictures. Lizzie was wearing a white, glittery tutu edged with marabou feathers. She discarded her crayon on the table and squirmed between Brett and me, breaking our hold onto each other, settling on my lap. I hugged her, asking, "Where did you get that tutu?"

"Lana brought it for me." Lizzie pointed to Brett's cousin. "They cut up my other tutu," she pouted. I smiled and held up her arm, lined with My Little Pony Band-aids, just as Brett had described.

"They cut my clothes too. Did you get some cuts?" I asked her, gliding my hand on her arm, ever so carefully over her row of Band-aids.

"Yeah." Her eyes focused on my forehead. "Mommy, you've got a big ouchie. You need a really big Band-aid. They have so many here. Maybe you could get a sparkly one." She paused, "Do you need a kiss?"

"Yes, sweetie. I think I do," I said. She leaned up to my forehead and kissed my temple, near the wound, but not on it, and then squirmed off my lap, back to her coloring book.

I looked up at Brett and said, "I want to see Claire."

"I've got to get back. The sitter could only stay until one," Sammy said, releasing the handles of the wheelchair, nudging it toward Brett to take over. She kissed me on the top of my head.

Brett grabbed hold of the wheelchair. "Alex, I have to warn you," he said, wheeling me to the ICU. "Claire isn't doing well. Claire was hit directly. Her skull cracked."

"I need to see her." We stopped moving before large steel double doors. Brett picked up a phone on the wall and indicated we were Claire Porter's parents. The doors flung open automatically, as if opened by ghosts, and Brett wheeled me in. I was accosted with harsh, repetitive beeping and the whir of machines. Sterile and cold. Little islands of machinery and beds were scattered around the silver room. Brett turned the wheelchair left and stopped me in front of where a nurse hovered over my sleeping baby. An air-filled heated blanket, like an inflatable pool mat, draped over her little body. Claire was naked, but for a diaper. Brett carefully pulled me to stand. My legs were unsteady, and I gripped the side of Claire's bed.

She lay on the raised small bed, lifeless, motionless—everything *less*—and my stomach clenched. She had several rows of staples—rows of teeth in a shark's mouth—punched into her forehead, each row holding her skin together. Below the bottom row, which stopped an inch above her eyebrow, her face was perfect. But for a little swelling, exactly as before. As beautiful as before.

And a scab on her lip. Her body was untouched, not a scratch or a cut. Her skin was pulled taut from swelling. Otherwise, perfect. Her outie bellybutton, that I had kissed each time she'd come out of a bath, was the same. Perfect.

Brett pointed at a monitor and explained, "This number tells us what level her brain pressure's at. Normal is somewhere around twelve. Her brain pressure was at 75 earlier, but it's down to 40 now. It needs to keep coming down."

I nodded that I understood, but couldn't take my eyes from Claire's sleeping, peaceful face as I reached for her hand. It lay tiny and limp inside mine. I wanted to get closer, to hold her, but wires and tubes and IVs weaved around her. I inched closer, but the nurse turned around and said, "You can't hold her." She must have realized how rigid she sounded because she continued, softer, "She's not in any pain. She's highly medicated and she's being kept asleep, to help reduce the brain pressure." I nodded again like a child, and the nurse turned to check the IV solution.

I felt so useless. All I could do was hold her hand. If only I could extend my aching body, give her a light kiss on her perfect rosy cheek.

Of course she was going to be okay. I wanted to talk to her, soothe her, but I found my voice wouldn't even come. After standing there silent for what seemed like an hour, I broke down, the weak weeping mother, the only noise that reached her ears was my gushed sobs. Brett caught me as I started to fall, then helped me back into the wheelchair. How could I have let this happen? Brett wheeled me back through the large, steel doors, out of the ICU.

I couldn't stay in this place. I couldn't help. My body ached. I wanted to burrow into my bed, pull the sheets over my head, and sleep, sleep as if today never happened. As the doors clamped shut, my voice finally came, "Take me home."

We got Lizzie from the waiting room, Brett rolled me out to his car. We left, leaving Claire alone in the hard, cold hospital.

Lizzie went right to bed, and Brett left to travel the hour back to the hospital. Minutes after he left, Sammy arrived at my front door. She put a chair before the bathroom sink, where I sat and leaned my head back, the counter's edge digging into my neck, while warm water rushed through my hair and Sammy's fingers carefully massaged shampoo into my hair.

She toweled my hair and helped me into bed. I acquiesced and followed her, like a child afraid on a dark night. She sat in the reading chair in my room, lit only by the lamp, and read aloud while I tried to drift to sleep. She'd planned to leave after I fell asleep, to go back to her kids. But I couldn't sleep. I couldn't shake the image of Claire's helpless body being forced to sleep. After nearly an hour, I feigned sleeping, focusing on breathing at rhythmic intervals, so she could leave. She closed the book, turned the lamp off, and crept out of my room.

My eyes flicked open after she left. I couldn't stay in this bed. I knew I wouldn't sleep—lying on my right side, then stomach, then left side, then back—only to start the rotation over again. I didn't have the peace, or the blank mind, that sleep required. I rolled out of bed and made my way across the dark hallway into Claire's room. The light glowed from the living room.

Sitting on the carpet in Claire's room, just a slither of light spilling in from the living room, I stared into the open closet, looking up at her line of clothes, trying to figure out by process of elimination what clothes I'd put on Claire yesterday morning. Which carefully chosen outfit had been cut off her today, matted with blood, lying in a trashcan somewhere?

It had seemed like years ago. I couldn't remember, and I finally gave up. I wanted to dissolve, to disintegrate into the floor. I rolled myself into fetal position and, tears dripping onto the carpet, wept loud sobs and clawed at the carpet. The wretched noises I heard escaping my body seemed detached from me.

The hallway light flicked on, and I froze. Sammy rushed in and knelt by my side. As I wept, she rocked me back and forth. I was a baby, being rocked to sleep. I whispered over and over from the dark corner of the room, where the light from the hallway couldn't reach, "I can't lose my baby."

I woke up in my bed the next morning and remembered Claire would not be calling to me from her crib.

Brett's cousin swung by the house early to take me back to the hospital. A neighbor was watching Lizzie. I packed a bag of books that Claire liked; I wanted to read to her. Today, I would be stronger.

Little had changed. Her brain pressure was a little better. My mother had flown in from Seattle that morning. Without feeling, I hugged her, like a corpse, my eyes glazed over. Some of Brett's aunts and cousins were scattered throughout the waiting room.

When I saw Claire still lying in her induced sleep, a different nurse looming above her, I pulled the picture books out of my bag and attempted to read to her. I sang songs she knew from bedtime, a fall-time song my mother's grandmother used to sing to her, which she sang to me as a child. *Come said the wind to the leaves one day. Come over the meadow with me and play. Put on your cloak of red and gold. Nights are long and days are cold. Fa-la-la-la-la.* My voice thin and squeaking, I felt exposed and defeated in front of the omnipresent nurse. It came to nothing. They were simply empty words and lullabies, unheard and useless.

I'd wanted Claire's brain pressure to change, even a little, when Claire heard my voice. She would try to wake, break through the drugs that kept her sleeping. Maybe even reach those soft little fingers up to me, to hold her. As I stood there, listening to the rhythmic beeping of the life-support machine and her assisted breathing, I tried to break through the blackness and remember what had happened at the intersection. I could only remember the song that was playing in the car, Lizzie and Claire both singing. Nothing else would come. I realized no one had even told me what had happened. Did I pull out in front of the other car? Was it a green light, yellow, red? Did the other car run a red light? Did I?

What did it matter? No knowledge was going to change that I was now waiting in a hospital, to find out whether or not my daughter was going to live, whether or not she would go to preschool one day or ever ride a bike. As I grappled for these visions, my arms swung above me, and I was grabbing at little bits of paper. Each with a separate dream I had for her, a hopeful future moment, an expectation. The wind blew these folded pages from me, higher to where I couldn't reach them. I jumped and ran, but these fluttered up to the sky like butterflies, dangling just out of reach. Unobtainable, fleeting.

I wasn't sure how long I'd dozed off. Probably just a moment. But at that moment, I knew. As I looked into her still face, it held no future. I had the strangest feeling that she was there, hovering around her body, but not inside it. Her heart may still be beating, but she wasn't there.

Brett was so hopeful that she was going to pull through, so I didn't tell him. But I knew. I slept by her side, on and off throughout the day. Each time I awoke, I hoped something changed. Nothing did.

My sister arrived the next day. She coddled me, brought me things, held food to my mouth, kept her arm around me, but I stood upright and hard, a statue. Not knowing what to say, what to do.

I awoke that morning after drifting off in the hospital with one of my eyes sealed shut with mucus. When I cleared it all away, with the help of my sister, I realized a surfacing tiny grain of glass was dislodged and loose in my eye. I couldn't swipe it out. Brett tried to flush it out with saline, but it sat there, obscuring my view, making me cry. It reminded me of a fairytale, The Snow Queen, I had read to Lizzie. In it, the young boy Kay was plunged in the heart—causing half his heart to freeze—by a shattered piece of magic mirror that caused good things reflected in it to become small and mean, and bad things to become magnified and worse, every flaw apparent. He'd also had a speck of it in his eye, changing how he viewed the world. I wondered if some glass had unknowingly plunged through my heart as well. I felt like it had.

Claire's brain pressure increased.

The doctors requested a "meeting." Three doctors, my mom, Brett's parents, and Brett and I sat on hard chairs as the doctors explained in hushed tones, "Your baby is dying. We think it's time. On the chance she does pull through this—though we think it's highly unlikely—she would have no brain function. But ultimately, it's your decision. You tell us what you want to do."

Brett's parents asked some questions, about the likelihood of her recovering if we kept the machines going. The answer was something low. I couldn't listen. I just gazed ahead at them—these experts coming in with their life-shattering expert opinions.

After a while, the doctors filed out, while we sat on the hard vinyl chairs.

"Alex," Brett put his hand on my knee, rubbed back and forth a minute, then pulled his hand back into his lap. "I can't read you. Did you hear what they said?"

"I just want to hold my baby," I said. I needed her in my arms at that moment. Nothing else mattered.

"You know the nurses won't let you." He moved his head in front of my face so I'd see him instead of the vinyl floor. I blurred him out too and rubbed my left eye, then my right. "Do you want to keep hoping?" he said. "I think she could still pull through. I think we should give it another night."

Brett's parents and my mom stood uncomfortably and shuffled out the door, leaving us to talk.

"This needs to end," I said. "Her body's been through enough. Can't you tell she's not there anymore?" Finally turning my head and looking into his eyes. "I just want to hold her. Now." Brett dropped his head, looking down at his hands resting on his lap.

"Okay. I'll tell them." He stood to leave. He paused with his hand on the knob, as if he were going to say something, then turned the knob and shook his head slowly. He left through the door, leaving me trapped in the room alone, sterile and empty and cold like the icy walls of the Snow Queen's palace.

An hour later, as Brett and I stood side-by-side, silent and just watching Claire, the nurse brought in a rocking chair. She motioned me toward it. And I sat. When Claire was born, I'd sat in a nearly identical wooden rocking chair at the hospital to nurse her for the first time. I remembered the nurse bringing Claire to me then, crying and alert, begging for food. Now the nurse brought Claire's sleeping body to me, still attached to tubes. And I rocked her dead weight, back and forth. Her body still and heavy. Her eyes closed. I held her body close to me. I kissed her cheek, her nose, her chin. I whispered, "I love you, my little Bear," still not giving up on the idea that the words would break through the frozen barrier, penetrate, that she would hear me and wake.

The machine was still breathing for her. I held her as I did when she was newborn, cradled in the crook of my arm. She'd never let me hold her like that when she was awake, always wiggling out of my arms. But occasionally, she would fall asleep in my arms, and I'd hold her still, afraid to move so I wouldn't wake her. Now I wished I could wake her. But memory came over me, and I rocked her, a fluid motion back and forth, smooth as water.

Our families came in. They walked in timidly and circled around us. A neighbor had driven Lizzie to the hospital, and now Lizzie tagged along with the bereavement lady, who had no doubt been paged to be with us when the machines stopped. Lizzie followed her and "helped" create a hand mold from Claire's swollen fingers, dipping her hand in a creamy plaster while it dangled motionless from where I held her. Like an ice sculpture of her swollen hand that would never melt.

Maybe when they released the cords, I thought, Claire would breathe on her own, beating the machines, the doctors' assessment. But she didn't take one breath on her own. And just like that, I was holding my child's corpse. The rosy hue drained from her cheeks. The rocker creaked slowly to nothing. Still.

Chapter Seven

Shock numbed me through those first days. Not the pain killers. Not tranquilizers, which I refused when the doctor suggested them. I floated through those blistering days—as if I wasn't contained in my own body, my reflection in the mirror not recognizable.

I sifted through stacks of sympathy cards from neighbors, friends of my parents, cousins I hadn't seen since childhood—everyone dutifully signing and stamping an envelope, with sympathy. Some even sent helpful reading material, books and pamphlets about support groups I could join, how to cope with loss, grief. *When Bad Things Happen to Good People.* That stuff. I put them aside, stacked them away on shelves, in niches, for later.

Plants and flowers overtook my house, hanging green leaves, pumping oxygen into the air between the blank walls I stared at all day.

And the nights were unbearable, torturing me with the image of Claire's emotionless face and motionless body lying in the hospital.

But mostly my head filled with questions of everything I'd done as a mother—wondering why I hadn't done things differently. I shouldn't have lain in bed, waiting for her pleading screams to silence as she settled back to sleep in the darkest minutes of the night. They were vacant moments passed on by a selfish mother. If only I'd been a different type of mother.

At the beginning, Brett cried with me. We lay in bed, our faces inches apart, his breath cool on my wet cheeks, our knees tucked up and touching. "Do you remember when we found

Claire's shoes in the refrigerator? She was hysterical when she realized they were gone—wouldn't listen to her bedtime stories, wouldn't go to bed until we found them. She was more attached to those shoes than any stuffed animal in her crib. She couldn't sleep without them."

I smiled through tears, and said, "We searched the entire house. And there they were, tucked in with the cheese sticks in the dairy drawer. I still don't know how they got there."

Normally scorning sentimentality, I had nothing else to share with Brett. It was either this or hatred for whatever unfeeling god did this to me.

We talked about the futile teeth that had just poked through Claire's gums days before the accident, the way she woke up in the morning shouting happily from her crib most mornings, always carrying those silly pink shoes to me to put on so that she could take them right off again.

On nights when my crying was especially loud, sobbing, like a baby wakened in a black night anxious for a mother's reaching arms, Brett would pull me from the bed and lead me through the house, careful to not bump into anything, and tried to go quietly into the night. I curled up in Brett's lap, and cried, the crying sucking all my energy with its sheer volume, leaving me not enough energy to sit up. After the heaving ceased, Brett guided me back through the dark house into bed, tucked me into cold sheets.

It felt like a punishment that we had to prepare a funeral service at the most cluttered, unclear days of my life. There were also appointments at the mortuary. The first time we walked through the cold glass doors into the over-air-conditioned foyer, a white-haired man wearing a stuffy pin-striped gray suit led us into a room and showed us several pages in a catalogue of tiny caskets. A tragedy that these several pages had to be created at all.

We chose a white wooden casket with fluted edges. Two feet long should be the right size, the mortuary worker assured us. "I need this satin in white, no flowers." I couldn't imagine anyone using the obnoxious print pictured with the casket in the catalogue. "And the casket will be closed," I said, bracing Brett with my eyes.

I'd always felt intrusive snatching a glimpse of a body lying in a casket at the few funerals I'd been to—my great grandmother when I was a kid, great Uncle Rich. It seemed unfeeling, sick. Almost as bad as the throngs of people crowding around to see a person hanged or guillotined. Morbid. No one would be gawking at my baby.

Before we left, the man asked us if we wanted to dress Claire. "Yes," I answered shaking my head no to whatever unfeeling mortuary worker would be putting his hands on her if I said no. I wouldn't let a stranger dress her. "I want to be the one to do it. We'll do it."

We returned the next day. Early that morning, I'd stood at the mouth of her closet, fingering the soft pink and yellow and lavender clothes hanging useless from their hangers, like mocking reproductions of my daughter, arms and legs dangling, their ruffles and bows drooping. It was unnatural that these inanimate, stained pieces of cloth outlived Claire.

I'd plucked a simple cotton dress with a single pleat, sage green with the tiniest white dots, from the closet. The hanger fell from the dress; it slid onto the floor and left a jagged mark on the perfect vacuum lines in the carpet. A phantom was cleaning the house since we returned from the hospital. There was a small oval stain on the fabric of the dress, just above the pleat, a subtle deeper shade of green—where Claire had dropped some food the last time she wore it. I think it was the cherries I'd pitted and squeezed into the blender, my fingertips bleeding the juice. She loved cherries. This cherry stain held proof that she'd existed, she'd eaten. Yes, that was the right dress.

Several hours later at the mortuary, we were guided to a room where Claire's body was lying on a table. I walked to her and looked down, touched her fingers, almost expecting them to tighten around mine. When they didn't, I stroked her cold palm. I looked at her face, eyes shut, which could have been her napping but for the orange make-up smeared on her face. "We said closed casket," I told Brett, as I stood rigid above Claire.

Brett pulled the dress from my bag and laid it softly on the table, pulling the snaps open. He lifted her body, a porcelain doll. I turned toward him and put my arms underneath, trying to help support her.

This was quite unlike the way we dressed her a week ago—more like dressing a doll, unbending arms and legs and torso. We couldn't pull the dress over her head and work down, but instead had to work our way up. Holding her brick body at an angle, we pulled the dress over her legs and continued up, struggling to get the arms through the sleeves. Then laid her back onto the table.

I pulled a soft-bristled brush from the bag and stroked her fine, short brown hair. Then added a little pink barrette near her forehead and put the pink shoes on her feet—the same ones she carried around the house and slept with at night. Brett had found them discarded beneath the seat in our car after it had been towed to the junkyard.

We worked in silence. Brett nudged me and gestured to the casket resting on a table in the corner. I opened it and winced. The bright floral print covered the interior. "I am not laying my baby in this," I told Brett. "Go get someone."

He left the room and returned with a different, younger man—yet still in a suit—who said he'd take care of the problem right away. He carted the casket out of the room. We stood near Claire's body and waited. No words. Just looked at her.

He returned with a different fabric, with tiny yellow flowers. "I said I wanted a solid white satin. This isn't what I asked for. Do I have to go do it myself?"

Brett glared at me, then spoke calmly to the man, "I'm sorry. Do you have white satin?" I stood with my arms across my chest and shook my head as the man took the casket out again.

When the casket was returned, I said nothing, nodded approval of the white, and waited for the man to leave before Brett and I lifted Claire's body together. He held her shoulders and I her lower legs, and placed her inside. Her legs barely fit into the casket. We had to push on her feet, bend her knees, cramped, to make her fit inside. I turned away. When I turned back, Brett saw the anger in my face and his eyes bore into me, pleading with me to relax. I flattened her little dress, so that it laid perfectly, as if readying her for a photo. I wrapped a blanket, her purple chenille blanket, around her waist and tucked it under her legs and feet. Methodically, like a mother does to keep the baby's feet warm, keep the baby from kicking a blanket off during sleep. But I did it anyway. I didn't know any other way.

I kissed her cheek before I left and waited for Brett in the hallway, the chill still lingering on my lips. I wish I had known then how I'd be tormented about Claire's cramped legs. If I had known I'd dream of digging up her coffin to switch it out—mud in my fingernails, her face just as I remembered it, but her arms and legs just bones—I would have demanded a larger casket right then.

The evening before the funeral, a kid came by our house and knocked on the door. He was young, early 20s, and had long blond hair tied in the back and wore Wranglers with cowboy boots. I opened the door, and he walked in clutching a fistful of flowers held together by a paper ribbon, his mouth clenched together and his face red, as if scrubbed with a Brillo pad by his mother. He handed the flowers to me, looking around the house, probably trying to take in who we were, who this kind of stuff happens to. "I'm Mike. I was at the accident scene."

I led him into the family room and gestured toward the couch, "Sit down, please." I sat opposite him. He nodded and waved toward the hallway while Lizzie peered around the corner from her room. My mother had been reading a book to her, putting her to bed. Lizzie never could ignore a knock on the door, always needing to know who was there. "Good night, Lizzie." She ran over and hugged me, kissed me on the face, then ran back to her room.

He sat fidgeting, looking around the house, nodded over to Brett and his father and some of his cousins who were sitting in the kitchen, picking at a deli tray.

"I'm sorry about your daughter," he said. He was staring at a framed picture of Lizzie and Claire from Christmas, in matching velvet burgundy dresses. "I stuck around after I saw those two trucks plow into you. I wanted to help. I used to be an EMT. I opened your baby's air passage before the paramedics came."

I pursed my lips, watched his nervous eyes darting. He saw Claire while she was still alive. This punk kid, cowboy wannabe, a stranger, was one of the last people Claire saw before she fell asleep and never woke again. I choked out several words, "I don't remember—anything."

"You don't remember? Yeah, I was at that intersection, waiting at the red light, and I saw these two trucks, both of 'em speeding, one in the suicide lane, trying to merge over, the other wouldn't let 'em, racing, and the one in the middle lane had to get over, but didn't in time, hit you on the driver's side, spun you around, then the other truck ran into the side where your baby was." He stopped to take a much-needed breath. "I didn't know then, that there was a baby there, but when the light turned green, I pulled over, like I said, and got out, thought I might be some help, you know with my EMT training, and that's when I saw your baby. How she couldn't breathe, then I just opened her mouth, cleared the passage, and waited till the paramedics came."

"Was she awake?" I asked.

"No. But I did see her open her eyes once, let out a whimper, then pass back out. She had real pretty eyes. She sure was pretty," he said and nodded up to the picture hanging on the wall.

"Yeah, she was." I wanted to get away from him. I should have appreciated him, that he cared to come by the house, offer a token, but I just wanted him out of my house. "I need to use the restroom. Are you hungry? Want a sandwich?" I gestured toward the kitchen where Brett and the others sat talking quietly.

"Don't mind if I do," he said. He sauntered to the kitchen. I rushed out of the room before I heard him introduce himself to Brett and locked myself in the closet, between my long dresses and unused suits, for the next hour. I heard them talking, but I didn't come out until I heard the front door squeal open. I tiptoed out and looked around the corner, like Lizzie had an hour before. The kid saw me and said again, "I sure am sorry."

"Thanks." He walked several steps toward me, which startled me, and threw his arms around my shoulders. I hugged him, because he needed it. I found out the next day at the funeral I had to hug a lot of people because *they* needed it.

I sat through the ceremony stone-faced. The room was stuffed with overbearing, fragrant flowers and lush plants. People offered little gifts, more flowers and the softest stuffed bears, to me as they passed. So glad it wasn't them, not their kids. I felt eyes burning into the back of my head. Everyone talking about Claire as if they really knew her, but they didn't understand. Their lives weren't going to change. I was mourning myself too, knew I could never be the same person. That person was being buried along with Claire.

While the pastor spoke, I stared straight ahead, watching him and not listening, as if the mute button had been pressed. I didn't cry. Perhaps I was just dehydrated from crying on the back patio late last night.

After the service, we were ushered out to the hearse for the short drive to the cemetery in town. Climbing out of the hearse, I scoffed at the gray, foreboding rain clouds gathering overhead. Smirking as the man from the mortuary handed me, Brett, and Lizzie each a white rose. The rain fell on our heads as the priest said a few final remarks near the pre-dug hole.

The pastor opened his Bible and said, "Let us read from Job: 'Naked came I out of my mother's womb, and naked shall I return thither: the Lord gave, and the Lord hath taken away; blessed be the name of the Lord.'" I couldn't listen to this. How could we stand here and bless the Lord for taking my baby away from me?

I looked around with disgust. At the flowers, the people, the rainclouds. This moment was a cliché—dripping sky, dark umbrellas hovering over cautiously dressed people, standing semi-circled near a hole in the ground. We tossed the roses onto the casket before we left.

Sammy had a luncheon at her house after the funeral. I stood in her kitchen, chewing on a piece of ham, slowly, as if it was too much effort for the reward of eating. Sammy stayed nearby, observed random people offering their services to me. Over and over, can't we help, what can we do? After an exuberant neighbor implored again for something to do, Sammy whispered, "When the next person comes by begging for some way to help, tell her that you'd really like to have Claire's name spelled out in only pink roses, from all your arrangements." I thought of their shocked expressions—or better yet, at picturing a couple old church ladies plucking pink rose after pink rose from the vast flower arrangements—and tried to laugh, but nothing would come. Not even a smile. I could already feel my approaching days void of laughter.

I went home and lay in bed after the lunch, but didn't sleep.

Finally frustrated with even the attempt of sleep, I crawled from my bed. The house was still. So many people slept on our couches, extra beds, and even our floors in the last several days that the house was rarely empty. I lurked around the house, turning corners, and found no one. I walked to the window in the front room and looked out onto the cul-de-sac. Brett was sitting on the lawn in the corner of our yard, obscured by a tree, talking with someone. It was a friend from his work—pretty, blonde Jen. A woman he worked closely with. I knew that Brett and she were friends. I stood staring out the window for a moment, then walked into the kitchen, sat on a barstool, and studied the grain in the countertop until the door creaked opened.

At the beginning, the doorbell rang nonstop. Random people darkened the door stoop—some I knew well, some acquaintances, some people I'd never seen before. The amount of Bible-thumping women in my neighborhood, all crawling out of the woodwork now, was nauseating. They'd balance plates of paper-thin chocolate chip cookies or undercooked brownies in their palms. Shifting from side to side, they'd linger on my front step, so long that eventually I'd invite them in, to keep the flies out. They'd sit, perfectly upright like they were working on their posture, feet together, rolling a ring round and round on a finger while they asked, "How are you doing?" with their thin over-lined lips firmly pressed together.

I'd repeat, "The best I can," uncomfortable, laughing, "At least I'm getting out of bed each morning," then they'd audibly sigh.

After we exhausted all reasonable conversation, the surface talk, they'd stutter-step to the front door, to the safety outside. I'd thank whoever it was for caring and for bringing comestibles. Then close the front door, turn the lock, and promptly toss the cookies or brownies or whatever into the trashcan. Smelling its rotting odor several days later as I lugged the garbage outside.

A woman from a couple houses down appeared at the doorstep one afternoon. We didn't know each other well, I took to simply waving to her—to most of my neighbors—while gardening or out at the mailbox. She wore a lavender cotton jumper and her hair ashy blond, curled perfectly under at her shoulders, her bangs thick and ending at her eyebrows. After she was uncomfortably seated across from me and had given her deepest condolences, she asked, "What do you want?"

Startled by her question, I answered slowly, unsure, "I want my baby back." That was all I wanted. I felt the aching emptiness of my arms, their uselessness, yearning to feel the warm weight of my baby against them.

She shook off my answer with impatience, obviously not the answer she hoped for, and asked again, "Dig deeper into your soul. She can't come back now. What do you want from God?"

I didn't want anything else from God but to have my baby back, but I knew that repeating the truth would irritate the woman. What did she want me to say? *Just tell me what you want me to say*, I thought, *and I'll say it, then usher you promptly to the front door.* "I guess peace."

Bingo. "Yes, peace. You need to pray. God can give you peace." She smiled smugly, with the self-importance of a child knowing all the correct answers. She nodded, reiterating, "Get down on your knees, and peace will come."

"Yes, that should do it." I saw Lizzie walk from her room where she'd been playing. "Lizzie, are you hungry? I'm sorry, I've got to get Lizzie her afternoon snack. Thanks for stopping by." I stood, signaling the end of this conversation. She shuffled to my front door satisfied. I could imagine her bragging to her friends at their weekly Bible study group that she'd saved me, that she was my crutch in this ailing journey, those would be her words. I could already hear her squeaky, self-righteous voice over weak coffee and stale shortbread cookies with raspberry filling.

One by one everyone left. They left their flowers and plants and cakes, and they moved on. I found Claire's room empty and clean—all of her things stashed away in a plastic bin in the attic. My mom's idea, to stay busy. She and my sister would just clean out the room, help me out, save me from having to put them away, save me from having to deal with it. This was just like my mom. She was doing was she needed, but what about what I needed? I needed to see Claire still here. I needed pieces of her around my house. The more this brewed in my mind, the more I despised my mother for sweeping up the last Cheerios Claire had thrown onto the floor, picking up the toys she'd left out, putting away the crib, washing the dirty clothes left in her laundry basket. I wanted to drown in her dirty clothes and smell them, leave them forever untouched. I wanted her to stop picking up the mess and return home. She finally did.

I stayed curled in my bed long after Brett left for work. My days were filled walking back and forth through my house like it was the first time I'd been there. Bumping into furniture that was molded into the carpet from years of being there. My eyes glazed over, not focusing. Clumsy numb footsteps. Sometimes I'd climb up into the attic and sift through Claire's toys, her unworn clothes—some still bearing store tags—touching things she'd touched.

Lizzie was gone. Neighbors offered to watch her after most of the family left. At friend's houses, play dates, I wasn't sure. Every once in a while, she came home and expected things from me, like a snack or time. I sat on the floor and looked beyond her. Doing dishes, I stared out the kitchen window at the passing cars while she rolled Play-Doh into little round balls. I heard the thud, a Play-Doh ball dropping against the tile floor, and I knew she sat waiting for my reaction, to pick it up, but I couldn't look beyond my absent watching, out the window. I left it lying stubborn and changed, stuck to the floor. Eventually, she ambled to her room and closed the door.

By dark, after Lizzie was asleep, I was relieved to have stumbled through another day. Although my days wouldn't end come night. My mind was wild while I lay still in bed, searching my memory for details about the accident, trying to focus and bring back even one of the seconds I'd lost. I wondered how I would have reacted had I not blacked out, seeing the blood masking my baby's unconscious face. I thought about Lizzie screaming because she wasn't lucky enough to have been knocked unconscious, uninvited into our black world.

Brett had already gone back to work, coming home so late that I would lie stock-still, trying to feign sleep, when he ambled in at 2 am. He had begun painting again, had made a make-shift art studio in the garage where my car used to sit. I could hear him out there when I got up in the middle of the night to fill my empty glass of water, could see the slit of light filing in through the edges of the door. Just another way to be in our room less often. I was angry while he was away or out in the garage, but even angrier when he finally came to bed.

If Brett tried to talk to me or hold me, I'd slink away. I didn't want to be near him. I didn't even want his arm resting near me while he slept, or his foot grazing my leg as he shifted in bed. When he did come to bed, I rolled to the edge and would lie on my side for hours, so he wouldn't know I was awake. I'd get out of bed the next morning with a stiff shoulder.

The last time I'd been this sleep deprived was the first several months of Claire's life, when she wanted to nurse round the clock, wanting to eat more at night than day. I thought of her when she was fragile and unable to lift her neck. I'd cradled her carefully in my arms, rocking, rocking, helpless and tiny. But this time, the sleep deprivation had no reward, no smiling toddler or preschooler at the conclusion of the sleepless nights. My arms would still be empty at the end, if an end ever came.

I stumbled through days that first week, knocking and banging into nights and mornings, meals. The week could have been a month or an hour, time not acknowledged.

When I looked into the mirror, I should have been surprised with what I saw but wasn't. My forehead was a grotesque map of skin and blood and a few loose blue strings from stitches the doctor missed. I couldn't see anything but the deep crimson mass. I couldn't see myself beneath that wound and couldn't feel myself inside my body as I pulled out the scissors and dug into the wound, clipping the leftover blue threads.

Chapter Eight

The doorbell was quieter now than it had ever been. People forgot, life continued for everyone else. Even the church ladies. I watched them speeding by in their cars, taking their children to soccer or school or the park. Although I didn't want them to come by, I didn't want them to not come by. My mind was a contradiction, and I couldn't wrap it around anything.

Little pleasures from before the accident—the event that would forever bisect my life—no longer held any satisfaction. I couldn't sit and read a book, although before I'd read four to five books at any given time, stocking them each in different rooms, like an alcoholic stashing bottles around the house, to get a fix. Now I ran my eyes across the black type and found no meaning in the letters, only empty words drifting through my head and disappearing. The characters seemed flat and unfeeling, the plots mundane.

An old friend from high school sent me a spiraled notebook with chairs littering the cover, and I attempted journal writing. But a cohesive, chronological account of the last couple weeks was more than I was capable of and stopped after the first paragraph. No words fit. If I stared at the words that finally planted themselves on the page long enough, they were merely scribbled lines. I did find slight comfort in detailing morbid dreams or fragmented thoughts that flashed through my head.

A dream woke me.
It was like an old film,
grainy and silent.

I looked down
into the glass coffee table.
She had crawled underneath
and looked up at me,
smiling, a game we used to play.
I picked her up.
An odd feeling of happiness
triggered my memory,
brought back reality.
My memory killed her, there
in my arms.
She turned cold, stiff,
her eyes rolled back into her
head and she decayed in my arms.
Just a corpse from some movie.

I wandered the house. Keep moving, that's what I told myself. I rearranged the furniture. From the west side of my house to the east, I gutted each room one at a time. When one stood naked and empty, all but the pock marks left in the carpet, I began anew, bringing in one piece at a time—hauling back the couches, overstuffed chairs, bulky tables, and trunks. My own convoluted game of musical chairs. When I didn't recognize the room, it was complete and I moved on to the next.

Brett never knew what he was going to walk into—a room he'd known for years, imprinted like the lines on his palm, changed. He didn't seem to mind, probably grateful I didn't ask him to move the furniture.

Reverse.
Another dream tonight.
I found a lump at the bottom of a sleeping bag.
I panicked, knew it was Claire,
and flailed, wailed, groped her arm, pulled,
yanked her limp body
from the stifling, airless cave.
She was no longer dead.
She crawled away,
to play.

Brett decided therapy would fix me. I assumed somebody at work suggested it, perhaps his friend Jen. I knew it was meant for me, not him. Instead, I suggested a support group and found a group that met at the Red River community building on Tuesdays at six. We were one of five couples who'd lost children in the past year. Lost, as if we had misplaced or lost track of them. As if Claire had crawled off at the park or a carnival. Lost. I was the one who was lost. But I knew where the community building was. As I swept into the foyer several minutes after seven on the first night, I overheard a bewildered couple arguing. "I'm just going to ask someone where room 210 is," said a plump woman with frizzy blond hair and large round glasses that had slipped to the edge of her nose.

"No," the man said. "I know where we're going. We need the elevator. It's gotta be on the second floor. 210. Now, where's the elevator?"

I walked to the information desk and asked, "The family services room?"

The woman pointed to a set of doors on the edge of the building, "The stairs and elevator are through those doors. It's the second door on your right upstairs."

I thanked her and hurried toward the doors. The couple perked up when they heard the word elevator and scooted after me, followed me all the way, rode up the elevator with me so self-assured, as if they were showing me the way.

Ken, the husband, had a military quality—buzzed hair, cold gray eyes. He sat rigid and square, his gut hanging over his belt, while his wife continually nudged her glasses back up the hill of her nose. They sat close together and held hands during the sessions.

I couldn't remember her name, the wife, but took to thinking of her as Kendra because she didn't seem to have any thoughts of her own, she was always echoing Ken's. She was usually silent and would nod her head in agreement as Ken made blunt comments about their existing children misbehaving. Their six-year-old foster child, a boy named Tyler, strangled himself from twisting the swing around and around in the back yard. The family had some biological children, but more foster children. Ken told about losing their house because they couldn't cover their mortgage payment with losing the state money Tyler didn't bring in any longer. I decided they were in the wrong support group.

Two other couples had lost babies—one a stillborn, the other just weeks old following heart surgery. Alison, the mother of the baby born with a heart problem, explained that her whole pregnancy seemed like a dream. It was her first baby. Neither she nor the father spoke often, but when they did, they used their words sparingly, as if each were precious. You could glean more meaning from their pauses than their words.

Like a first-grade school class going around the room telling what the students did on summer vacation, we circled the room telling our child's story. When telling how they lost their child, Vivian stammered through her sentences, unable to articulate a word through her clamped jaw, her face flushed, tears flowing, chin quivering, then spit out how she found her baby girl dead in her crib early one morning. Her husband broke apart the same way. But they both looked past each other, not noticing each other sitting inches away, not responding to other's outbreaks. Staring right through.

Leslie and Richard lost their 12-year-old daughter, their only child, from leukemia after years of treatment. They didn't return after the first week.

A chaplain from State Children's Hospital drove to Red River and monitored the group. He was a skinny white-haired man named Frank who would fold his hands between his knees, stare at us with grave eyes, and make comments like "So, you're feeling sad" or "Now you think your life has changed."

"This guy's a master of the obvious," Brett once commented under his breath.

The sessions were strained and punctuated with long silences while everyone fidgeted with Kleenexes; several boxes were positioned strategically about the room. The only helpful conversations transpired after the meeting ended when several of us would walk out together on the way to our cars. We'd tell more truth during the several minutes out in the parking lot than the entire hour inside.

One week, inside the room, I told the faces what I remembered about the accident—the helicopters and the sirens—while they left their finger prints on a photograph of Claire that was making the rounds.

Ken bluntly said, "I'll bet you're glad to still be alive."

"No, I wish I could have gone too."

I guess people still don't know what to say, even when it happens to them.

An awkward hush permeated the room. I looked to Brett for reassurance. He smiled uncomfortably. I continued, "I don't mean that I'm suicidal. I'm not. This isn't a cry for help. I just don't see the point in doing this day-to-day stuff anymore. I'm not afraid of dying. It seems like the easy alternative. I don't rush across the street anymore when a car's coming. I don't wear my seatbelt."

No one spoke. I shrugged and continued twisting a Kleenex over and over until it became a hard little ball. I stood and tossed it in the trash, then grabbed a new one.

We suffered through six weeks of this, sitting down on the hard plastic chairs, munching brownie bites, waiting like Prometheus to be disemboweled, week after week after week. I was always sadder on my drive home than I was on the drive there.

But I was one of those people who never missed a class at school, so I never missed a session. Perfect attendance. I was relieved when the six weeks ended, but I didn't feel a bit more fixed. Lying in bed with Brett afterward, the still silence was sucking minutes like a waiting storm. I needed something. I reached over and slid my hand into his. He didn't speak. Several moments later, he disentangled his hand from mine and rolled away. We weren't fixed either.

My Guilt List

My friend Sammy suggested I make a list of all the things I felt guilty about and rip it up, then I'd never have to think about them again. The guilt couldn't eat me like the acid I'd used years ago in high-school science experiments. I don't think this is going to work. Maybe it would be better if I burn the list, have a bonfire out back. Would that do it?

1. I should never have signed Lizzie up for ballet.
2. I should have pulled a couple more weeds, gotten there a couple minutes late. Why do I always have to be on time to everything?
3. I could have taken a back road.
4. I should have kept Claire on the life support for one more night.
5. I wish I had rocked her to sleep every night, picked her up every time she cried.
6. I wish I had been a better mother.
7. Maybe I never should have married.

Lizzie went off to play with a friend one morning, so I spent my time sprawled on the floor under a blanket, watching early reruns of *Facts of Life*, so early that Tootie was still on roller skates. It was a better day, with an actual activity, watching television. I blocked out pleas from my sister on the answering machine to "pick up," and turned up the TV's volume. Lizzie returned home around lunchtime. "How was your play date?" I asked.

"Good," she said, shrugging off her jacket and haphazardly kicking off her boots by the door. She skipped off to her room. I followed her. She was crouched on the floor, arranging her Care Bears by color, then size. Working patterns out in her head.

"What did you play?"

"I don't remember."

"You don't remember? Did you play dress-ups?"

"Yeah."

"Did you have a snack?" I sat on her meticulously made bed, just on the edge, so that straightening the comforter when I got up wouldn't be difficult.

"Mom?"

"Yes, hon?"

"Olivia's little sister was trying to play with us. We didn't want her to, so we shut her out of Olivia's room."

"You should be nice to her."

"Why does Olivia still have her little sister?"

Silence.

"Why did Claire have to die?"

"I don't know."

"I wish Olivia's little sister would die too."

I knew what I should have said—what the right "mom" response to this should be, but I couldn't say it. I stared at a light area of paint directly underneath the windowsill where I could see some of the original paint color from when we moved in. Yes, I should have painted that spot one more time. I wondered if I still had some leftover paint in the garage.

An old high-school teacher
Sent a package, a silver heart charm.
Inside it was a gaping hole.
A sickeningly sweet poem to go with it.
This tired cliché—a hole,
a hole in the heart isn't enough.

*People live with physical holes in their heart
for years, unknown to anyone, even themselves.
Losing Claire was my amputation.
At least people can stare.*

Brett packed up his paints and brushes and canvases and finished pieces and stacked them in the corner of the garage to make room for the new car. The replacement, a Volvo wagon. Sounds safe, doesn't it?

One night, the three of us drove to the cemetery in the new car. When we arrived, I pulled a scratchy brown-and-white Mexican blanket from under the backseat, which I put there for trips to the cemetery. I spread the blanket out next to the spot of yellowed grass. The headstone was ordered but hadn't been cemented into the earth yet.

I sat on the blanket while Lizzie danced around the cemetery in her satiny pink and lavender fairy dress, oversized heeled shoes, and plastic, dangling clip-on earrings. Brett sat next to me, staring straight ahead. We didn't speak. I looked down at my stained t-shirt and pajama bottoms. I'd been wearing this for the past three days. Not changing to go to the grocery store or even to throw it in the wash. I knew how I must appear to Brett, but I didn't care. We sat listening to the few remaining birds stalling their migratory journey this fall and the crunching leaves underneath Lizzie's dancing feet.

Suddenly, Lizzie let out a gravelly cough, then it became screams, and she fell onto the ground. Lizzie cried, "Mom, mommy."

She was coughing and spitting into her cupped hands when I reached her. "What's wrong? What happened?" She held her open palm toward me, a piece of her plastic earring floated in a pool of mucus mixed with blood. "You had this in your mouth?"

I hooked my finger and dabbed at her throat, trying to fish the rest of the earring out.

I shouted, "Brett, we've got to go now," as I picked Lizzie up. Brett grabbed the blanket, and we drove but didn't know where we were going. "I think we should take her to the emergency room," I said.

The coughing ceased, and she cried. When she heard that fateful word "emergency room," she stammered, "Mommy, am I going to die?"

"No, Lizzie. You're not going to die. We just need to get the earring out."

Brett said, "I don't think we need to take her to the emergency room. Let's stop by Michelle Davis's house on our way home." Michelle was our neighbor and an RN and nice enough that she didn't mind everyone in the cul-de-sac asking her medical opinion or bringing by their fevered children.

I carried Lizzie in my arms, like an oversized baby, up Michelle's front walk to the door, but no one answered my frantic knocks. I climbed into the back seat of the car, not wanting to put Lizzie back in her car seat. I'd just hold her. "She's not there. Should we go to the hospital?"

"The coughing's stopped," Brett said. Lizzie began to breathe out forced coughs, still needing to be babied for a while longer. I tucked her head under my chin and stroked her hair, pulling out several pieces of brittle leaves that were stuck in her hair.

"We might still want to go, just in case," I said.

"What are they going to do? Let's just give her some water at home, and it'll pass to her stomach. The piece will come out in the next couple days. That's probably all they'd do at the ER is give her something to push it down." I looked straight ahead, knowing he'd made up his mind. I wiped the tears from Lizzie's tear-streaked dirty face as we drove the couple houses down to our house.

In the kitchen, I poured a large glass of water for Lizzie, sat her on the barstool, and watched her drink it. "I'm done," she said. "I can't drink anymore."

"Can you still feel it in your throat?"

"Yes. It's right here," she said, dabbing at her neck.

Brett stood watching. I went to Brett and whispered, "I don't want to take a chance. I want to take her to the hospital."

"They're not going to do anything. Seriously, Alex."

I turned and walked away, leaving Lizzie seated on the stool, and mumbled, "You want this one to die too?" I don't know why I said it. I knew she was probably okay by her regular breathing, but maybe I just needed to feel something. Even if it was just anger. Heading straight into my bedroom, I slammed the door behind me, went to the closet and pulled a pair of shorts and shirt from the closet. I was going to change clothes and take Lizzie to the hospital.

I left my old t-shirt crumpled on the floor and had just slipped a blue shirt over my head when Brett banged through the door and stood in front of me. Too close. He pointed his finger at my face and shouted, "Don't you dare imply I don't care about my child." I was wearing just my bra, my arms caged in the shirt.

He was crowding me, waiting for my response. I pushed past him and wriggled the shirt on. "Get away from me."

"How dare you accuse me of not caring? Lizzie's the only thing I have left."

"The only thing?"

"Come on, Alex. You're barely here. You sleep here and live here, but you're not here. You don't see me. You think I can't tell?"

"How can you stand here and make this all about you? I lost my baby!"

"So did I. And I couldn't do anything about it. It wasn't *my* fault."

"Are you saying it was my fault?"

"You were driving. Why don't you ask the police whose fault it was?"

I stomped into the bathroom and slammed the door behind me.

Brett burst in after me. Again. Ever since we were married, on the occasions we fought, it was always like this. I'd need a moment to cool, collect myself, but he would follow me from room to room, willing me to fight him. Argue. Yell. "Just stay away from me," I shouted and pushed his arm away from me. But this time, he pushed me back. Hard. With both hands. I staggered against the sink and fell onto the tile floor. He'd never touched me before, not like this.

"Mommy!" Lizzie cried from the doorway, where she stood watching. She was too scared to come nearer.

I climbed onto my feet, rushed to Lizzie, and ushered her into her bedroom, where I set her on top of her bed and lay next to her shaking, while we cried. Tears ran in torrents down my face, onto Lizzie's hair and pillow. She didn't notice; she had fallen asleep.

Holding Lizzie, I was still registering the shock that Brett blamed me for Claire's death. I'd never known what had happened. One moment I was driving, the next moment I was waking up in a punctured and shattered car. I had no defense.

I looked down at my hands, shiny from tears, and studied the lines and creases on my hands. The anti-Midas hands. I ruined everything I touched. I was given two perfect beautiful baby girls—one I killed in the accident and if the other one didn't die from swallowing this plastic earring, I would turn her into an emotional wreck. I held Lizzie tighter and closed my eyes.

I'm not sure how long I was lying next to her, but I woke when the streetlights shone in through the window. I tucked Lizzie into her sheets and kissed her forehead. The house felt strange and still when I staggered into the dark hallway. My bedroom was empty. I slipped between the sheets and just lay watching the ceiling fan swing round and round.

An hour later, I heard Brett shuffle into the room. I felt the bed sink when he sat on it. My eyes still followed the fan blades. After several minutes, he pulled himself off the bed, mumbled, 'I'm sorry,' and walked out. He slept in the guest room that night, then came back the next night without ever speaking a word about it.

Lizzie didn't complain about swallowing the plastic earring until she wanted to wear it again. The plastic must have swum the course through her body and made its way out.

Lizzie carried a baby doll around the house with her, dragging it by the arm. This doll had peach plastic arms, legs, and head, with an unmatched pink plush body. She wasn't wearing any clothes; Lizzie had lost them months before. She called the doll Claire and put her in Claire's chair next to her at the table. She buckled her into the seat in the car where Claire used to sit. She brought that doll everywhere. Playdates, in her backpack to take to pre-school. Lizzie talked to Claire with a high-pitched voice, her baby voice. She'd pretend to play games with this plastic doll. I wasn't sure what Lizzie saw, but I couldn't look past this plastic mold's constant emotionless smile and dead blue eyes.

She insisted on bringing her into the store, seating her into the shopping cart beside her.

"Lizzie, why don't you leave Claire out here while we go in?"
"Mommy, you know we can't leave a baby in the car."

I'm a rare exotic wild animal,
on display at the zoo. In a cage.

I can hear the teacher's clear voice,
ushering the children through on their field trip,
saying, "Class, pay attention. Class, look at this.
This mother's baby died.
Look at the way the animal sits, still,
staring at the wall.
Look at deep slope of its shoulders.
Look at it.
Come along, now. We must hurry along
if we want to see all the animals today."

I feel on display each time I run into someone I know,
at the grocery store, passing by on the street,
walking to my mailbox.
Anyone I know, who knows what happened.
As if they're studying me, "See the way
she slowly drags her feet, while she pushes the shopping cart
through the aisles lined with canned soup, bread, dry pasta."
"See the distance in her eyes.
She's not even buying the things on her list."
I could still hear the school-teacher's voice,
"Take notes."
"See the difference."
"Pay attention."
"Look closely."
"Don't poke your fingers into the cage."

    I found a tiny sock of Claire's, brown on the bottom, in my library bag. The sock was white with an embroidered pink daisy on the ankle. It held a secret. Like the secret a conch shell whispers of the sea. It was unwashed, a treasure, for when I put my nose into the sock and inhaled, it smelled of lavender and of Claire. It held just a moment of my lost life. I kept the sock on my nightstand. Every night before lying down to sleep, I smelled the sock and closed my eyes and pretended just for a moment that Claire was still there. One morning, I found a slightly larger sized bright pink sock next to Claire's on the window ledge.

I'm constantly tormented
with dreams.

No rest. Last night,
my dream was dark, and wet.
It was raining, I was driving, Lizzie in back,
I watched a car smash
into us, slow motion, silent,
car exploded into the backseat
where she sat.
Yes, she died.

History couldn't repeat itself,
But it does.
Over and over again
every night
from the safety of my own bed,
in my wrecked mind.

I loved Lizzie. Of course I did. While I was pregnant with Claire and felt her fluttering movements, I never believed that Claire could stack up to Lizzie. I accepted that I would love the new baby less than I loved Lizzie, for no other reason than she just wasn't Lizzie.

And she wasn't much like Lizzie at all—looks, temperament, her husky voice. I heard the deep tone in her cry the moment after her first breath. But I adored Claire. She was her own little person—she liked carrots cooked in chicken broth but wouldn't touch pureed carrots in a little glass jar, she'd kick me in the side after nursing at night until I returned her to her crib.

Now I looked at Lizzie, and I knew I was miles from her. I'd tell her I love her with an echo in my voice, as if I were telling her from across a rift, or in a cave, where my words bounced off jagged edges until they settled into a lump on the ground. They meant nothing. I couldn't quite love her enough because she wasn't Claire.

My Birthday.
Celebrating nothing.
Candles, candy,
Nothing.
Thanks for remembering.
It's just a day.
Another empty day.

Only grief.
No Claire.
No diapers, or naps, or baths.
Just me.
A shell.

Going out with the people from Brett's work felt like a punishment. We met his friends at an Italian restaurant in Portland. A restaurant in a house, tables spread throughout what used to be someone's living room and bedrooms. A vase of magnolias in the center of our table. I ordered a half order of the spinach gnocchi. "I'm not that hungry," I said under the rumble of their talking about some television show that seemed to be *the thing to watch*. I sat quietly in this group that I wasn't familiar with—Jen with her wispy, blonde hair and her sparkly look-at-me shirt, balding David whose office was next to Brett's, and Jill who was average—dark wavy hair, unremarkable face, and boobs that were so obviously manufactured I could barely pull my gaze up to eye level.

Jen sat next to Brett, and I numbly watched her place her hand on Brett's arm as they joked and discussed things "you had to be there" to understand. I couldn't pull my thoughts into their raucous world and let my mind drift to Claire's body, enclosed in that airless box underground. I thought about how her soft skin was now decaying and how her short hair would keep growing and growing. When was it that the worms started to take over?

Pulling my fixed gazed up from the magnolias, I looked right into the dark brown eyes of a man several tables away. His hair was peppered. He looked smart, clean, good-looking in an authoritative way. Like a college professor. He wore a button-down shirt with khaki pants. He probably thought I was the one at this table without a date; because to any observer, Brett was with Jen. Periodically while eating my five tiny dumplings, I'd look over to see if he was still glancing my way and he usually was. The woman at his table didn't seem to notice, nor did anyone at mine.

All through dinner, I waited for someone to acknowledge my daughter, but no one did. The absence of Claire's name at the table haunted me. Left me unfilled, just like the gnocchi. When the server brought the check, I stood and told Brett I would be in the bookstore next door. I was careful not to touch Brett, as

Jen had been all night. I felt the peppered-haired man's eyes following me out the door.

A bell clanged as I walked in bookstore. I browsed through a number of books on a round, sensible table. I was leafing through the pages of a book when I heard the bell cling again, then footsteps behind me. I looked up into the mahogany eyes belonging to the man from the restaurant. Eyes much softer and startling than I could tell from before. He crossed over to one of the bookshelves and plucked a book from its place on the wall. I eyed him and stepped to the window to see if Brett's car was waiting for me. It wasn't. The man looked up from the book he held in both hands, and stated matter-of-factly, "You're unhappy."

"Yes," I agreed and looked back down into the opened pages.

"What are you doing with them?"

"I don't know," I said without looking up. A morsel of truth I hadn't even admitted to my husband. I saw the flash of headlights through the window and hastily added, 'I've got to go.' I set down the book and tripped back through the ringing door, ducked into the waiting car.

We drove to the show—rather it was a soliloquy, just a man standing on a stage talking about the differences between men and women. He was a middle-aged, balding, overweight man who would rotate between standing, then sit on an over-stuffed recliner when his feet were tired. His monologue was about the hunter—or man—and the gatherer—the woman. It was funny, sure, if you were in the right mood for it. I wasn't. Jen sat on the other side of Brett and nudged him throughout the entire show, laughing with him.

As we left the theatre, I saw the man—that same man from the restaurant—in the lobby. This had to be a coincidence, as the show had been sold out for weeks. He looked at me that way when I knew someone thought I was pretty, couldn't pull his eyes away. I felt his eyes on me, like a warm spot from the sun. I knew I'd never see him again, didn't want to, but it felt nice to have eyes look at me like I was there, really there.

On the ride home, I thought about the man, about what he'd said to me. How he'd been able to see inside me, my sorrow. Why was everyone else around me ignoring it? Maybe he was trying to pick up on me, but I knew it was more than that. I knew he could see that I didn't belong with anyone. Not the man sitting next to me. How could he comment how odd I looked there, that I didn't blend in, and Brett—the man I slept next to every night—couldn't muster a couple words about my despondency or even notice it was sitting right there between us?

> *I had another dream last night.*
> *I was a kid*
> *at some kind of summer camp—*
> *soccer or 4-H.*
> *I found myself naked, like so many childhood dreams,*
> *But had the body of an adult and the hardened memory.*
> *I walked around with my arms pressing down on my breasts,*
> *hard, smashed against me, to cover.*
> *Milk started streaming down my chest,*
> *flowing like a spilled drink.*
> *Waking, I felt the letdown.*

One morning, as Lizzie tugged on my arm again, to "please wake up." I mumbled that I needed to sleep, just go. "I know," she said to herself and skipped out of the room. I slept on, until I heard a crash that brought me to my feet.

Lizzie was nowhere, but shards of a glass bowl lay on the kitchen floor, milk reaching out on all sides, under the oven, the refrigerator, into the pantry. "Lizzie!" I shouted, "Get in here!" I grabbed paper towels and tried to sop up the streams of milk. When I followed the stretched finger of milk flowing underneath the pantry door, I discovered Lizzie lying with her face hidden on the cold tile, her arms over her head.

"Lizzie, what were you doing? You know you're not supposed to use these bowls. You have plastic ones."

She didn't respond, just whimpered, from where she was balled, like a pile of dirty laundry.

"Answer me! What were you doing?"

She said nothing. The milk had run to her plaid flannel pajamas; she had moved her legs into it and smeared it along the pantry floor. Blood from where the bowl must have sliced her foot channeling into the river of milk, swirling pink.

"Lizzie!" I screamed again. "You have to help me clean this mess." I tried lifting her body with both my arms, like you would a cat that didn't want to go into a pet carrier. She tried to keep her body shut tight, and I fell to the ground next to her, trying to peer underneath her arms to see her face.

"I'm sorry, mommy. I'm sorry. I'm sorry," she said softly, not stopping, not wanting to hear my response. I lay her back on the ground and gathered a clean paper towel, blotting at her cut. It wasn't so deep she needed stitches and the bleeding stopped immediately. I folded the paper towel over and continued swiping up the rivulets of milk.

"Lizzie, it's okay," I whispered. "I just wish you'd—"

Then I noticed the wooden bed tray lying against the refrigerator and the image of Brett bringing me breakfast in bed on my birthday came back—Brett carrying the tray and Lizzie trailing him with a smile so bright. I stroked her back and the tears flowed from my eyes too. I huddled on the milky floor, trying to hold her, although her body was still tight. We lay there until our clothes were sticky, our eyes dry, the blood scabbed over on her foot, and Lizzie felt safe enough to come out of her turtle shell.

I knew that no matter how long I curled around her in the pantry closet, my daughter was afraid of me. She didn't know me, and she was so afraid of me that she had created this barrier with her body to keep me out.

Those last remaining weeks were jumbled, bleak, fuzzy, cold. I forgot things I'd done the day before, couldn't remember if I'd fed Lizzie lunch most days. Usually I had to ask. I stopped caring what day of the week it was, which month. It didn't matter. I became too tired to move, to stoop to pick up Lizzie's toys, to do the dishes, all futile. I didn't want any responsibility—including the domestic jobs around the house—and I couldn't take care of Lizzie anymore. I didn't have enough energy to take care of both of us.

I stared out of my windows with anger. The neighbors' meaningless chatter on the front lawn, after picking up the mail, bothered me. My neighbor with her ripe, pregnant belly mushrooming from her loose top. How could they be standing around talking about groceries and preschool?

Why were people still having babies?

I didn't want to live in this house anymore.

I didn't want to see these people anymore.

I didn't want to live this life anymore.

I wanted to disappear, to dissolve, dissipate, leave. I thought voraciously of the unopened bottle of sleeping pills my doctor prescribed. I could take them all. End it now. Go wherever it was Claire went. Or just cease. Somehow that felt more comforting.

I considered this in the black of my closet, while hiding from Lizzie's pleas to play games or dolls. It would be so easy.

No. I needed to suffer for what I did. No mindless sleeping, quiet death. Too easy. I needed the torture, the wakeful pain, the ceaseless stinging of grief. I owed that to Claire. There was only one other way.

I devised my escape plan while reading *Tess of the D'Ubervilles*, an old favorite I'd read in college, as Brett and Lizzie sat on her bed across the hall reading Curious George or some fairytale. They'd started this several weeks ago—reading together before bed. Then Brett helped her into pajamas, filled her cup with water and placed it on the nightstand, and tucked her into bed. I sat in my room with the door closed but could hear them. I tried to block out their voices while I read. I finally reached a point where I could read again, but only books about unhappy people who had lost things—children, husbands, best friends. That's why I picked up Tess. I remembered she had lost a baby, and I wanted to go back and look on her with new eyes. But I felt contempt for her now, my old friend, for not truly mourning over her lost baby, Sorrow. I related with her in one way at least—her desire to leave, get away, start over. I read two sentences over and over until I had enough courage to follow her:

"Yet even now Tess felt the pulse of hopeful life still warm within her; she might be happy in some nook which had no memories. To escape the past and all that appertained thereto was to annihilate it, and to do that she would have to get away."

Christmas season came. Everyone was happy. Joy to the world. Our doorbell rang again—neighbors and friends bearing little gifts for Christmas. Candles, fudge, snowflake mugs. Happy little notes attached. Merry Christmas.

I opened a box of Christmas decorations that Lizzie had begged for and unburied Claire's blue velvet stocking amongst the tree skirt and jolly Santa Claus figurines, elves.

Most of the other decorations landed in a giant heap on the floor, then eventually found their place.

Of course, there would be presents under the tree for Lizzie on Christmas morning. If you were thoughtless enough, you could say this year would be easier than last—fewer presents to buy.

I couldn't bear the cheerful Christmas carols; didn't want to be wrist-deep in cookie dough, gleefully stamping out Santa Claus- and reindeer-shaped cookies; didn't want to take gifts to my neighbors; didn't want to think about others and make them happy. Why should everyone else get to be happy at Christmastime when I couldn't? No matter what was under the Christmas tree or left on my front door.

I sat before the fire, watching absentmindedly as the flames flickered and twisted. If a passer-by were looking into my window now, he'd see the stockings dangling from the mantel, the Christmas tree lit, but he wouldn't know how I was rotting inside. He wouldn't know that I was planning to steal off into the night, leaving my Lizzie sleeping in her warm bed, while she dreamed— surely not—of sugar plums.

The doorbell rang and woke me from my wicked thoughts. I opened the door, expecting another cheerful acquaintance pressing a plate of Christmas cookies into my hand. Instead it was the FedEx guy, complete with brown polyester uniform and crew cut, holding out a slim cardboard envelope. I signed my name on the digital display chart; it came out jagged and scarcely resembled my signature. I brought the envelope inside and opened it, sitting with my back against the front door. I knew what it was. Brett and I had signed the settlement agreement from the car-insurance company several weeks before. I pulled out the check. It was made out to the Estate of Claire Porter, Brett or Alexandria Porter, in the amount of $100,000.

Brett and I had actually spoken about the guilt we felt knowing this money was en route—some cruel payment for losing our daughter. But here it was, and I trembled, knowing my decision was made. I tucked the check safely into my purse, and later that afternoon, I deposited it into a shiny, new bank account.

I hugged Lizzie more that day than I had the previous three months. She shied away from me, unused to this misplaced affection. However, when Brett didn't make it home before bed, she graciously accepted my offer to read books before bed. She chose all her favorites—*Madeline, Olivia, Angelina Ballerina, Where the Wild Things Are*. She fell asleep, her head against my arm while I read, her breathing steady, a high whistle in her nose, then a heavy breath out her mouth. I kissed her gently on the nose, laid her head onto her pillow, and pulled the sheets over her shoulders. Set her brown fuzzy teddy bear, Tara, on the pillow next to her head. I turned off the light, then walked out and shut the door.

In my bed, I waited for Brett's breathing to become slow, regular, heavy. I drifted off and woke with a start several minutes later. I didn't hear the constant heavy breaths from Brett, and I reached over and gently laid my arm on his. It was clammy and cold and hard and still. Like a corpse. Like his body had been washed up onto shore, lifeless white.

We were dead together. If I didn't leave now, it would be my corpse lying next to his, flung from above, two dead lovers lying side-by-side, cold and useless. I crept from the bed and noiselessly grabbed a couple pair of jeans, shirts and sweaters, underwear, socks, toiletries, and threw them in a duffle bag. I added my worn paperback copy of *Tess of the D'Ubervilles* and my journal. Hastily grabbed a stack of photos. And Claire's sock.

In the garage, I unbuckled Lizzie's car seat and set it on the concrete floor next to Brett's car and drove away, as simply as I'd tossed Lizzie's proffered hand-picked dandelion bouquets into the garbage months before.

Chapter Nine

As I drove away, I knew I should have handled it better. I should have given them both a proper goodbye. Maybe written a letter and left it on the kitchen island for Brett to find when he noticed I wasn't lying next to him as the sun crept over the hill the next morning. But I knew I couldn't have talked to him. Brett would have tried to convince me to stay in a life I was never meant to live, surrounded by walls that clung to memories of the life that was supposed to be mine. Or worse, he might have agreed that leaving was the best thing.

And I couldn't face Lizzie. She needed a mother. Could I really leave her? Could I be that person—the mother who abandoned her family? Lizzie would think I didn't love her. Maybe she already did. I could still go back home. I'll just say I needed some time to think, if anyone even noticed I was gone. Then I'd fall back into my role, my place, my numb existence, my incomplete family. Like a puzzle, with one small piece missing. One misplaced piece leaves the whole thing useless. Fit for garbage.

No. I knew what I was leaving, but I couldn't stay another day.

I drove for several hours, not knowing where I was headed. I drove circles through the back roads, driving away but never getting too far. When the gaslight glowed empty, I pulled my car into a lonely country gas station a few towns over, its lights shining that it was open. I filled the tank and walked into the building to use the restroom. On my way back through, I hesitated in one aisle for nearly ten minutes before I clutched at a bag of traditional Doritos.

Within those few minutes, while I stood pondering whether I felt more like Cool Ranch or Nacho, I made a decision—not only about what to eat, but where I was going. My friend Sammy had a small, seldom used cottage in Astoria, at the mouth of the Columbia River near the Oregon coast. Because she and I had spent a weekend there a couple summers ago, I knew where the house key was kept. No one needed to know. Astoria was just another couple hour's drive.

Leafing through a magazine rack near the cashier, I found an atlas and added it to the pile of my Doritos and a Diet Coke from the fountain in front of the cashier. I used my debit card to pay, half-hoping Brett would use it to track me down.

Late-night talk radio filled the car—something about aliens declaring war on the United States, hovering over us in their UFOs. I listened half-heartedly but kept thoughts of Brett and Lizzie tucked in the corner, to pull out and sift through when my mind wandered. When I pulled into hilly Astoria just after five in the morning, the sky was still dark. I parked my car on the street, grabbed my bag, and hiked the million concrete steps to the little blue house, no street having access to it on its steep hill.

I pulled the door key from inside an artificial rock in the front flowerbed and let myself in through the back door into the kitchen, where Sammy had started renovations. The front room was crowded with the kitchen's upper cabinets. Several buckets of paint were stacked neatly along the inside wall in the living room. The stove was the only source of heat in the house, and the wood supply was down to three pieces. Not wanting to waste wood on a fire now since I was just going to sleep, I trudged up the stairs and grabbed some blankets from the bedroom closet and piled them on the bed. After climbing underneath, I slept long and hard.

I woke in the middle of the afternoon with light streaming in narrow slanted streaks through the bamboo shades. I lay on my back with Claire sleeping on me—her heaviness warmed my chest, her ankles dangled against my wrists. I froze, wanting to keep this feeling for as long as I could. To feel I was still her mother and she needed me, close enough to fall asleep on me. The feeling lifted, and I remembered where I was, staring up at the white ceiling.

In the dream that brought Claire to me, I had been back at home. A neighbor walked a stroller to my front door and knocked. She held Claire in her arms. She told me she'd taken care of her all these months. I reached my arms toward Claire, but she clutched onto my friend, not wanting me. Claire had changed. She was older and her hair was long, blond, and curly, but her piercing emerald eyes had remained the same. A pair of broken sunglasses hung precariously on her nose. I asked if she remembered me, and she answered "yes," too clearly and much too quickly as if she were an adult and finally came to me. But moments later, like a baby, she fell asleep in my arms, her head quiescent on my chest, leaving her imprint on me when I woke.

The foreign room where I lay now was bare except for an old wooden rocking chair in the corner, where I had stashed my bag in the darkness that morning. I sat up and panicked, thinking irrationally that no one would know where I was to give Claire back to me. Then rationally, I ached, knowing Lizzie did not find me in my bed this morning. I couldn't knock the vision of Lizzie staggering into my bedroom—hair matted and tangled, her pajamas draping over her slight shoulders, eyes sleepy but bright—out of my head. She'd feel around my bed and find only the absence of me. She'd probably look around the house and settle by the window to wait for me to return, as she had when I jogged in the mornings.

I pictured the walls of our house, with its window eyes and taupe skin, watching the demise of our family. Maybe Brett would let Lizzie sleep in his bed, needing something within arm's length to love, someone he really loved. Their mornings would be quiet, but rushed no doubt. Lizzie's legs would swing in rhythm, dangling from the bar stools, as she and Brett ate cereal together before he left for work. They would read their bedtime stories together every night.

Downstairs, I entered the musty bathroom, opening the window to let in some cold but fresh air. This room was next on the renovation list, Sammy had said. The bathroom was small, and cream bead-board surrounded a dingy wall-mounted sink, toilet, and claw-foot tub. I used the toilet, then shut the door behind me. I didn't want the house any colder.

I found a half-empty box of stale Froot Loops in one of the lower kitchen cabinets and nibbled on them dry. I'd have to go buy some groceries. Standing with my hand in the box of cereal, I stared out the front window toward the bottom of the hill. Houses stair-stepped all the way down until they stopped at the Columbia River. I could see the docks and a barge on the river from here. I stood for a while, just watching, an empty quiet moment.

Dropping the cereal box on the couch, I picked up the remaining pieces of firewood and arranged them into the mouth of the stove. A stack of last month's newspapers sat in the corner. I crumpled some of them, stuffed them in the stove, and dug around in the kitchen drawers until I found matches. After the first attempt failed, a small fire took and I collapsed onto the couch and resumed munching Froot Loops, watching the fire take and grow. The stillness of the house, the silence, felt so unusual. I wondered if Brett was searching for me, but he wouldn't think to look here. I felt mostly safe here—safe from Brett, safe from anyone who knew me or what had happened. Just not safe from me—my head had become my fiercest enemy.

Upstairs again, I dumped the clothes from my bag into the seat of the rocking chair, filing through until I found some sweats and put them on. Slowly, my timid feet took me across the landing to the other bedroom. I opened the closed door and entered. The paneled wooden walls were freshly painted white, the new paint smell trapped inside. A sand-dollar chandelier, with seashell necklaces draped like jewels from the lights, hung from the ceiling. Sammy's original work. The room's matching twin beds were on each side under the sloping ceiling with the window overlooking the river between.

A crib was tucked away in one corner of the room. What was it about a crib? Just seeing a crib. Just knowing that a baby slept there. I resolved not to think about how most people got to watch their babies grow up—watch them go from the crib to a twin bed to a college dorm bed. I shut the door behind me and kept it that way for the rest of my time here.

Up and down, up and down. I found myself downstairs again and perused the bookshelf under the window seat in the front room and plucked out several books to read—*Catcher in the Rye, The Bell Jar, Jude the Obscure, Beloved*. Although I'd read these books before, I at least knew they were worthy of my time. And I felt like drowning myself in my sorrow. I was getting to the point where I had little tolerance with books, throwing down one book after another if it was poorly written or just plain stupid. I didn't have the energy to read through every book I picked up anymore. Safe books were good for my uncertain days here, and I needed something to pass the time, keep me occupied.

After reading the first couple chapters of *Beloved*, I locked up the house and walked several blocks to the neighborhood market. I was there for food essentials—bread, peanut butter, bagels, fruit, and a small satchel of wood, at least enough for a couple of days. I kept my head down at the store, the hooded jacket shielding my face. Chances of running into someone I knew in Astoria weren't likely, but I was only 300 miles from my home. It could happen.

The little blue house seemed to mesh into me, like I belonged in there, secluded, a hermit in my shell. I couldn't hide my stay here though; the chimney smoke whispered of my presence. It wouldn't be anything unusual for someone to be staying there, as I knew Sammy lent the house out to pretty much whoever wanted to use it. "As long as they clean up before they leave," she always said.

I went to bed when the moon loomed overhead and woke when the sun peeked through the window.

Although it was still dark, I left the house around seven each morning and walked to the docks and along the Riverwalk, by the trolley tracks. I listened to the cranes and seagulls and relished the crisp cold air on my face, welcoming the subtle smell of fish and salt and morning. I could see the cliffs from Long Island Peninsula in Washington across the water. Passing the fisheries, I eyed the mottled fish traveling lifelessly up the conveyor belt. Their smell strong—discarded and rotting somewhere nearby. Dead. And why? Perhaps they weren't large enough to send away to restaurants or grocers. Small fish killed needlessly. I held my breath as I walked by and looked beyond, toward the river.

The river always captured my gaze during these morning walks. Somewhere open to focus. The water was jerky, deep velvet blue and silver, and reflected a chopped lazy morning sun, unsettled and restless, when it finally ascended into the sky. Often I would stop, rest my elbows on the railing, and watch the ships pass by. Each ship with its predetermined destination, on its course, while I stood by wondering where I'd be next week.

Except for my early mornings by the water, I stayed inside the cabin, reading mostly and staring out the window. My time here was limited, and I knew I would leave before the weekend. Only two more days, and there would be more decisions to make.

One afternoon, I went for a drive. It was the only time I got in my car that week. I drove across the four-mile bridge, over to Washington, and drove the 101. It was a nice foggy day and complemented my dreary mood. I passed Black Lake, Dismal

Nitch, Cape Disappointment—all named for me. I wondered what tragedy had happened here. After an hour, I turned back.

When I made it back to the house, I leafed through a thick book on Lewis and Clark that had been left on the coffee table and found the answers I was looking for, about the disappointing names of the historical spots I'd seen. I should have known. Astoria was thick with history about Lewis and Clark. I read about the members of the discovery camp being stranded in the winter storm for six days, wondering if they were going to survive. Their goal not completed, but within reach. They knew how close they were, but there was nothing they could do, just wait.

And after they reached the Pacific Ocean, they had to turn around and start all over, head back to their starting point near St. Louis. Mission over. This place was inundated with Lewis and Clark. Signs everywhere. Lewis and Clark Trail.

Before bed that last night, I turned on the faucet and watched water thunder into the bathtub's streaked porcelain. The water had filled the tub nearly three quarters when I turned it off. I closed the toilet lid, undressed methodically, folding each piece of clothing and stacking them on the toilet seat.

I turned out the light and opened the window. The steaming water rose as I dipped my foot in. The water was hot, too hot, but I sank in. The pain of the hot water only temporary, until my body resigned to it. Closing my eyes, I sank further in the water until the water cupped my face—ending at my chin and the corners of my eyes. Several air bubbles traveled to the surface from my ears, and I heard the rhythmic beat of my pulse, my heart's song, pounding music into the water. One beat after another, proving my body could live much beyond my will to.

Dropping even further, my face immersed, I continued listening and realized how easy it would be to listen to that pulse slowly crawl to nothing.

No one here to stop me.

Or find me.

Just me and this water.

My out.

Tap, tap, tap, like something was knocking. Was something knocking?

Panicked, I opened my eyes through the water, then came hurriedly up for air, gasping. I listened and heard nothing. All was silent but for the barking of dogs far off in the night.

I relaxed, feeling the breeze cool my face and inhaled the smell of smoke from outside.

I wouldn't linger on the cowardly idea of suicide anymore. I had to move on.

I heard the light strum of rain before I saw water pooling on the windowsill. I lay listening to its steady beat before I pulled myself out of the tub.

In bed that night, I tossed, wondering if my car would take me back home tomorrow. I couldn't go back. Lizzie was better off without me. I was hurting her. If I just left, I wouldn't keep pulling her down into my abyss, misery, dread, until she was under too. She wasn't strong enough to tread water and hold me up, and it wasn't fair to ask her to.

At first light, I walked down to the river and watched the ships go by one last time. Seagulls flew overhead. I gazed at the murals painted to look like the inside of the mills on buildings along the trolley tracks and walked past the Wet Dog Café, aptly named for the smell along the Riverwalk. At the end of my walk, I hiked up the steps to the house and packed my bag. I tried to leave everything as it was—the dishes washed and put away, garbage vanished, and hair rinsed from the tub and sink. No proof I had been here. I packed up all the food but left the wood. It could have been anyone, the last guests. I locked the house, put the key in the artificial rock, and sunk down each step to my car.

Chapter Ten

When I left, I followed the Lewis and Clark trail signs since that somehow made sense. The signs were every couple miles or so and were brown-and-white silhouetted pictures of Lewis and Clark pointing. I drove past the freeway exit where I could have turned to go back home, but passed it wearily, my trembling hands gripping the steering wheel.

With Lewis and Clark to guide me, I let waves of memories drift through my head. I thought back on my life when it was normal. I hadn't known I was happy. How was I supposed to know? The simple satisfaction of turning around in the car and seeing Claire in her car seat, sleeping or shaking a rattle, sucking on a toy. Lizzie would be singing along to some much-too-loud kid music. Brett driving. We'd be out doing some leisure shopping on an ordinary Saturday afternoon. Nothing special.

I thought about Claire as an infant, when I nursed her into the night, her warm body nestled in against me, head resting on my arm as she slept. Then I'd feel her restless knees nudging my side, the sign that Claire wanted her crib. I'd quietly pad across the hallway into her room where she'd sleep until morning. But Lizzie wasn't that way; she'd stay in my bed until morning, lying there so still and noiseless I'd wake up just to make sure she was still breathing.

Memories of Claire's first birthday streamed through my head. The chocolate birthday cake smashed to her face, a chocolaty goatee, a pointy birthday hat. Lizzie thought Claire was being so funny and liked the way Brett and I were laughing that she smeared chocolate cake on her own face and hands.

I shuffled through the few details my mind held from the night before the accident—how she had walked around outside, up and down the steps on the deck. Up and down, back and forth, a game of practicing having her feet and knees beneath her.

It was some time before I realized I hadn't seen a brown sign. When had they stopped? Had I left the path? Well, I knew where Lewis and Clark ended up, around St. Louis, and I kept going.

As I passed over Idaho's state line, I leaned in, pulled the curled atlas from its nest in the glove compartment, and found St. Louis on the map. I didn't know much about it—except that's where the arch was and the Cardinals baseball team, and I could see quite clearly that the Mississippi River ran alongside it on the map. I studied the atlas for the surest way there—Interstate 70—and plotted my course.

A little after midnight, I passed a green sign welcoming me to Boise, Idaho. My eyes were burning and heavy, and I willed them to stay open. I rolled the window down to let the cold air keep me awake, uncomfortable but awake.

A crude neon light flashed "Vacancy" at a cheap hotel off the freeway where I got a room for the night. Once inside, I flopped onto the bed, pushing the dirty floral comforter to the floor. I slept, hard and dreamless, until morning.

I woke from hunger pains. After stumbling outside, I grabbed my bag from the back seat of my car. Then threw on a pair of jeans and a lambs' wool sweater and tied my hair back in a ponytail. I had to get breakfast and swung by the first fast-food restaurant I saw. Across the street, while I waited for the cashier to hand me back some change, I noticed a shiny car, a Mercedes convertible, parked next to a couple other cars in an open field. For sale. They were all for sale.

When the lady with the visor and headphone handed me my bag with a breakfast croissant and orange juice, I pulled into a spot in the parking lot and ate. I stared at the car, my mind wild with irrational thoughts of driving along in a Mercedes, the wind tossing my hair behind. I liked the idea of breaking out of my life, my personality, all that I thought I'd turned into, not caring about what other people thought. Goodness, after Lizzie was born I rarely pulled a comb through my hair, so sure that people didn't see me anymore. All they noticed was the baby. Now I was alone. I didn't have the distraction of children. I was anxious with the insidious idea of putting myself in this car, enjoying its smooth ride. I could already imagine its rich leather smell and the many gadgets on the dash, most of which I wouldn't know how to use.

I watched as a car stopped in front of the open field and a man stepped toward the car. I wasn't sure if he was looking at the cars or owned one of them, but I stuffed the rest of the hash brown patty into my mouth, started my car, and drove across the street. I parked behind his car and got out, taking a sip of my orange juice.

The man had opened the door to the for-sale Jetta parked over from the Mercedes. "Do you own any of these cars?" I asked when he looked up.

"Just the Jetta. You interested?"

I gestured toward the Mercedes. "What about this one?"

"It's not mine, it belongs to Joe. I know him. You want me to call?"

"Could you?" He nodded and pulled a cell phone from his jacket pocket. A little over ten minutes later, Joel drove up. He let me drive it around the block. I paid him with a cashier's check from the insurance money. And he suggested I take my Volvo to a car lot about ten miles away that would pay for trade-ins with no strings attached. Of course I didn't get what the Volvo was worth, but I didn't care.

As I drove the black Mercedes down the street, I accepted that I'd made this decision consciously, knowing I'd purchased a temporary happiness, that it wouldn't last, but it had been so long since I'd had any joy that I was willing to spend the money even if it was short-lived. So, I owned a sleek, not-so-kid-friendly car and gladly left the memories of the last couple months in the Volvo wagon abandoned back at the lot, just another used car.

Despite the fleeting happiness, I did feel prettier when I caught a glimpse of myself in the mirror as I drove down the street. With this new-found energy, I decided I'd keep the momentum going while I could and get a haircut. I stopped at the first salon I saw and had my long hair cut chin length, with side-swept bangs to cover the still-visible scar, and even changed my dark hair to blonde. My reflection would be another thing I wouldn't recognize—along with the car, the strange streets, and the bed where I slept. I would force any reminders of my past out of my thoughts. It was a new beginning. I was a new person. I tossed out my old, worn-out life for a new one, like simply changing my clothes, leaving the old ones deserted in a wrinkly pile on the motel floor.

    I stayed in that motel room another night. Around seven the next morning, I got in my car and drove. I forged my way into St. Louis, but when I got there, I kept driving. I was afraid to stop. Everything looked so busy and demanding. Not a single reminder of Lewis and Clark anywhere, I noted with distaste.

    When I found myself crossing a bridge over the Mississippi River and into Illinois, I determined I had to pull off somewhere. At this rate, I'd end up in North Carolina—too afraid to actually make a commitment. I veered off onto a smaller highway and exited on a less-demanding road, the cars driving just a bit slower here, and I arrived in the small town of Hanover, where a green sign touted a population of 4,240.

    I pulled into a gas station, filled up the tank, and yanked a St. Louis Post Dispatch from the dispenser, then got back into my car and drove through a historic street lined with antique stores and small mom-and-pop shops and steepled churches, like you see in black-and-white photos of old villages. People strolled down the street, waving to each other, stopping to chat. Some even waved to me as I passed. The little town seemed to beckon me, smiling, opening its outstretched arms.

    The Courthouse Diner sat directly behind the small stone edifice complete with Ionic columns framing the entrance and was my first stop in this little town. It was late afternoon, which meant the diner was empty save for an older couple sipping black coffee, perhaps having an early-bird dinner of roast turkey and mashed potatoes. I ordered a chicken-salad sandwich and a Diet Coke.

    While I waited for my food, I stared up at the walls and strolled over to a bulletin board near the entrance. I read tacked-on pages about local happenings—a Hanover High School basketball schedule, several fundraisers for the high-school band, and cars for sale. My eyes trailed over the clippings until I saw a yellow piece of lined paper, hung at an angle, just one tack in the corner, that read:

Studio Apartment For Rent
237 Main Street
$400/month
Call Debbie 555-7896

I didn't have a pen, so I yanked the page from its place, folded it neatly, and tucked it into my back pocket. No one else would need this anyway.

Back at my table, I gazed out the window, which looked out onto the courtyard and watched several squirrels scampering up and down some trees until my food arrived. After the first bite, I dug out the "Wanted" classifieds from the newspaper and found several ads for writers or editors, even though I knew my experience was outdated and useless. I even circled a couple ads for assistants and secretaries, hoping I wouldn't have to use them. I'd put myself through college as a legal secretary, and although it was a high-paying job for a college student, I never wanted to feel the way I did when I worked there—the attorneys always looking down on you, degrading you while you typed on and on, fingers ceaselessly tapping keys like a woodpecker making tiny little dents in the bark of a tree. But I could fall back on that, if I had to. I folded the classifieds several times and stuffed it into the pocket of my jacket. Then I read through international events, the arts and movies, sports, ads—anything to keep myself from feeling so solitary at this table long after the early-bird couple left.

I left the diner and drove to the address on the paper I'd pocketed. The house was a large white Victorian perched on the edge of Main Street, across the street from a motel. An octagonal tower with gables perched above the rest of the house, overlooking the steep rooflines that slanted down every which way in chaotic order. The house exterior was painted many shades of blue and grays. The house was wrapped with a wrought iron fence, curled in geometric designs with a fleur-de-lis at every post. I walked through the gate and knocked on the front door. It had a brass knocker, but I never quite knew if those things were just for decoration or if people were actually supposed to use them.

As I waited, I took in the wicker furniture on the oversized porch. I could see myself here on crisp summer nights, sipping iced tea and watching cars drive slowly past with people waving, to me.

Looking down at my hand, I stared at the innocuous wedding ring still hugging my finger. I heard footsteps coming to the door and the knob turning, and I quickly twisted the ring off my finger and slid it into my jeans pocket. The door opened to a woman with bouffant-styled white hair, a young face, a kind smile, and much too much light pink lipstick.

I held up the crinkled ad about the studio for rent, "I'm here about the studio apartment." She shuffled out the door and stood next to me on the porch. She was slight, the top of her bouffant coming up to my neck, and I always figured I was short at 5'4". "Is it still available?" I asked.

"Yes, it is. You're going to love it. The last tenant was my niece, and she moved out a couple weeks ago. She's getting married, and they're moving into his place. I did a couple repairs—you know, fixed some of the plumbing, replaced the sink—but it's ready to move in now." She gestured to me to follow her as she began walking down the steps from the porch. I ambled beside her along the side of the house to the backyard. The bare, twiggy branches of rose bushes huddled in clumps around the edge of the house, no blossoms—they were hibernating for the winter—and I took a simple satisfaction in seeing their nearly dead form.

She turned back and said, "I'm sorry I didn't introduce myself before. I'm Debbie." While we walked, she extended a surprisingly smooth hand—it looked ten years younger than Debbie did—which I grasped for an awkward moment, then released.

"I'm Alex, uh, Andria. Alexandria. But I go by Andria." I blurted this out hastily. I hadn't decided before this moment to change my name, but perhaps a new name would allow me to metamorphose into someone new. Leave my name in the past, along with my previous life.

"There's a rear entrance to the studio." She motioned ahead at an outdoor two-story spiral staircase that went right up to the attic. "I think you'll like this apartment. It's perfect for a single woman. I assume you're single?"

"Yes," my voice trailed behind me low and hollow. We circled up the stairs. Debbie clutched onto the staircase railings and I walked slowly behind her, my arms ready to steady her if she misstepped. She turned a key in the door at the top of the stairs, which creaked a bit as she opened it.

The studio apartment was surprisingly spacious; the entire apartment was open, no walls to break it up besides the bathroom and a rectangular opening that led out into the tower room with a window seat to look out from its circle of windows. It had slanted walls, dormer window niches on two sides, hardwood floors, and the best part was the picture moldings on the walls, with the old-time hooks intact. The kitchen was small, containing freestanding shelves on the walls in lieu of cabinets, but it was enough space. It had a microwave and refrigerator and stove.

"I think this will work," I said.

"I know I should probably have some sort of application for you to fill out, but I'm not all that official. Do you have any references?"

I hadn't thought about trying to scrounge up references and realized that I didn't have any. I didn't have anyone who could vouch for me. No one here, not anyone she could contact back home. I had no one. "Actually, I've lived in a house for the last five years with my husband. I don't have any current references, but I'd rather you not call him."

"Oh, did you leave him? You poor thing. I was married to one of them before. Thought he could push me around just because his meat loaf wasn't warm enough or have enough sauce." She shook her head and placed her hand on my arm. "Good for you, for leaving. I wish I had. I stuck around far too long, until he died of a stroke about ten years ago. I wouldn't say this to anyone else, but that was a relief. Back in my day, we were just supposed to grin and bear it. That's the way the ball bounces, they'd say. After Harold died, I sold our house and bought this one when it went to the auction. I'd always admired it as I drove by, so I did it with his life insurance money. The only thing he was ever good for. I thought I'd rent out this apartment to help me pay the mortgage. I prefer a renter to him any day."

I nodded as she spoke, allowing her to assume that yes, I was running from a wife beater. "How much do I owe you now? I can write a check or if you need cash," I began digging in my bag.

"A check is fine. Three hundred for a deposit and $400 for this month. My full name's Debbie Watkins. Just make the check out to me. Here, you can have this key." I wrote out the check and handed it to her; she placed the key attached to a shiny smiling sun keychain in my hand in exchange for the check. She looked at it for a moment. "Alex, huh? Looks like you've come a long way, Andria, dear. But don't worry, your secret is safe with me." She smiled and shook her head—as if only imagining what my husband could have done to make me leave. "You're gonna like it here. Let me know if you need help moving anything in. Several of our neighbors are real friendly. They'll help out with that kind of stuff. Even helped me move a piano in downstairs. Nice guys. They're always coming around, but I don't mind 'em."

"I don't really have anything. I guess I should go out looking for something to fill in this place. At least a bed."

"Starting over," she muttered as she walked toward the door and smiled back at me—as if we were in some kind of club together. A conspiracy against men. But I didn't hate Brett. I still loved him. He was grieving. He'd lost Claire too. I caught myself and tried to force the thoughts from my head. I took a long look around the bare apartment and felt a twinge of anxiety—I was perched at the brink of something completely foreign—and then headed out the door.

Debbie suggested I go across the river where they had "real stores" to shop. I picked up a new laptop computer I'd need for updating my resume and looking for a job. I also bought a mattress that Frank and Lennie, who Debbie called over from next door, maneuvered up my narrow circular staircase. A cigarette hung from Frank's lips as he agreed to help, "Surely." A nice guy and so scrawny he reminded me of a twisted pretzel stick, wearing a plaid button-down shirt, several white chest hairs searching for their way out from the top of his shirt.

I also picked up some new bed sheets and pulled the quilt I had from the car, the one I'd used since I was a child. I slept with the mattress in the center of the apartment for several nights. My bed an island, until I brought back more furniture a little at a time over the next several years.

I'd noticed a bookstore on Main Street, Maggie's Corner Book Shop, and went by, picked up several books to hold me over since I didn't have a job or a television. This was a strange feeling, being still, doing for myself, only making enough food for one. So different from the way I lived before.

My resume went out for the job listings I'd marked. During the next week, I got an interview. It was for a marketing writer position, in a company so filled to the brim with testosterone that I didn't see a woman in the entire place. Wearing my gray suit and a scarf tying my hair back, I felt overdressed for this interview conducted by three t-shirt wearing frat boys. It would have been more appropriate if I'd worn a miniskirt and an extra coat of mascara. I didn't get a call back and felt more out-of-touch than ever.

I lived off the insurance money for months, had an interview here and there, but had no jobs offers. Frustrated at not being able to work, I lived hour-to-hour, day-to-day, locked up in my tower.

Debbie played the piano in the afternoons. Right at two o'clock. When I heard the melancholy notes reverberating through the house, I'd lie down and press my ear against the cool wood, feeling the vibration and listening to her Nocturnes by Chopin or Beethoven's Sonatas or her favorite, Clair de Lune. The melodies lured tears from my closed eyes that would meander across my nose and drip onto the floor. The music drew seldom-visited memories of Claire and Lizzie and Brett from the dark cave where I kept them. Then I'd wipe up the little puddle of tears after the last note sounded through the floor.

Sometimes, after her solitary performances, Debbie would invite me for coffee or tea, and she'd tell me about her mother who ached for her to be a concert pianist, but Debbie would sit on that piano bench when she was a little girl, refusing to play. "She knocked me right off several times. But I'd smirk and plant myself right back on, not even touching my fingers to the keys, like they disgusted me," Debbie said. "She finally gave up."

"But you play beautifully," I said.

"Now I do. My mother died when I was ten, of a heart attack. I was her only child. After a couple years of neglect, my father sent me away to live with my Aunt Mary and her four boys. They had an un-tuned piano there that nobody ever played. I played my heart out. Hours and hours before and after school, hoping that all my practicing would bring my mother back. But of course it didn't. I got pretty good after all," she said with a sad smile.

I brought the tea cup up to my face and took a drink, wiping away the innocent tear that had formed in the crook of my eye so that Debbie wouldn't notice while she surreptitiously wiped her own.

It was December, almost a full year since I'd left Oregon, and I was still without a job. Without family at Christmas. It wasn't really the money I needed; I wanted to be busy. Maggie—who I'd come to know well from frequent trips to the Corner Book Store—had a part-time holiday position, so I worked there in December. The first week in January, my break came and I found the job where I'd stay for the next four years. Technical writing. I missed hearing Debbie's daily concerts but was glad to have a job. It was shortly after that when I found the cemetery and gave myself the liberty to wallow in the memories of my lost girls, my abandoned husband there where it symbolized the death of my entire family. I went there when I needed it, more some months, less some. I stayed in the quiet studio apartment, upstairs from Debbie, and worked at the technical writing firm for years.

Each day from the moment I arrived in Hanover, I anticipated the phone call or knock on my door from Brett or my mother and sisters, perhaps even my friend Sammy. I thought they would have found me by now as I had written checks, got a job using my social security number and previous work references, hooked up utilities under my given name. I plodded on each day grateful but sad that no one had found me. Did I really want to be lured home? After a while, I stopped expecting to be found. I was alone in the world, but by now, it was oddly comforting in a solitary way. I lived for myself now. This was the life I chose.

Part Three

✤ ✤ ✤

The Pulse of Hopeful Life

2004

Chapter Eleven

I told him everything. Then I lay there feeling both restless and fearless from lack of sleep. The dull light pulsing through the curtains told of the sun's rising, dragging morning along with it.

"You just left," Quentin said softly, slowly, as if trying to dissect the words and place exactly where it fractured my life, filling in the holes he'd noticed in me. His dark hair mussed from the sleepless night, he stared up at the ceiling, his arms resting behind his neck, like wings.

I wanted to respond, defend myself, but let my heavy eyelids win for the moment. I awoke minutes later from the howling wind alive outside, clawing at the windows. Sometimes at night, I still heard Claire's cries in the wind beating against those splintered windows. I'd lie and listen, frozen and unsure, tears seeping through shut lids the way the rickety windows let water squeeze through and puddle on the sill during a thunderstorm. Tonight I listened again to Claire's pleas in the wind.

I lay frozen with dread knowing that I had let everything tumble out, everything I'd taken such care to keep hidden inside. Had I actually said those words to Quentin—told him the story I hadn't uttered before? I rolled to my side, inching closer to him—a question of acceptance I needed answered. I curled my knees against his leg. He stretched his hand over to my face, brushed the tears from my cheek. I felt him push my bangs to the side on my forehead and tenderly rub his fingers over my scar, where my skin was once gaping and mangled. He combed his fingers through my hair. My forehead nestled inside the gap under his collarbone.

In the void between waking and sleep, I felt the mattress shift as he slid off the bed, then rustled around while I feigned sleep. Perhaps he was looking for his glasses or coat, then paused next to the door before leaving. I listened to the sound of his shoes tapping down the stairs. I pried opened my eyes and stroked Hero who had curled into Quentin's leftover warmth.

My head pounded, the physical reality that last night had not been a dream as it seemed to be. I crawled out of bed to fill up my empty glass with water and saw the note he'd left on the counter.

Andria,
I didn't want to wake you this morning.
Thanks for trusting me last night.
I want to see you tonight. Seven?
Quentin

I spent an anxious day wondering whether Quentin would act differently, but I felt a naïve relief at having released the words. This was a huge step—a leap from my third-floor apartment window felt more like it. Where would I land? And would I be able to pick myself up, brush off my knees, and walk away?

Midmorning, an innocent vase of burnt-orange chrysanthemums was delivered to my office. I opened the envelope. "I can't stop thinking about you. Quentin."

They were beautiful, and six years ago, I would have fawned over them. But I couldn't have these oblivious heads peering over my shoulder all day. Plucking the vase from my desk, I pocketed the card and strolled into Abby's office. Abby worked alongside me for years, the closest thing I had to a friend around there. I set the vase onto her desk. "Happy Birthday," I said and turned to leave.

Abby said, "Hold up. My birthday's in June."

"It feels like your birthday," I said and turned back.

"It's not," she said and eyed me suspiciously, scooting the vase forward to get a better look at them and to officially take ownership. "But I never turn flowers away. Today can be my birthday."

"Happy birthday," I said again as I turned the corner, stifling a laugh. Well, along with my leap from last night, I'd made a baby step in the flower department. A month ago, I wouldn't have hesitated throwing them in the garbage, amidst empty soda cans and crumpled paper and rotting half-eaten sandwiches.

At seven, Quentin knocked on my door carrying a bag with take-out Thai. We sat on my floor, my grandmother's quilt spread beneath us, and ate from little boxes filled with panang and mussaman curry and laab. The spicy food tasted better, more alive, than food had tasted to me for years.

We talked easily of everyday stuff—the weather, which was full of dripping snow again; some projects at work; even basketball which was playing on the seldom-used 12-inch television peeking from my armoire—skirting the issue we both knew was hovering.

I had been euphoric earlier realizing that I'd finally released my secret, but now I felt ashamed of my naked skeletons while they dangled in the open, feeling the cool air and the bright light after years of stifling darkness. I'd offered him my past as if I'd poured him a glass of wine. Now he'd drained the glass, we eyed each other, waiting. I looked quickly away, back at the television. I knew how it seemed, if I could have looked at it from the outside in. Most people would react differently in my situation—being grateful one child had lived—but instead, I left my remaining child. I could have spoiled her with toys and pretty little ruffled dresses and endless kisses, but I chose instead to walk away. I watched the basketball passing from player to player on the television screen, panicking. I wanted to disappear. I wore my shame like a bad sweater, hoping he wouldn't notice how it bunched in the shoulders and the hole near my elbow.

"I feel like I should say something about last night."

He focused his eyes on the quilt beneath us—its pattern of white and pink and blue triangles hand-stitched by my grandmother years ago. As if he'd had a response ready and waited for the green light, he said, "Do you miss your life?"

"That hasn't been my life for a long time." I looked into my plate and mixed the curry gravy into the rice. "I could never have imagined leaving, but I just did it. At first, I had these thoughts—they kept crawling back into my mind—about what I would be doing at certain times of the day, if I had stayed. You know, like cleaning the house, making dinner, playing with the girls. But I thought about my life before the accident, never after—you know, with two children, not just one. And when I pictured us together, it was all of us together." I paused, took a bite of the laab, and then continued, "But I made a decision that I wouldn't think about them anymore, and I tried to move beyond the memories as best I could." I paused again, the words dangling in my mind and knowing how they must sound, like I was some kind of robot without emotions or feelings. "I had to squash all those thoughts or I'd kill myself with the pain, realizing what I'd done. How could I sit around and think about what Brett and Lizzie were doing each day? If I lingered on what Lizzie would have for breakfast—oatmeal or cereal or toast—or what she'd wear or what toys she'd play with or which books she'd read, it would have driven me mad. It still does, to think about it, even now, although I have no idea what's in her closet or which books line her bookshelf."

Quentin didn't speak. He nodded but let me keep talking, my words pouring out from an endless source like a channel to the ocean. Maybe this was what I needed, to say them aloud.

"I really did want to stay there with them. So much. But I wanted to be the mom and wife they needed, and I couldn't be either of those things. I had no patience with Lizzie. I'd yell at her every day for the smallest things, like getting out toys while I was cleaning or spilling a glass of milk. I'd blow up every time anything spilled. I was so cruel, and she would cry and tell me that she loved me. Or that she missed Claire too." I thought of her as she was when she was three. No matter what I did, she was so ready to be folded back into my arms if I offered her a place there.

But the worst part, which I didn't dare tell Quentin, was the way she tried to protect me. If I were talking to someone and cried, she would distract us, ask for something or even demand the person leave. She just wanted her normal mother back, but that mother had died too. And a three-year-old child shouldn't be protecting the mother. It wasn't fair. And it wasn't fair that I couldn't change it all back to the way things should have been.

"I wonder what she's like now," I whispered as an afterthought.

"What about Brett?" he asked with what could have been a jealous-boyfriend question, but wasn't.

"I miss him. I miss what we once had together before everything changed. But after that, neither of us was the same. We had changed into two people who couldn't possibly be together. We coexisted. Our love was dead. It wasn't even friendship. If I had stayed, I'd be swallowing anti-depressant pills every day, dwindling into nothing. I didn't want to live that life. I felt my only option was escape. I figured we all would be better off that way." I paused for a moment. "I know how it sounds, so selfish, but I didn't think either of them deserved to be stuck with who I'd become." I wondered if he felt the hollowness of the words that I did as I said them.

He stroked my arm, without words, and I leaned in toward him. Then he asked, "Do you ever think of going back?"

"No. I don't even know where they are or if they still live in Oregon. I broke all ties with anyone who would know."

"Aren't you curious?"

"I suppose. But the cost of finding out isn't worth it."

I knew this conversation wasn't over but felt relieved when Quentin snatched up the remaining food boxes, closed the tops, pulled himself off the ground, and carried them to the refrigerator. "Hey, it's nine and I have a standing date for a stroll through Hanover."

"I think walking in the slush sounds like fun tonight. Suits my mood." We layered on our hooded sweatshirts and coats and boots and stomped down the stairs to wander through the night.

Our feet continued plodding through January's slush, then February's. All the while, Quentin came around more often. We didn't bother waiting around leaning on lampposts anymore. Our walks nearly always included a shared, thrown-together dinner before or a lazy movie afterward.

One night, after explaining to Quentin on another cold walk about how my sister Anna and I used to huddle in the same bed on Christmas Eve—we continued on with the tradition until she got married and moved away—I returned to my apartment alone, changed into dry clothes and layered blankets over myself to warm up. I couldn't shake the vision of Anna from my head—our pillows bunched together lopsided and side-by-side, the darkness overlaying the blankets as we huddled together with the anticipation of what the next morning had in store. Even as two college kids, we squeezed into her twin bed and worried about how we'd done on our philosophy or biology finals. The image of us together wouldn't leave. I ached for her as I'd never before. Maybe I was wrong cutting everyone off. Maybe I did need to be loved. Maybe she could still love me, without expecting too much back. I wanted her back in my life. Well, at least on the other end of the telephone.

Maybe now, maybe enough time had passed and we could get over what everyone would want to talk about—me leaving, Claire dying, and Lizzie, poor Lizzie.

Anna would hate me. I shouldn't have left without telling her.

Lying under my blankets, I played back the film of my memories with Anna. I remembered when she was the big sister coming home for summers in college and I wanted to be near her, following her from room to room like a puppy. I asked her millions of questions, trying to glean information about college life—what classes she was taking, about her professors, what it was like to live with roommates—while we walked down the tree-canopied street behind our house at dusk. The pinks and oranges and purples of the setting sun just barely visible through the shade trees.

I thought about the first time in high school I had a drink of alcohol. I was thirteen. My friends and I filled up on some bitter, dark whiskey sleeping in a thick brown glass bottle under the counter in my junior-high-friend's basement. Then we staggered through town to a party and made our debut as giggly drunks. After a half hour of laughing and kissing some boy whose name I didn't know, I was pulled out of a dark closet by Anna and ushered home. She tucked me into bed and was careful to keep Mom away while I slept it off. Protecting me.

An unfamiliar spontaneity came over me. I picked up the phone and listened to the level-headed zinging of the dial tone. My heart beat, and I pressed down the receiver.

It was 10:30 in the evening, 8:30 in California. If the number I knew was still hers. I picked the phone up again and began dialing the numbers I'd neatly tucked away in my head for years but pressed the receiver again midway through. I couldn't do this. What would I say? It probably wasn't her number anymore. Maybe I'd just dial and see what happened, see if it rang at all.

I dialed the phone with a trembling hand and let the phone ring, clenching my teeth as I waited, ring after ring after—"Hello?" her familiar voice said, her voice so like my own it startled me.

I paused, frightened. I hadn't spoken to her in years. No contact. Not even a Christmas card. I never let her know I was okay. Nothing. She said "hello" again with a little irritation.

"Hi, Anna. It's me, Alex," I said, hearing my name and feeling so detached from it. As different from the person I had become as a childhood photo. She was silent. "Anna, are you there?"

"Yes. I don't believe it's you." Her voice was flat, but then cracked over the "you," and she stopped. I could tell she was crying, from that and a muffled sniff. A tear rolled down my face and then another. Our mom had always been a crier. The three of us would all sit around the television watching *Little House on the Prairie* or some sentimental *Folgers* or long-distance commercial and laugh at each other for our red eyes and noses and tear-streaked cheeks. Crying had been as contagious at our house as the flu.

Anna croaked out, "Where are you?"

"I'm in St. Louis. I live here."

"St. Louis? Why? I mean, why there? What have you been doing?" Her voice sped up, not giving me time to answer. She continued without waiting for a response, "We were sick about you leaving, not knowing where you were. Brett was a mess."

"I didn't think he would even care," I said, sort of to myself but out loud.

"Alex, he lost his baby and then you. I've been so angry with you—well, after I found out your body hadn't washed up on the edge of some river. What happened?" Of course, she'd ask. Her voice was tinged with anger. I deserved this. She was my sister; she wouldn't let me off easy.

"Oh Anna, I just couldn't do it anymore. I had to get out. I kept driving until I came to a place where no one would know me or—pity me. I couldn't be that person everyone averted their eyes from." But I sounded unreasonable now, unjustified.

"I can't believe you could leave Lizzie. How do you leave a child? Your family? I never thought you'd be capable of that, until Brett told me he knew where you were and that you were okay. But he wouldn't tell us where. He was adamant about that. I pestered him for months trying to find out."

"How did he know?" My thoughts were rumbling from my lips low into the receiver. I wasn't waiting for an answer. She didn't know. I sat up rigid on the bed and tried to will the pattern on my bed to explain this to me, how Brett knew all this time where I was and didn't contact me. She let me sit and stew over this for a while, probably knew that I needed to think it through. After a deep breath, I asked, "Anna, do you still see them? How are they?"

"No, I haven't seen them in years. Mom has. Lizzie stays with her every once in a while. Brett and Lizzie moved, a year after you left. They're still in Oregon, but I think they moved to . . . ummm, Red River? I hadn't heard from them until last year. They sent a Christmas card. It had a picture of Lizzie. I can't believe how much older she is. I guess she would be eight now, huh?"

I did quick math in my head, astonished that I hadn't been following the years, and put numbers with both Claire and Lizzie,

6 and 8. "She'll be nine next month," I said. The only picture I had in my head was a three-year-old Lizzie with that chubby, cherubic baby face and apple cheeks.

Anna said, "I don't know if Brett got remarried or what, but the Christmas card was signed Brett, Jen, and Lizzie." She spoke each word slowly so that I'd understand what these names meant.

"Jen? You don't think—" I tapered off, my mind racing. Jen. It couldn't be the Jen that Brett used to work with, the marketing director. Tall, pretty blonde Jen with her constant laughing and touching his arm while I was nearby.

"How are Mom and Beth?" I asked. I didn't want to think about Jen right then, especially if this was the Jen I pictured.

"They're fine. Mom finally retired. But she's teaching a preschool class out of her house now."

"What about you?"

"I'm on number three now. Three boys. I didn't know how to reach you, to tell you about Jackson when he was born. He's two now." We went through everyone in the family, little details about her children and cousins, even Dad who checked in now and then.

We talked until after eleven. Before she hung up, though, she said, "Alex, you'd better call mom." She used the bossy voice I'd been obeying since I was a toddler—getting her things for her, staying out of her room.

"I don't know. But wait, before you go, can I ask you a favor?"

"Sure, if you promise to call mom. Or I'll just give her your phone number myself. And you know I'm going to call you on this number too. It better be yours," she said, her voice stern.

"It is. You can call me here. Do you still have that Christmas card of Lizzie? Would you send it to me?" I forced myself to give her my address, accepting that I was officially out of hiding now. I might as well be listed in the phone book, my location as clear as the black-and-white type on those beige recycled pages.

"I'll see if I can dig it up tomorrow from the Christmas boxes."

I obeyed her demand and called my mother the next night and felt the same trepidation dialing as I had the night before, only worse. My mom could be so severe, as she had when I was younger. Always expecting the best from me, too much. I sort of wished I had told Anna to just give my phone number to her, but I knew she'd be hurt that I didn't call her. And I wanted to be in control. At least for a little while. When she answered the phone, she sounded older, her "Hello" drawn out and slower.

"Mom, it's me," I said. "I'm sorry." I just said it up front, knowing I'd have to apologize over and over to her, which is why I had called Anna first. So much for having control of the phone call.

My mother had always seen the world in black and white; things were either right or wrong, and there was very little wiggle room. And I was so far black that I knew I'd have a long struggle back. It felt impossible. I remembered Lizzie mixing a bunch of watercolors together to create black—she'd learned it in preschool, along with blue and yellow make green, red and yellow make orange—but there was no reverse after the colors were mixed and lay fixed, drying.

"Alexandria, what took you so long?" I could feel relief in her words, as if five years of worry had melted away by the end of the sentence. But I was shocked by how pulled together she was, no quiet sobbing on the other end like I had expected.

"I don't know, mom. I was just trying to stay afloat."

"I don't call leaving Brett and Lizzie staying afloat. How could you? Poor little Lizzie. And right after Claire's—" she hesitated, maybe afraid to say the words, even though she'd always been blunt.

"It's okay. You can say it, Mom. Claire's death. I know she's not coming back. You can say it out loud." My voice was already irritated. Why couldn't she just be happy to hear from me?

"Well, you sure got away quickly. I can't believe my own daughter could do something like that."

"Mom, please, not now. I'm sorry. I just want you to know I'm all right. And I love you."

The silence that hung on the line was unnerving. Of course my mother loved me. Of course she did, I thought while I waited for her to confirm this. "I love you too, Alexandria, but why did you have to go and—" she said with little warmth in her voice.

"I can't explain why. I had to get away. I couldn't stay in that house. Please don't make me live through it again. I just wanted you to know where I am, and that I'm okay."

A half hour later, Quentin knocked on my door. It was after nine. I told my mother goodbye and promised to call again soon. "Hey," I said as I opened the door. I was sitting on a small chair I kept by the front door and slid on my tennis shoes.

When I reached my arms out toward him, he grabbed onto them and pulled me from my chair.

"Are you okay?" he asked.

"So, I called my sister last night, and I just got off the phone with my mom." I opened the door and began stepping lightly down the steps. The night air was cold and heavy and smelled of wood-burning fires, and the sky seemed heavy and pregnant with snow. I wondered when the snow would start falling.

"I'll bet they were happy to hear from you."

"Yeah, I guess so. Well, Anna was. There's something about a sister, how she just lets you back in, just like that, just for calling. But my mother was so intent on telling me how wrong I was. Maybe I shouldn't have called her. She just drives me crazy," I said, facing straight ahead, walking straight to the sidewalk.

Shame flushed my face as we walked through the streets. I felt so much guilt for walking out, and my mother had just confirmed that I should be ashamed. I guess I needed Quentin to see me for who I was—the kind of person who could just walk out on my family, without looking back. He had been so forgiving, I felt like I needed him to condemn me too. If Quentin wouldn't do it willingly, perhaps I would have to call him on it. I sifted this over in my mind until I blurted, "How can you not judge me for what I did?"

He sighed and, looking down, whispered, "Andria, you went through something horrible, something no one should ever have to face. I'm not going to say you should have done this or that because I just don't know. Who can say what one person would do in the same situation? You can't until you've been there."

His patience and understanding baffled me. Of course that was the ideal answer, especially from someone I cared about, but it irritated me that he was just that forgiving. I wanted more from him. I didn't know what, but something else, some type of urgency or anger or incredulity. I looked into his face and he smiled his understanding smile. I stiffened my shoulders, took a deep breath, exhaled in a steaming cloud of breath, and kept walking. After a while, the steady motion soothed me.

I said, "You know, I'd never told anyone before. I mean, I wouldn't let myself get too close to anyone. I worried about how people would look at me, what they'd say."

Getting all sentimental like this just wasn't me. I felt like some dull character out of a Nicholas Sparks novel, someone in love, and I shook my head, trying to snap out of it. Back to my anger. Or was it shame?

I logically couldn't be in love with this person. I was confusing comfort with love. Yes, I felt content when I was with him, I felt more alive, more willing to be myself, whatever that was anymore. Perhaps I was in love. Perhaps it was the idea of loving someone and being loved again. I inched closer to him as we walked, let my arm hang near his.

I asked, "Can we go somewhere different tonight? You can be my invited guest now, back to the cemetery where you saw me." I had thought about taking him to my cemetery with me, now that he knew what had spurned my emotional breakdown that he'd witnessed so long before. It was time to explain what he'd seen. Tonight was the night.

"Are you sure?"

"Yeah."

Acting upon an uncharacteristic surge of confidence, I snatched his hand, feeling tense and exhilarated at our hands touching, through the thin fabric of our gloves. I felt reassured as his hand tightened around mine. I led him down a dark unlit street, then a gravelly back one. We turned into the dark clearing.

"Here we are. Looks different at night," I said, referring back to the morning he'd been here. We shuffled through the trail, matted with thick weeds and foliage wearing a crown of two-day-old snow. This was the trail I always took. I'd been to this small, old cemetery often, many times at night when the wind beckoned me from my fitful sleep.

"This is my place. My thinking spot, I guess you could call it." I pulled him over to the edge of the cemetery on the little hill that was built on top of the mausoleum. From there, you could see all the sparkling lights of Hanover and follow them beyond to most of St. Louis. The myriad twinkling white lights, shining like a fairy village, fanned out before us.

"It's great up here."

"I found it years ago and I came here when I needed to think about Claire or Lizzie. When I'm here, I let myself feast on their memories and not hold back. When I'm here, I feel like Claire's with me. Sounds crazy, I know, but even as I sit here now, I can feel a heaviness, like she's in my arms again." We both looked out over the glittering lights, and Quentin pulled me close to him. Almost an embrace.

"You can see everything from here," he said. He pointed toward the chain of lights on the horizon that faded into the deep velvet sky.

We stood watching for a while, our hands gripping each other's in the cold.

"Lizzie's here too. But I when I picture now, she's stopped aging in my mind, the same way Claire has. I can't picture her any other way than she was when I left." I stopped talking and looked toward Quentin while he was turned toward the light show. "I was here on the Fourth of July one year. You can see all the fireworks, even downtown. There's the arch." I pointed to where the arch was just a firm white horseshoe, so small, like the hoop in a croquet game. "I'm here every year. Best seat in town."

"Maybe I'll come with you this year."

I could feel the warmth of his breath on my face.

"I'm glad you trusted me," he said into my ear as we stood looking out.

"Me too," I said. Maybe it was the night, or the lights, or my cemetery, but I felt completely absolved right then. I wanted to melt into him and live happily, openly, with him next to me.

He must have felt something too because he said, "I think I'm falling in love with you."

He leaned down and kissed me. I held onto his neck, my fingers grasping through my gloves and traveling up to the strong line of his jaw. His lips were as cold as mine, wet and icy, and I shivered, not from cold but from elation. I didn't want to let him go. The kiss didn't last long. He kissed me on the forehead and ducked his head down, kissed me quickly on the lips again.

Without words, he grabbed my hand and we began walking back.

We didn't talk much on the walk home. Just walked, with the comfortable silence that I'd appreciated from some of the earliest walks we'd taken. A moment from my phone conversation with my mother was eating at my happiness, at my calm from minutes before. When my mother was talking about Lizzie, wishing I could return home to domestic bliss, she was disappointed that I couldn't, that Brett was with someone else now. I'd asked her if Brett was remarried. She'd said, "Honey, you and I both know he couldn't have remarried. You two never divorced."

I was clutching the phone. I guess she was right. We had never divorced. I couldn't believe that I had never let it enter my mind. Surely it didn't count for anything. Surely he had somehow ended the marriage—wasn't there some kind of abandonment law? But maybe we were still married.

My face felt hot even in the cold night air, and my shoulders ached as I walked beside Quentin. I felt so transparent, but he didn't seem to notice. He didn't know that I could still be married to Brett. Even though Brett had moved on, divorce or no.

I woke the next morning wide-eyed and excited, dreamily re-enacting my kiss with Quentin, the way I had after my first kiss with Bobby Harris in sixth grade, over and over in my head while my math teacher Mr. Martin rambled on and on about fractions. I jumped out of bed to shower and skipped through my apartment with a feeling I had forgotten existed.

I flew through my daily commute and work, in a daze, anxious to see Quentin again. He left a message on my voice mail at work, asking to meet at a German restaurant called The Danube Bistro, the only sit-down restaurant in Hanover, at six thirty.

As I left my apartment to meet Quentin that evening, I checked my mailbox. A white envelope sat inside, donning big swoopy letters, a familiar handwriting I hadn't seen in years, my sister Anna's. The envelope was addressed to Alex Porter.

I climbed into my car and sighed, to prepare myself for this moment, then eagerly slid my finger along the seam and pulled out the Christmas card. It was a photo of Lizzie. Lizzie was distinctly the same child I knew as a baby and preschooler—older and ganglier than the picture of her I'd kept in my head all these years, but unmistakably my daughter. Lizzie's white blond hair had deepened to a dark blonde, but she still had those beautiful wispy white highlights that kids have from playing in the sun. Shoulder-length hair, flipped out, which framed her heart-shaped face. Her blue-green eyes were still the same—blue on the outer rim with a star of green surrounding the pupil. I would never forget them, though the photo didn't show her up close. Her features were the same, though matured, and I could see the little girl I spent almost four years with inside this face. She wore a red dress with embroidered gold flowers and ribbon around the empire waistline. She sat in front of a lit hearth I didn't recognize, holding a long-haired white kitten with golden eyes.

She smiled up toward something or someone, probably behind the camera. I wondered if it was Brett or maybe the mysterious Jen. Jealousy grounded me as I thought about this woman hugging my daughter and stroking her hair, putting a band-aid on her knee. I scorned the happiness in my child's smile.

The inscription read: Happy Holidays Love, Brett, Jen, and Lizzie. I studied the photograph, bringing it closer to my face, wishing I could smell something of the place from where it came.

I imagined unrealized memories while I stared at her face. Lizzie's first day of school, waiting on the street for the stretched yellow school bus to come by and extend its arms, bidding her in. A backpack weighing her down—loaded with a fistful of sharpened yellow number-two pencils and folders and notebooks, a lunch box with a peanut butter and strawberry jelly sandwich. I pictured her tiny legs stretching in order to climb those tall steps meant for bigger kids. She was so eager to learn, even at three. My precocious daughter. She would sit, leaning her head on my shoulder, snuggled into a blanket with me, on nights when she couldn't sleep, and I'd read to her whatever book I was reading, until her breaths were long and loud and regular, and I would carry her to her bed.

And then Lizzie coming home from the first day of school, so anxious to talk about her day, the kids, her new teacher. I wasn't there on good days. Or the bad—for her to fall into, to sink into my arms, to hold her and tell her that everything was okay. I was away, selfishly thinking that I was doing her a favor by not being there. My sacrifice. I gasped for air, my nose tingly and stinging the way it always was before I cried, at the thought that she most certainly thought I left because I didn't love her.

I played through my mind other days—Lizzie going to the doctor's when she had an ear infection. Who took her there when she was sick? Whose hand did she hold while the doctor poked the light into her ear or when she got a shot? While I was miles away, administering to my own pain, closing myself up, letting my wounds heal while gouging new wounds into her fair, fragile skin. I wiped the tears from my face and swallowed, tucking the card into my bag. I drove slowly to the restaurant, trying to allow enough time for my splotchy red face to fade back.

Quentin was waiting in the foyer of the restaurant. Frazzled, I walked through the door as he held it open. While we waited to be seated, he rested his hand on the small of my back—a new intimacy we now shared. The hostess led us to a booth. I glanced distractedly at the menu and shut it, then gazed out the window, drumming my fingertips on the checkered tablecloth. A pink carnation sat lonely in a small vase in the center of the table. I studied it a moment, then pushed it aside behind the salt and pepper shakers so I didn't have to look into its fringy eye.

A stringy-blond woman with a wrinkled face came to take our order. Her name was Gwendolyn, her plastic name badge showed. She asked what we'd have. After she walked off with our menus, I peered around the restaurant, scouring the tables for people who were sitting within hearing distance. Lowering my voice, I mumbled, "I got something in the mail today." I slid my hand into my bag, set the card on the table, and nudged it toward him. "This is Lizzie—now." I toyed with the cloth napkin while he looked at the picture. "She's grown up," I said.

He looked up, and I grabbed back the photo, returned it to the safety of my purse.

"I can see you in her."

"Yes," I said. Several minutes later, Gwendolyn left our meals, setting a brie and Gruyère fondue pot before me. I dipped braunbrot into the fondue and bit into a gherkin and watched the small blue flame lick the pot.

Quentin neglected his steaming pork chop and potatoes, not even picking up his fork. He just looked at me, waiting for me to say something, and finally asked, "What do you want to say?"

It hit me so suddenly. As I sat there, I knew I needed to close out the old chapters of my life, a thousand unfinished books—each extended, lying open, scattered over tables, counters, and cluttering the floor. I felt overwhelmed by the tiny missing details, the plot arcs I never saw completed. If I didn't close all these books, I would never be able to start a new book with Quentin, or anyone.

"I have to go back." Hearing it startled me. I wanted to find Lizzie, stroke her hair, kiss her head. Tell her I'm sorry for leaving. I hadn't decided this before. It just came flying out, like roused bats from a disturbed attic.

"For good?"

"No, not to stay. But I want to go there, see Lizzie, talk to her." I was too afraid to tell him I needed to go back to get a divorce as well.

"I think—going back could help you." He spoke slowly. He finally took a bite of his chop, which relieved me. He chewed, took a drink, then continued, "It's going to be very difficult."

"I don't even know what I'll do," I said.

"You'll figure it out." His voice was reassuring. I wished I could take his optimism with me. It was easy to sit hundreds of miles away and say it will all be okay.

After several quiet moments, Quentin took a drink of his soda and whispered, "Are you still in love with him?"

"No, of course not. But I think I may still be married to him."

"Oh." He drew it out as he was saying it, hesitated, then nodded. "Yes, you should probably go. But I want you to know," and his eyes locked deeply into mine, "that I'm not saying I want you to try to fit back into their world. I think this could stop your dizzying habit of tormenting yourself. Go back there, get what you need, and then you'll be free to move on." He reached his hand across the table. His hand was shaking as he tried to squeeze mine, like it was supposed to be reassuring to me, but maybe not to him. His understanding nature, that I'd scorned last night, was exactly the reassurance that I needed tonight.

Yes. It seemed so simple from the safety of these walls and the safety of the arms of someone who thought he loved me. Perhaps this is what I needed so that I could stop hiding and find some sort of solace in the world, in other people, in myself.

"I wish you could go with me and hold my hand," I said, knowing that this was something I had to do on my own.

"You'll be fine. You're stronger than you give yourself credit for. And I'll be reachable, if you need me."

"I'm not convinced I'm ready for this." I looked at my food. How was I supposed to eat when my stomach was in knots from thinking about confronting my past?

When we had finished, Gwendolyn cleared our plates. My cup was empty. We didn't move. I was scared. I could feel more stones tumbling down from the wall I had so carefully built around me.

We sat at our booth for a while after we finished eating. Gwendolyn continued filling our glasses. The other workers noisily rolled silverware inside cloth napkins, joking and laughing, in preparation for tomorrow's round of meals. We were the only patrons left in the restaurant. When we finally walked out, my legs were stiff.

It was snowing and windy. I'd heard thunder rumbling during dinner, which during winters in St. Louis have been known to foretell heavy snowfalls. As we stepped outside, the snow fell in big round flakes. I walked alongside Quentin to my car. "Come to my apartment," I said, rushed, shielding my face from the snow. He agreed. Driving through Main Street, I watched his headlights behind me in the rear-view mirror while my tires gripped the snow-covered street.

I thought about how I'd told myself what I had needed when I first arrived here—to be alone, to be exempt from feeling. If I just didn't put myself in a position to get hurt again, then I was safe. Now I had put myself back into a vulnerable position. I was walking in front of a dartboard while several drunks threw darts blindfolded, knowing it was a matter of time before I was sure to feel the sharp point of a dart in my skin. But for now, it felt like some absurd extreme sport. I ran past smiling, full of adrenaline. I needed to have Quentin. I was ready.

We hiked up the stairs to my apartment, then shook off our coats and shoes and left them scattered on the floor. We settled into the stiff formal chairs in my apartment, although I felt anxious to be closer to him, to run my fingers through his snow glistened hair.

"So, it was chance that brought you here," he said as if he'd been tossing the idea back and forth in his head on the drive here.

"Yeah, I guess so."

"When do you think you'll go?"

"I don't know, I don't—," I said. I looked down at my hands fidgeting in my lap. "I need to do this. Brett's living with someone, and this will free us both. And I want to see Lizzie. I want to know who she is, and I want her to know who I am. I don't expect her to understand why I left, but I want her to know it wasn't her fault, that I loved her, that I still do. That that's *why* I left."

"You're going to go there." His voice was slow and pensive, as if he were thinking out loud. His eyes turned serious and solemn, penetrating me. "Things might not go exactly the way you hope." He treaded on these words delicately, as if they were a smooth sheet of ice.

I kept seeing her face in the photo that was tucked away in my bag. "I know. But when I think about her, I can't believe I left her. I shouldn't have been allowed to make any decisions then—shouldn't have been allowed to pick what color to paint a wall. I left so absentmindedly. I'd shut out the fact that my daughter is off miles away growing up. I tried for so long not to let memories of her creep into my thoughts. Almost as if she'd never even existed. Worse than if she'd died too."

The room was silent, but the air was heavy. I made up my mind. I was going. As silence hovered, I stood and went to him, grabbed his hand, and pulled him slowly up from the chair. He stood and I crept into his arms, needing them around me, needing to be held. I hooked my arms around his waist and held on, like a child afraid in the water, holding to the edge of the pool.

Chapter Twelve

Lizzie's picture took up permanent residence in the bag I toted everywhere with me so I could pull it out whenever I thought about canceling my trip and just staying here, where I'd molded my life to the shape I needed. Maybe I didn't need to go back. Did I really need a divorce? Maybe Quentin would be perfectly happy with me not having to *officially* move on. Didn't Brett do it?

Perhaps I would call Brett first and see how he'd respond to me on the other end. But in my mind, it didn't go well. I'd already taken the cowardly route, and now I needed to stand up and face it. If Brett chose to pelt me with stones from a snarling crowd, I had to stand up straight, look him right in the eye, and take it, owning my decision to leave.

My mother—although it pained me to ask her—gave me Brett's phone number and address. I scribbled it into my planner and tucked it away in my suitcase. Still, I was curious to see where Brett was now, what he was doing, so I googled him. Brett Porter was a common name, and the search engine returned with several hundred options—including a golf pro, an engineer, and a movie agent. I didn't have the time or patience to sift through all of them. I looked up his company's name, but the URL didn't work. I shut down my laptop, guilty that I'd even looked. Brett and Lizzie lived in Red River now, so even if I didn't call him to let him know I was coming, I knew where to go. I wasn't ready to call him.

Anxious and eager to know what the upcoming weeks had in store, I thought of little else. When I envisioned how it would all play out, I got nothing more than a little closure and summers with Lizzie. I'd return to Hanover and Quentin would tell me how he needed me in his life and we'd be married. He'd treat Lizzie just like his own daughter, and we'd take her to movies on Saturdays like a regular family. Of course he'd have to understand I didn't want to have other children. But that wouldn't matter. Our love would be strong enough. Yeah, okay, I realized this was some fairytale life that wasn't mine, but it was the constant dream I tucked in my head to keep me motivated. I wasn't too far gone; deep down I knew it wouldn't go this well.

On Monday, I waited in the conference room for a quick overview with my boss Carol, who was heading the Compaq project, and the rest of the Compaq team. After each of us writers gave a summary about how far we were along in our sections and how they were coming together, I lingered while the others filed out. Carol was gathering her papers together when I asked, "Can I have a quick word with you?"

"Of course, Andria. Come into my office." We walked together, our shoes clicking out-of-sync on the hard floor as we made our way to her office. She shut the door behind me.

I sat in the brown leather chair across from her desk. As Carol sat at her desk and swiveled the chair toward me, I said, "I know this isn't the best timing, but I need to take a couple days off." I took a deep breath and waited. I don't know why this was so difficult for me. I'd worked here for four years and had never asked for time off, never took my vacation days, never was sick. I had 14 vacation days each year that kept rolling over unused to the next year. Just to sit unused again. Like the rocks Lizzie used to collect and pile into a corner on the front porch during the summer. Always a couple more heaped on now and again, but never really played with. Just sitting useless in the corner.

"Most of my sections are finished for the Compaq project, but if I can get next week off, I'll have a couple days to finish them up, plus I can work over the weekend before the deadline."

She looked at me without speaking, just narrowed her eyes for a moment, I guessed trying to figure me out, then smiled and said, "It's about time. Of course, you go. You could use a break. And I know you'll have your chapters ready along with everyone else." She had turned toward her computer as I stood and made my way to the door, in the glow of her warm smile.

"Thanks, Carol."

"Enjoy your time," she said as her head bent over a file and began leafing through papers. "You can leave the door open."

I booked a flight that left on Sunday, with a short layover in Salt Lake City, and reserved a rental car to drive from Portland to Red River. My landlady, Debbie, agreed to check in on Hero every day, fill her food and water bowls, check her litter box, scratch behind her ear.

Saturday night, Quentin sat on my bed, stroking Hero's fur, while I packed my bag. I'd had this feeling before—nervousness mixed with excitement, apprehension, but eagerness. I think it was in grade school when I was riding the bus ride to 4-H camp, not knowing anyone and unsure if anyone would like me, but excited that this was a week away from home doing fun things—like swimming, hiking, telling campfire stories. And hopefully making friends. Oh, and there would be boys—across the way in the separate cluster of cabins.

I pulled open a drawer and filled my bag. Just chucking floppy folded shirts and pants into the open mouth of my bag, a baby bird waiting to be fed. When the bag was full, Quentin stood and put his arm around me.

"You're going to be fine," he said, so reassuringly that I believed him for a moment. He pulled five pair of pajama bottoms out of my bag. "I don't think you're going to need all these. I'd focus on jeans. Or maybe a pair of khakis."

Leaning my forehead onto his chest, I let out a snort of a laugh and said, "What would I do without you?" Then smiled up into his face, pulled his neck toward me, and kissed him.

I had to do this alone, but in so many ways I wished Quentin could come along—to calm me when I was jittery or frightened; put a faithful, steady hand on my shoulder to prod me along; give me another of his easy smiles. But I couldn't ask him to do that and wouldn't. I put myself here, and I had to find my own way out.

That night, Quentin stayed over. I needed him to keep his arms around me and hold me and make me feel that everything would be okay. But I couldn't sleep, hearing someone else breathing next to me. I'd become accustomed to sleeping on my own, which had been an adjustment on its own after I left Brett. Now it was hard to relax with another breathing body nearby. Despite the lack of sleep, his presence gave me an added strength, a boost, an invisible hand pushing me onto the airplane the next morning.

As I sat in my narrow seat and buckled the dingy seat belt, I panicked. I wasn't afraid of flying, never had been. I didn't have to drug myself, sleep the whole way with my arms wrapped around a disposable pillow. Not me. What scared me now was that I couldn't turn back. The air inside the plane already seemed too thin, and I started counting out breaths, remembering to breathe in and out again. I adjusted the vent so I could feel the air blowing on my face. Then I tried to read.

I eyed the large computer manual sleeping in my bag, but couldn't focus on work now. Instead, I yanked the flimsy softcover from my carry-on. As of late, my pleasure reading had been reduced to several pages while I scarfed down a ham and cheese sandwich at my desk or a couple drowsy pages before bed. I opened the book and held it open while my eyes wandered out the small window to my left and watched the ground move farther and farther away until I couldn't see anything but white—the plane was engulfed in a puffy, cheerful, suffocating cloud.

Several bags of peanuts, two Diet Cokes, two short naps, and a layover later, the plane circled above Portland. I looked down into the city, surrounded by a green expanse of forest. My stomach flipped at the thought of being back here, smelling its comforting scent, seeing its raw beauty again. I had loved living in the Northwest. My life had been here, my happiness. My eyes followed the tiny streets, snaking along, imagining what it felt like for a spirit to look down on people still living. Did they actually look down from above? Do they really float around? Looking down from a place we hope exists, this heaven that had made me feel an insignificant amount better when Claire died? As we descended to the runway, the cars and the streets grew larger, like those sped-up videos of a plant sprouting, a flower blooming and then dying in mere seconds. Time fast forwarded.

Walking along the airport corridor with a suitcase and carry-on tugging on my shoulders, I looked around and realized everything was the same. It seemed like nothing had changed, like I was coming back home from a weekend trip. I remembered the airport, remembered where everything was, so that my body just moved in the right direction. I didn't follow the arrowed signs. My hands were playing a song on the piano I hadn't played in years. Mechanically fingering the rhythm. I was standing before the car rental kiosk, like I didn't remember I hadn't coursed my way through this song in five years. I'd have to be careful not to just drive to the house where Brett and I had lived. I could imagine myself driving up, being frustrated that my garage door opener wasn't in the car and my key didn't fit into the front door.

I rented a white Ford Taurus and lobbed my bag into the trunk. Before long, I was driving Route 20, the two-lane highway that cut through the forest along an ambling river. I knew the route well. The Ponderosa pine trees stretched up to the sky, looming deep green, creating a narrow tunnel, beckoning me home to a place that once held everything I loved. I focused rather on the green wall it created beyond the road, a wall of trees.

As I drove, I worked on convincing myself that I had to come here, that I had no choice. I kept the windows sealed, unwilling to let the scent of fresh pine lure me back to a life I'd abandoned. I refused to be mesmerized by the sound of rushing water from the river. When I crossed over the pass, the ground beneath the dense forest was packed with snow. The snow usually stayed year-round. My eyes focused on several burned areas, where only the largest pines remained, their trunks charred. Some stumps remained, reminding me of the trees they once were. Everything else—the smaller pines, shrubs, and even the grass—were gone, just empty spaces. Hollow.

I drove to Red River and parked my car at the Best Western. I hadn't made arrangements beforehand, just figured there'd be some vacancies and, of course, there were. I got a room on the second floor. After I set my bag down on the floor and collapsed onto the bed, I realized I hadn't eaten a real meal all day, just the peanuts on the plane. Despite my queasiness at being back here, the hunger persisted so I ordered in a pizza. I sat on the bed cross-legged and watched the local news—it thrilled me that I still remembered some of the news reporters' faces—and licked grease and cheese off my fingers. I wanted to relax tonight. Tomorrow I'd begin.

Dressed in flannel pajama bottoms and a t-shirt, I slid between the sheets and flipped through three or four television shows—an old rerun, a detective show, and a home decorating show—nothing held my interest. I stayed up until after midnight and fell asleep with the sound of the television my only companion.

The next morning, I woke startled about my foreign surroundings. Pale light stamped the walls and I looked around, recognizing the generic hotel furniture from yesterday. I jumped out of bed. While dressing, I considered how I would face Brett and Lizzie. Perhaps I could just hang around town for a while, hope I'd run into them. I might choose to be somewhere they'd be. I didn't want to be a stalker. But let's face it: I would have to use some stalker qualities to find them that way.

And I didn't want to just show up on their front step. I'd wait, though, and use the address as a last resort.

Lizzie should be in school. Maybe I could swing by the elementary school—Lizzie would be in third or fourth grade by now. I was disheartened that I didn't even know which grade my own child was in. But finding Lizzie without Brett's consent would be counterproductive. And I didn't want to pounce on her. Yes, I would talk to Brett first, to be fair.

It was a typical winter day in Oregon, cloudy and murky and dull. From inside my motionless car, hands grasped onto the steering wheel, I hesitated. I had no plan. Where would I go? I could start with food. That was easy enough. I stopped for breakfast at a drive-through. While I waited in my car, my eyes followed a sandy-haired girl holding her father's hand as they walked along the sidewalk. I wondered where they were going, maybe to the dentist or a doctor's appointment. I regretted missing these simple mundane acts with Lizzie. Engrossed in watching the girl and her dad, I hadn't counted out the change and was scrambling for money, dropping coins onto the floor as the visored worker held her cupped hand out to me.

Nibbling my sausage egg biscuit, I drove the highway toward Addison, the town where I'd lived. It was a twenty-minute drive, and the car took me straight to my old neighborhood. Driving by my old house, its familiarity stung me with regret and little changes stood out, which seemed so obviously wrong. A swing had been added to the front porch and a group of baby pine trees lined the front beds. The exterior of the house was the same— the same deep red brick, which Brett and I had compromised on when we'd built the house. I'd wanted a gray brick, and he'd wanted stone. I remembered lazy afternoons on this grass when Brett called to say he'd be coming home late, and I'd herd the girls outside to give us a change of scenery. It always worked. I'd spread a blanket in the front yard and read to them or let them hunt for bugs or rocks.

It was time to move on. As a former member of the neighborhood watch program here, I knew I'd be calling attention to myself as a "lurker" if I lingered too long. I drove on through familiar streets that made me yearn to hold Claire and fold Lizzie in my arms. I had to find Lizzie.

Parking the car in front of another house I remembered well, I got out and knocked on the front door. I wasn't sure if Sammy—my old best friend—would still be here. After all, it had been five years. No harm checking. I waited. A dog barked through the door but no one came. Looking around at the houses on the other side of the street, I finally heard faint footsteps approaching the door. Sammy swung open the wooden door. She was still pretty, older, shorter hair. A white-blond girl squeezed under her arm and stood looking up at me, backed against her mom for protection.

"Sammy?" I said. She studied me, squinting her eyes, looking hard into my face. Of course she remembered me.

"Alex, come in. It's been forever." She hugged me quickly and hard, then led me inside, not letting go of my arm, directing me to the couch, locking her arm with mine.

"I hope it's okay I just stopped by."

"Of course!"

We caught up with each other for nearly an hour. Mostly my whereabouts and how her family was doing, how she was. How I was. I felt such comfort in the warmth of her concern. Always my most blunt friend, she asked what had been hovering in her mind when first appeared on her front step, "What are you doing here now?"

"Trying to make things right," I said naively. "I want to see Lizzie. And I guess Brett and I should probably make things official—you know, since we're not together and probably shouldn't still be married."

"Have you seen them?" she asked while she brushed her fingers through her daughter's tangled sleep hair to try to clean her up. The girl whimpered that it hurt and leaned away, pulling from her mother's arms and scurried off.

"No. Not yet. I just got here last night. I know they don't live in Addison anymore. They moved to Red River, I hear. I'm not quite ready for that yet, so I was driving around and my car just brought me here."

"I've wondered about you. I called your house and left a bunch of messages before I knew you'd left. Finally, Brett answered the phone and told me. His mother was there from

Washington to help take care of Lizzie until he found a day care. But I didn't hear much after that. I saw your house was for sale a year or so later. It's so good to see you again."

We talked a little longer, about people we both knew, mutual acquaintances. Who had divorced, who had moved, who ran off with whom. Little pieces of gossip. I got nearly five year's worth of information in an hour. Finally I stood and said, "I guess I should go and do what I came here to do." We drifted toward the front door. "I don't know how to do this. Do you think I should just show up at their house? Like I did to you?"

"I don't know. I should call Stephanie. Didn't her husband and Brett used to play basketball together on some league? Maybe they still stay in contact or something." I nodded in agreement. She picked up the phone and dialed. I tried to appear nonchalant, studying a framed photograph of her family, while my stomach turned anxious circles. I tried to make out words, but couldn't hear well. She sidled up to me a moment later. She was smiling proudly, like a preschooler who'd put together her first puzzle all by herself.

"So?"

"Well, Stephanie said her husband's company put in the data and phone lines at Brett's office. Or Internet, I'm not sure. She's going to call her husband to see where the office is; she couldn't remember it off the top of her head. She's calling right back." Sammy rubbed my arm and said, "You want a Diet Coke?"

"Sure."

She sauntered off to the kitchen and brought back a can. The phone rang. Stephanie relayed to Sammy, then to me, the name of Brett's company, which was NOS Software. His office was in Red River. "In those professional buildings, the gray multistory office buildings on the edge of town. Down and across the street from The Stacked Deli. Do you know where that is?" Sammy asked.

"I'll find it." I checked my watch and left the unopened soda can on the kitchen counter. "I'm staying at the Best Western in Red River. Let's get together again while I'm here." I had missed the comfort of friendship with a woman, the friendship Sammy and I had, the type of relationship I'd refused to have since.

As I drove out of my neighborhood, I contemplated the best course to take. Popping in on Brett at work might not be the best idea. I needed a quiet place to think. I drove to the cemetery where Claire was buried and parked my car up alongside where wilted flowers had once drooped over the newly shoveled ground. At that time, nothing marked her place but a patch of dead yellow grass. Now all the grass was a yellowish green, and crunchy from the cold, the same. I climbed out from the car and walked to her headstone. I hadn't seen it before. Brett and I planned what we wanted, but it hadn't been placed before I left. The headstone was a small pink granite rectangle. Her name was chiseled into the stone, along with a little picture of an angel and a bear, for her nickname, Claire Bear. I chose the picture out of a binder with different types of angels and random child toys. Below her name and the dates was the quote we agreed on: "Farewell! Thou art too dear for my possessing." I'd borrowed it from one of Shakespeare's sonnets.

A faded pinwheel poked out of the ground nearby and spun lazy circles in the chilled wind. Nylon orange, pink, and white daisies sat in a cup, windblown and dirty. I wondered when Brett and Lizzie had last been here. They probably couldn't visit as often now that they moved to Red River. Although it was chilly, I slipped my sweater off and spread it on the ground directly in front of her headstone, then kneeled on it and bent over, grazing the shiny granite surface and tracing each letter of her name with my index finger.

Then I sat down, cross-legged, back straight and rigid, staring ahead. A harsh gust of wind whipped my hair into my eyes, stinging, ready tears blurring the words I mouthed over and over "thou art too dear . . . ." Tears dripped into my mouth, tasting of the sea. I didn't attempt to wipe the hair from my face. Just sat there, resigned and helpless. And lazy, like the neglected daisies being bullied by the wind, their petals flapping.

The wind nudged me, pushed me away, told me to leave. I wasn't wanted there.

Crumbling onto the wet, frozen ground, I cried. How could Lizzie want me here? I tried to remember her as a baby, as I'd held her in my arms and remembered the way she'd smile up at me. Her trusting smile. But the face I saw wasn't Lizzie's, it was Claire's. "Help me do this, Claire," I whispered into the grass, its prickly tops scratching at my face.

I'd been there nearly an hour, ignoring the cars and people passing through. When I pulled my body up off the ground, my back and legs and shoulders ached. I stumbled to the car and cranked up the heat for the drive back to Red River.

I still hadn't decided how I was going to connect with Brett. I couldn't just saunter up to the front desk and request to see him, as any business contact would do. If the Jen from the Christmas card is the Jen that Brett used to work with, she might be there. I didn't want to make things too uncomfortable. Bursting into his office would be selfish and cruel. Plus, that would blow this into a scandal. If there was one thing I was certain about, it was that my reappearance wouldn't exactly thrill Brett. I could simply call his office and try to arrange a time when we could meet, at his convenience. Of course, he could refuse to see me at all. The most passive, and thus the most appealing, option was to wait in the parking lot. Stalk him, wait until he left his office and talk to him. But what if he wasn't alone? What if Jen was with him? What if he was with a colleague discussing important business things and there I was, waltzing toward him? Magically appearing out of thin air after nearly five years. What if he was away, traveling or something, and I waited for useless hours?

I took each option, tasted them and rolled them around in my mouth, spit them out. Less optimistic than I'd been back in Hanover, when I acted each scenario out in my mind, it always ended the same way—Brett steaming with fury and shaking his head in disgust. "How could you?" I could hear him saying, "You're her mother."

Upon entering Red River, I drove through town to the office buildings Sammy had described and made my way through the parking lot until I saw the name of the company on a sign near the entrance of the building. I was surprised to see this was the only name for the entire building. The company had grown. Still hours before I expected him to walk out those doors, I stopped to get some lunch and went back to my hotel room to watch some television. I also took a hot bath; I needed to relax and to wash the smeared dirt off my face and skin from the lying on the ground at the cemetery. I turned the lights down, closed my eyes, and attempted to relax. I had nothing left to do but find Brett.

Chapter Thirteen

Arriving at the parking lot after three, I settled my car into a spot close to the building's front entrance. I had a decent view of who was walking in and out. Every time the doors swung open, I braced myself and watched from behind an open newspaper. I hadn't seen Brett in years, but I had spent five years waking up next to him. Of course I would recognize him when he walked out.

I didn't expect to see him for a while. I couldn't get him home before 6:30 or 7:00 when he was coming home to me. Always leaving his dinner warming in the oven while Lizzie, Claire, and I ate. We'd hear the garage door opening while we were eating, and Lizzie would rush off to hide behind the couch or underneath the table, a game she never tired of playing, and wait for him to find her.

After a half-hour of waiting, I was startled by the woman who emerged from the building—Jen, with her flaxen hair floating behind her. She wore a black pin-striped suit and power heels. My eyes penetrated her until she stepped into her car, a dark blue Toyota sedan, and drove away. I strained to see whether or not there was a car seat in the back of the car, then realized that Lizzie would be out of a car seat by now. I felt so out-of-touch as I sat there, alone, in the parking lot hidden behind my ink-printed mask.

Against my better judgment, I started the car and followed her. Was she going to a late lunch? It was 3:30 pm. But here was a dangling morsel, and I had to bite. After all, I was sitting in this empty parking lot, waiting for something, and here it was.

I rolled out after her and stayed several cars behind as she drove. She turned left and slowed, as the school lights blinked their 20 m.p.h. and the closer we came to the stout red-brick building, more kids swarmed in every direction in clusters, trailing backpacks and clutching lunchboxes. I pulled off to the side of the road, pretending to search for something in my glove compartment, as I watched from thirty feet away.

Jen's car stopped along the curb near a group of four girls, huddled together. A child with golden hair and a brown sweater—my child perhaps—looked up and said, "See you tomorrow!" The other little girls waved and said, "Bye Lizzie," before looking back down at something. Lizzie heaved her overloaded backpack from the ground onto her shoulder and tripped toward Jen's car, opened the door, and climbed in. Gripping the steering wheel, I watched unblinking while the car veered back into the moving traffic, continuing around the turnabout and out through the exit. My hands were shaking.

Putting my car in gear, I tried to edge back into the flow of cars and quickly pulled out, scared I was going to lose them. A car honked behind me, but I waved and pulled out anyway. I couldn't get too far behind. Keeping my eyes on the blue Toyota, I followed several cars behind. I was the only car behind her when the blue Toyota turned into a side street, a neighborhood entrance. It was a nice neighborhood with the houses spread quite far apart with many naked, but big-boned trees separating them.

I saw Jen turn her head back. Did she realize I was following her? She was probably just talking to the child in the back seat. That child was Lizzie, I knew, but I had to distance her in my head or I wouldn't be able to remain calm. Still, I braked and tried to stay behind a little farther. At the corner of a cul-de-sac, a garage door yawned open and the Toyota disappeared inside.

The house was enormous and stone—a looming three-story, Tudor-styled house with dormer windows and a Romeo-and-Juliet balcony and wrought-iron railings, a circular drive-way. I drove past and stopped several houses down. Lizzie must have gone inside, because I saw Jen stroll to the front of the house, to the mailbox, alone. The yard was manicured and pristine, and I thought snidely that Brett paid someone to manage his lawn, as he never had much interest in lawn care before. Jen sifted through the mail on her distracted walk back to the garage. I worried that she would see my car, but she didn't seem to notice. The garage door shut, closing me out. She wasn't heading back to work. I envied this woman, her intimacy with my daughter, her intimacy with my husband, her place in my family. How dare she step into my family as simply as if she were wearing a pair of jeans I'd left behind in my closet?

I pulled out my planner and double-checked the address my mother had given me with the number on the mailbox and the street. As I already knew, it matched—267 Magnolia Way. After a couple more moments of taking it all in, I drove back to the office parking lot, resuming my watch. Waiting for Brett.

Yes, I'd come here to get the divorce. That was my main reason for being here. And of course I'd wanted to see Lizzie. But as I sat there, I was anxious to get to Lizzie. Her ten-foot jaunt to the car kept playing in my mind. I couldn't think about anything else and felt such a sense of urgency as I sat in my car waiting, that my body trembled and I couldn't even hold the newspaper without rustling it from shaking. Finally, I flung the paper into the passenger seat and rested my head on the steering wheel, trying to steady myself.

After several more agonizing hours, Brett finally appeared. It was nearly 6:30 pm. I recognized his gait immediately, his familiar steps and shoulders in a white button-down shirt, unbuttoned at the top. His tie hung loosely around his neck. His steps echoed off the pavement. I opened the car door and sprang out, walked quickly toward him. As he reached for the handle of a black BMW M6, I croaked out his name, "Brett." My voice was shaking and cracked and didn't sound right in my own head.

He released the car door and stood there, unmoving, his eyes boring into me. Almost as if he were seeing or hearing a ghost. Frozen. Then he looked away, off into the sky, refusing to look back at me.

"Can I talk to you?" I said, stopping several feet away, afraid to come any closer.

He shook his head in a combination of disbelief and contempt. "I don't believe it." His voice was dry, stale. Then he started to smile, but the smile twisted into a disgusted scowl. "I don't believe you came back here."

"I don't expect you to welcome me back." I tried to keep my voice soft, so he'd know I wasn't here for an argument. "I thought we have some things to work out. And I'm sorry." I don't know why I said it, it just came out. But he still wouldn't look up. Instead, his head hung down, focusing now on the ground.

"What do you want?" His voice was ice and his bone-hard eyes held me, whittling me down to a flaky, useless leaf that had hung around much too long through the winter. I used to know this person as well as myself, my girls. He held himself away from me, miles away, as if we'd never met.

But still feeling the urgency, I blurted, "I want to see Lizzie."

Not a moment passed. "No." He opened the door to his car, as if to signify the end of the discussion.

"Brett, you can't just deny your daughter the chance to see her mother. What if she wants to see me? I'm her mother."

"No, you're not," he said, just like that. The truth of it hit me like a punch in the gut. He settled into the driver seat, but left the door open a crack. "You lost the right to say that four years ago."

"Please, Brett," I said, "just talk to me. We'll get some dinner or something, talk it over."

"I'm with someone else now." He started the engine.

"I know. I mean, I understand. I'm not asking for my life to be handed back to me. Please, just meet me for dinner. And I'm here to give you a divorce, so you can remarry or whatever it is you need to do. What about breakfast tomorrow? Meet me at Norris Cafe at 7:30. Just hear me out." He backed up and drove off, leaving me standing in a pool of lamplight. He didn't say no. I'd be there tomorrow morning, and I hoped he would be too.

But he wasn't. I sat alone at a booth designed for four, sipping weak coffee. I thought he would at least hear what I had to say—maybe he'd even be a little interested in where I'd been, what I'd been doing for the last five years. Did he really want to keep me away from Lizzie as if I were vermin, a danger, something to protect her from—as if I'd never changed her diaper, or fed her late into the night, or covered her in a soft blanket to keep her warm in the dark? I unfolded and refolded the sheet of paper I'd brought with me, where I'd written points about why I should be able to see Lizzie. I'd made the list the night before. Every point on this list would sound foolish when spoken aloud, I knew that. I searched the parking lot again for Brett's BMW again. Not there.

Maybe Brett went home last night and talked to Lizzie about it. Maybe she had already made a decision. Maybe it was Jen who didn't want him to come. Maybe it was him.

My stomach felt hollow and ached from hunger. After twenty minutes, I ordered a breakfast—sausage, eggs, bacon, biscuits with gravy, fruit bowl. I swallowed each bite greedily. I ate as if the food could fill the part of me that was most empty.

I followed Jen's car from the parking lot to pick Lizzie up from school again that afternoon. I needed a fix, just another glimpse. It was something about being back here, where I had lived most the time as a mother, and I couldn't shake the "mom" desire to fit my days into a schedule. Yes, I was here alone, but I had two activities etched into my schedule—following Jen to pick Lizzie up from school and waiting for Brett in the parking lot after work.

Following several cars behind Jen, I drove. I was a stalker. I felt exhilarated, the adrenaline pumping through me. I saw Lizzie again from afar. She was wearing a green sweater and jeans. Her hair fastened in a ponytail. She skipped excitedly to Jen's car and hopped in—almost identical to my memory from yesterday, stamped into my mind, making it bolder. I followed them to their neighborhood before turning back, then waited in the parking lot until Brett walked out the doors shortly after six.

I'd brought a book along this time and had settled my nerves enough to get through a couple of chapters when he appeared. Rain was drizzling. The light rain tapping on my car was peaceful and nostalgic, reminding me of a time when this was my home and it rained soft and reassuring like this nearly every day in the winter. I stepped out of the car onto the gleaming black pavement. Brett anticipated me tonight. He surveyed the remaining cars in the parking lot, willing me forward. I appeared, this time walking languidly toward him with my hands thrust into my jean pockets, an expected intruder.

"Hi," I offered matter-of-fact, as I splashed uncaring through shallow puddles. Let my shoes get wet, I didn't care. His blue button-down oxford was already speckled from the rain. He wore a diagonally striped tie, a classic yellow and navy, one I remembered from years before. Maybe he'd chosen that tie purposefully.

"You're here," he said.
"Where else would I be?"
"You could go back to wherever it is you came from."

I laughed, trying to downplay his anger and twist it into friendly badgering. His eyes were steady, hard, cold, hostile, burrowing into me until my smile faded.

"I know I deserve this."

"Yes, you do. And you don't deserve my time." He walked hard steps toward his car, while I followed behind.

"Brett, please," I begged him, then grabbed his arm. I knew before I did it that it was a mistake. He yanked his arm from my grasp, and I stood back. But it worked. He stopped and turned. He was staring at me with impenetrable gray-green eyes, narrowed and angry.

"It's funny really, Alex, the way you just appeared back here, as if I owe you something, as if you weren't the one who walked out on us." He stopped speaking, his eyes saying a million things, all of which I already knew deep inside of me. "I couldn't believe that you were actually that selfish."

"I left because I thought you two would have a better chance. I was spiraling down and was afraid I'd take you both with me. I thought I was helping."

His eyes held me. I felt smaller and smaller with each passing second. I looked up at the rain falling straight down from overhead and felt vertigo as I listened to Brett say, "You're not here for Lizzie. The only reason you're here is to redeem yourself, to make yourself feel better. And it's bullshit."

"No, Brett. I'm trying. I want to try to make things better. I want to apologize to her. I'll do anything."

"No! You can't do anything! Don't you understand that? You left us," he shouted, paused, then continued in a harsh whisper, and looked around the parking lot, to make sure no one passers-by were passing by, "You left us alone, as if we weren't mourning too. I lost my daughter too. Lizzie lost her sister. Then you just left. She thought she wasn't important enough to keep her own mother around. She longed for you, screaming out Mommy in the middle of the night. She wanted you, not me. And I was the only one there. You abandoned her when she needed you most. You abandoned *me*." He spoke the last words slowly, sadly, looking young and scared, as if admitting something he hadn't realized.

I didn't respond. We stood silently, staring into each other's faces, daring the other person to speak. I noticed the top of Brett's wavy dark hair shining from the mist of rain still falling.

The lamppost flickered on, then pooled light onto his face, casting shadows in ominous angles.

An overwhelming, unanticipated sense of longing came over me. I edged a bit closer to him, slowly, as if he were a strange dog smelling my hand before I could pet him. Then I reached toward him—I don't know why—but I felt like the years had slipped away and we were bickering over some domestic problem, like Brett refusing to pick up his clothes piled by the side of the bed. He winced as I touched his arm, but he didn't shrug me away this time. I let my arm drift down and off his arm. His eyes softened and he dropped his head, marking the end of this round. "I've hated you all this time. I couldn't even look at your picture. Lizzie knew how I felt, but she always insisted on talking about you, kept hoping that someday you'd come back. She carried photographs of you around with her. I know she's forgiven you, but I haven't. And I won't allow anyone—especially you—to hurt her anymore. Not if I can help it."

I was a fool, but this wasn't some sort of show and I couldn't keep the tears from falling. Of course I'd hurt her. I didn't deserve to cry the self-pitying tears, had no right to feel them dripping from my chin and mixing into the puddle below.

"Are you back for good?" he asked.

"I haven't exactly thought that far ahead," I said, not wanting to admit that my return flight was in five days. Instead, I tried the submission that used to work with him. I had to swallow my pride—always had to in our history of arguments—to get him to soften, to listen, to understand. "I'm here because I wanted to do the right thing. But you're right. My showing up here isn't the right thing for Lizzie. My reasons seem selfish now. I want to know who she is, what she's like now, what her favorite food is. I can't believe how naïve I've been. I wanted to know these things. I didn't think that showing up here might be hard for her. Still, I hoped she'd want to see me."

But the reality still stung. It was selfish, my coming here. How would this benefit Lizzie? My argument was over. He was right; I was an intruder here. "This was a mistake. Say the word, and I'll go." This jolting realization halted my tears.

He didn't speak.

I turned to leave.

"Do you still want to get something to eat?" His voice was nearly a whisper. I followed his gaze to his shoes. They were brown, pin-striped cloth shoes, sutured at the hem with chunky rope thread and lined with fur and thick with sole. They were reminiscent of his college days, so unusual. When I looked up into his eyes, his face had fallen and was relaxed, his eyes soft.

"Yeah."

"I'll meet you at Norris Cafe in ten minutes." I watched those shoes step into his car.

I waited in the entrance of Norris Café, uncertain and apprehensive, a little hopeful. Like I was going on a long-anticipated first date. Each of the million feelings coursing through me was conflicted. I sat down on a bench and picked up the Red River News and began reading about the gas company's price increase to calm my crowded head.

Brett was careful not to touch me when he walked in. He kept a professional, comfortable distance between us. It felt like a business meeting. We sat at a booth. "So, did you tell Jen where you are? And who you're with?"

"How do you know about Jen?"

I followed her home. I saw her pick Lizzie up from school. "I have your Christmas card. Jen was always into you, even when I was around. It doesn't shock me. I knew."

"I never thought about her like that, not when you were here. Nothing happened between us until well after you left."

I nodded, wanting to believe him, wanting to erase that picture of the two of them sitting on the front lawn the day of Claire's funeral, their heads close, something intimate had been happening, I could tell even if I hadn't been close enough to hear their words. He may not have cheated on me, but I knew he confided in her and not me during the raw, aching moments right after Claire died.

"You never cheated on me?"

Brett rested his menu on the table and shook his head. "No. We were friends and coworkers. But after you left, she was there all the time, trying to help, sacrificing everything. She'd pick Lizzie up from school and bring her to the office or drop her off at home or the daycare. She'd even take her out, to see a movie or for ice cream. She loves Lizzie. And Lizzie came to accept her and then like her. She realized that Jen was the closest thing to a mother she was going to get."

I shook off his words and said, "What about you? Do you love her?"

"She's been great and has sacrificed so much for us. She works part-time, so she can be there to pick Lizzie up every day after school. She helps Lizzie with her homework. She cooks for us." He could have been describing an employee or a nanny.

"But do you love her?"

"Yes. I do." His answer was stern. He picked up the menu, opened it, setting a fresh boundary between us—conversation over. I ordered a patty melt with French fries, and Brett ordered a Monte Cristo. After the server left, Brett confessed, "I guess I should tell you something."

"Go ahead." I went still.

"I followed you to Hanover." He laid it right there on the table, as if it were a napkin or a coffee cup.

"How?" I stared right into his face, focusing on his eyes.

"Are you kidding? You wrote checks. And you used your debit card all the way to Hanover. You weren't trying that hard, were you? I found you easily. It took me less than a day."

"So, you were actually there?" I tried to remember a day in the first while I was there, with a strange car parked along the street, but to no avail. The entire place was still strange to me then. How did I know different then when everything was new to me?

"Yeah. My plan was to talk you into coming home. I sat for hours parked in front of that old house. I watched you come and go, saw your light in the attic come on and off. I saw your silhouette through the window at night. But I couldn't do it. You had chosen a new life, one that didn't include Lizzie or me. I couldn't force you to come home." A small, fleeting smile pressed his lips. "Although I really had to hold myself back from marching up there and taking back the money you took."

"I didn't use all of it. I needed a bed, food, just to get on my feet until I got a job, which took a lot longer than I thought it would—people don't exactly love to hire stay-at-home moms, you know. Oh yeah, and I spent a little of the money on a car."

"Yeah, I saw your car." He lifted his eyebrows at me like a father would his daughter. Or the same way he had used to do when I spent too much on boutique dresses for the girls. I just wanted them to feel special. I never got extravagant clothes when I was a child—just hand-me-downs and bargain-store numbers.

"The money was just a token of security hiding under my bed. Some of it's still there, sitting in my bank account. You can have it."

"It's not about the money, Alex. I don't need the money."

"I can't believe you were there," I trailed off in thought. I felt trampled and small. "I'm sorry I didn't leave you a note or any explanation. I should have at least told you."

"Yes, you should have." He looked into me, and I stared back at him. His dark features were beautiful, the same I had admired when I was his. He hadn't changed much from before—just seemed a little older, a little more worn. His eyes a little deeper, creases under his eyes like he was tired. He sat across from me and I wondered how I could have ever left him. I had loved every part of him, and my life, and my girls.

"It was a mistake. I made too many mistakes," I repeated, trying to make my overused words sound new by over-inflecting.

The server set our food on the table. We ate. After several bites, I said, "Tell me about Lizzie. I want to know everything."

"She's great. Straight A's, happy all the time, has a ton of friends. She's almost nine—you know her birthday is next month. She started reading when she was four. Just taught herself. I figured it out one night as I read her bedtime story. The phone rang and I saw her pointing at some of the words, saying them aloud. When I asked her what a certain word was—I think it was apple or something—she knew." Brett took a couple bites of his sandwich, then continued, "It's popcorn shrimp, by the way, Lizzie's favorite food. She's miles ahead of the rest of her class in reading."

"I always hoped she'd inherit your brain." Brett had a photographic memory. He just had to hear or read something once, and he never forgot it. I, on the other hand, had to study hard, work hours and hours for every B I got in school.

"I guess she did. But what chance did she have? She had smart parents."

I nodded, remembering the film class we took together in college. Brett never did his assigned reading but managed a B+ over my B. It wasn't fair.

"Oh, and Lizzie loves ballet. That ballet class you signed her up for. That was just the beginning. She's really good, always gets the lead roles in the recitals. When we moved, I put a ballet barre in her room."

"Sounds like you spoil her."

"She's all I've got." I noticed that he forgot about Jen. This pleased me.

"Was it hard leaving our house?" I asked, picturing the red-brick house sans the intruding porch swing and new pine trees.

"A little. Mostly the memories of Claire. But I kind of needed a fresh start. I live in Red River now."

"Do you still get to the cemetery? I suppose it's a bit of a drive now."

"Lizzie and I go every Sunday. When Lizzie was smaller, she'd bring little gifts and leave them at her grave—painted rocks, Halloween candy, pictures she'd draw." I smiled thinking about the meaningful gifts offered from a four-year-old child.

"What ever happened to that ugly plastic-headed doll that Lizzie carried around the house, calling her Claire?"

"Lizzie just needed to say goodbye to Claire on her own terms. A year or so later, Lizzie decided it was time to put Claire away in the attic, when we boxed up a bunch of her toys. She was finally ready. That's how she dealt with losing her sister. I wish it had been that easy for me—or for you."

"I know," I said, pushing another cold fry from my plate into my mouth. "I guess I didn't do it the right way."

"What is the right way to handle losing a child?" Our eyes locked. In his eyes, I saw the depths of pain that he'd endured—alone. I should have been with him. I reflected back on the time right after the accident. I knew we had both been saturated, so filled with grief that there was nothing left for either of us to give to each other. And doubt and regret hung over me like a veil.

I fought an urge to touch him again. I settled instead on wiping a bit of ketchup from the corner of his mouth. He didn't wince this time, adjusting to an intimacy we used to share, accepting a small token.

Staring at the remaining pile of fries jumbled together, lying cold on the plate, I said, "I miss what we used to have—the four of us together."

"Alex, why did you leave?"

"I hoped you and Lizzie would have a better chance if I wasn't there to mess it up. I know that sounds like a cop out—like I'm trying to manipulate you into believing I sacrificed for you—but I truly felt I was harming Lizzie. I was yelling at her always, and for nothing. And you, we were barely coexisting. I didn't feel like you looked at me. And I couldn't bear to be the person everybody referred to as 'the one who lost the baby.' Everybody felt sorry for me, pitied me, and I just couldn't be that person. I wanted to get away from it all. Thought perhaps I could be happy if I just erased myself and started over."

"Did you find what you were looking for?"

"I wasn't looking for happiness. You have to put yourself out there to find happiness, and I hid everything from everyone. But I'm not happier than I was before the accident. I don't think I ever could be." This truth of this startled me as the words tumbled from my mouth.

The server came and collected our plates, brought our bill. "I'll pay," I said as I snatched the flimsy yellow paper. I scrolled my eyes over the numbers, making sure the bill was correct.

"I guess it's the least you can do, considering that you ran off with all that money. Looks like you haven't changed much," Brett said. "You always studied every single item on the grocery receipt, and you would march right back in if they overcharged you. I loved that about you, and so many other things. I never once doubted that our marriage would last—even after Claire died."

"Neither did I." And I hadn't—just moments before I left, I never thought I could leave.

"Then why?"

"I don't know."

Brett glanced at his watch. "It's eight already. I've got to get home to say goodnight to Lizzie before she goes to bed."

I didn't want to ask but knew I'd regret it if I didn't. And I wasn't sure when I'd see Brett again. "Will you reconsider—about letting me see Lizzie?"

He sighed and said, "Alex, I've told you. I can't do that. I'm not going to stand by and let her get hurt by falling in love with you again and then watching you walk away, get on a plane and leave."

"I just want to see her." I stood and gathered my jacket and bag. Brett didn't move. He sat, so I slid back into my seat.

Brett had been so casual tonight, even endearing, that what he said next struck me hard, a slap in the face. "I don't want to see you again." His face was clenched, his words biting and abrupt. "Don't wait for me in the parking lot after work again. Don't ask me if you can see her. I want you to leave. Leave our family as it is. You did it once before. You can do it again."

But it was my family.

Brett's sudden change jarred my memory and reminded me of the person he became the months before I left—hard, cold, miles away from me. Although I didn't blame him for keeping Lizzie from me and not wanting to see me, he'd turned on me so severely it stunned me to silence. And disappointed me, that I didn't hold the place I had—where I could always worm my way back in, even after our worst fights. Someone else held that place now. It wasn't Jen, but Lizzie. He was pushing me away to protect her. As her mother, I wanted to respect that. But the irony was that I, who was once her protector, was now the enemy, against whom she was now being protected.

I nodded okay and turned to walk away. As I paid the cashier at the front desk, I heard his footsteps behind me, then the door swing shut. Not a light touch on the shoulder or a simple wave goodbye, nothing.

The drizzle had turned into a downpour. Normally, I would have run to my car to keep from the wet, but I walked slowly and allowed myself to be slapped again—as if Brett had physically slapped me as his last words had—by jabbing darts of rain. I stepped into the car and pulled out onto the street, the headlights tunneling ahead, the wipers lunging back and forth, screeching, over and over. I watched, hypnotized, and knew I couldn't return to my hotel room. Not now. I mulled over the last hour. Brett had let me in, he'd softened, and now I was back where I had begun. I needed to drive. I drove through town, down backstreets, through neighborhoods and houses I didn't recognize—I'd most likely never seen them before, but wouldn't recognize them even if I had for the rain beating down on my windshield, forming an impressionistic view of these foreign-but-familiar neighborhoods. The rhythmic beating of the rain on my car roof lulled me somewhat.

I had several days left and felt that tonight had been my dead-end. What would I do with the rest of my time here? I drove through Red River and continued toward Addison, to my baby. Pulling into the cemetery entrance, the rocky gravel crunching under the tires, I realized I wasn't alone. I squinted through the blurred window and recognized Brett's car. I was an intruder. I decided to turn around, come back later. But still, I had to drive by, go around the circle, to get back out. When I passed him—kneeling in the mud, soaked, with his arms draped over the headstone—trying to hug the only tangible thing that represented Claire, I didn't think. I stopped the car, got out, and ran toward him. The rain still slapping down. His cries were horrible, it broke my heart to see him convulsing and weeping, a grown man.

He looked up as I approached, his face contorted and raw. I fell onto the ground and wrapped my arms around him. He covered me, his body over mine. I welcomed the pressure of his body against mine and after a while wondered if he was trying to crush me for the force behind his arms, but then sensed that his body was blocking mine from the harsh beatings from the rain. His body trembled through our wet clothes, and his crying tapered off.

When he was still, I whispered, "I didn't follow you. I didn't know you were here. I just needed to be here." Brett was silent, didn't move, then looked into my face, his eyes swollen and bloodshot, his hands gripping my neck. His grip was so tight that I wondered again if he meant me harm, if he was trying to strangle me. He leaned his forehead against mine, relaxing his grip, and said, "It was always you, Alex." And he kissed me. Hard and wet and violent—and familiar.

Being with him again felt natural to me, I didn't resist. The rain pelted our backs and faces, pooling onto our necks, ears. I wished we could be the same people from years before. I trembled from the cold, and he stopped, looked into my face, our lips raw and red. He pulled away, wiped the rain from his face and ran fingers through his wet hair. His tone changed when his flat words came, "I don't know what I want."

"I didn't ask," I said as I watched him stand up, walk to his car and leave without another word.

I sat alone—drenched and muddy—and cried for leaving Brett and Lizzie, for not getting to finish the life we'd started, for my Claire whose name was etched in the stone beside me. I found solace touching the cold, wet surface, the rigid stone on the granite scraping my arm. I cried to Claire and mumbled unintelligible words of endearment and wished I could stay all night with her.

Chapter Fourteen

A slow, sharp pain drilled into my eyes, waking me the next morning. I felt hung over. I lay in bed while the events of last night reeled through my head and could still taste Brett in my mouth. I pulled the pillow over my head, squeezed it tight, wishing I could block out my headache. The phone rang. I answered quickly, hopeful, but my voice was drained. "Hello."

"Good morning, Alex. It's Sammy." Her voice came bubbly over the line; she was much too sunshiny for me now.

"Hey."

"Sounds like you're still in bed."

"I'm thinking about getting out."

"So, I just dropped my kids off at school. I'm on the way to pick you up. We'll do breakfast. You're at the Best Western?"

"Yeah." Still, no energy.

"I'll be there in ten minutes. Watch for me."

"Okay, okay." I was talking into an empty phone, she'd already hung up. It was more for me anyway, trying to convince myself to get out of bed.

I crawled out and dressed, ran a brush through my hair, picked the sleep out of my eyes, brushed Brett's taste from my mouth. I grabbed my bag, shut the door behind me, and looked out over the balcony. I didn't know what kind of car Sammy drove. Minutes later, a white Suburban honked in the parking lot, and Sammy waved from the window. Taking slow steps, I held onto the rail on my way down and settled into the passenger side.

"I don't even know what time it is."

"It's almost nine. It looks like you had a rough night." She wore a taunting smile on her face as she drove from the parking lot.

"You could say that." Pulling down the passenger mirror, I looked at my face and flipped it up again. "Nine o'clock seems so much earlier than it used to be. I remember how early I used to start my days with the girls." I realized that I spoke about both my girls as if they were gone.

"Where do you want to go? I've got a couple hours to spare."

"I don't care as long as it's somewhere besides Norris Cafe. I ate there twice yesterday."

"Anything but Norris Cafe, huh?" Sammy turned into the parking lot of a small bakery. "It's not Norris Cafe."

The Baker's Dozen was a local bakery chain. There was one in Addison too. The building was small, but smelled sweet of yeast and sugar. The bakery had a small area in the front with several bistro tables. I ordered an apple fritter and some coffee. The bakery was deserted but for a man in a business suit ordering a couple dozen donuts to go. We sat at a table for nearly two hours, drinking a lot of coffee—my head still ached—and talked. We talked about her kids, the neighborhood, books, anything but what was actually on my mind.

She did eventually bring it up. "So, did you see Brett?"

"Yeah." Sammy used to be the one person I could confide in—I'd told her everything—but I was hesitant to speak of what happened last night. It was my secret and I wanted it all to myself, so as to not spread it thin. The thought that maybe Brett still loved me came and went as quickly as my next cup of coffee. I wouldn't bring that up. I said, "He doesn't want me to see Lizzie. I've been here several days now and have only seen her twice from afar. I came all this way, and I feel like my time is ticking away."

"Of course Brett's still angry with you."

"I know." I was at the verge of giving up. "Sammy, do you think I should just leave them alone?"

She had a forgive-me look in her eyes. "Probably."

The rest of the day was dedicated to Claire—no, the rest of this trip, I determined. She was the only one who wouldn't reject me. I bought a solar-powered lantern from the hardware store in

Addison and wedged it into the earth next to Claire's headstone. This was my offering, in lieu of the flowers I despised. The rain dried up and the clouds broke apart, giving me a momentary peek at the sun. I spent hours reading on a blanket—chilled when the clouds covered back over again, relieved when they split and the sun warmed my face again. Everything was so still, so quiet. I was filled with peace at the thought of giving up.

I fell asleep, my book discarded on the blanket. Through sleep, I felt a hand on my face, brushing a stray hair from my eyes and opened my eyes to find Brett kneeling above me, the sun crowning him but blinding me. I squinted. At first I thought it was a dream, then mumbled, "I didn't sleep well last night."

I sat up while he settled on my blanket.

"Neither did I," he said.

"What are you doing here?"

"I have a standing lunch date with Claire every Wednesday. And I come here sometimes if I need to get out of the office." He held up a white bag and a soda. He looked around, focusing in on the lantern I'd brought.

"I thought it'd be nice. I don't know if you spend much time here at night but thought you might like it too." I didn't want to bring up our meeting here last night. Brett unwrapped his sandwich and took a bite. I opened my book and tried to find where I had left off. I found the page and dog-eared it, then closed it again.

"How much longer will you be here?" he asked.

"I fly back on Saturday, late afternoon. I've got to be back at work on Monday."

"I talked with Mark, our in-house attorney, and he said he could do up the divorce papers."

Yes, of course, the divorce. I'd nearly forgotten. But bringing this up now felt like a punch in the stomach. I nodded.

"That is why you came here?" he asked.

"Yes."

He took several bites of his sandwich, and I opened my book to the dog-eared page, then snapped it shut again.

"I wanted to ask you the other night but just didn't get around to it. How's your company? I remember how many hours you put into it—your baby then. Do you remember going days without seeing each other—well, awake—when we were first married?" I remembered not the time we were apart, but about a time when my biggest problem was aching to see him again. I could still see the scribbled love notes tacked sloppily onto the refrigerator for me to find.

"I guess you could say it paid off," Brett said. "Three years ago, an overseas company offered to buy us. They paid millions. I sold, but under the condition that I stay and run it, which they wanted me to do anyway. Not much has changed. Some of the staff is the same. Except they changed the name. It's NOS now, Networking Office Software."

"That and I guess you made a little money from the sale."

"Yeah. But I'm so beyond the point where I thought money could make me happy. I had all this money, all I had ever hoped for from the company, and it wasn't enough. Not now."

Like Brett, I'd realized the futility of money when the insurance company was paying us. It was funny how I used to think having a lot of money would make me happy. Every topic seemed to come back to Claire.

"So, does Jen know I'm here?"

"Yeah. I told her the first night. But we both agreed it's not in Lizzie's best interest to see you."

I released a sarcastic laugh, shaking my head in disbelief. "I love it. I can't believe some woman I don't even know is keeping me from my daughter."

"Alex, it's not just Jen. I don't think you should see her either. You're not *trying* to understand. You know that if you saw her just for a couple days, it would injure Lizzie much more than it would help. Maybe it would help you to see her—release some of your guilt—but it would only recreate the questions in her mind about why you left. You're acting like a child, not listening to what I'm saying."

"I don't know why I'm sitting here letting you two decide. I am her mother. I'm sure I have the right to see her." I knew my voice sounded hostile. I stood up quickly, unable to sit anymore. On the defensive, or was it the offensive? I wasn't even sure anymore I was so upset.

"What are you going to do? Go get a lawyer and go to court?" Brett asked. "No judge in his right mind would let you see her. You abandoned her. Anyway, you couldn't do it in three days." Brett hastily threw his food wrappers into the paper bag and punched it into a ball, then stood and walked away.

"You have to understand that I want to see her. Can't *you* try to understand?" I yelled after him, following behind.

He stopped mid-step, his back toward me. Then he turned around to face me and said, "I'm trying, but Lizzie comes first." He stood for a moment, not speaking, and I wasn't sure whether he was waiting for me to respond or just unable to move. Then he continued, "I'm going to give you one chance. And I mean, you see her—not the other way around. Got it?"

I nodded agreement like a docile child.

"She's in this play of Little Red Riding Hood for her third-grade class. It's at the elementary school. You have to promise me that you will watch, then leave, nothing more."

"When is it?"

"Tomorrow night at 7:30."

"I'll be there." He left me, climbed in his car, and drove away. I tried to read longer but couldn't concentrate from chewing on this bone Brett finally threw to me. I picked up my book and headed back to the hotel room.

At the elementary school that afternoon, I stopped my car on the side of the road, as if I were waiting to drive a child home. I needed another peek of Lizzie. Like glimpses of Lizzie was food that would sustain me for just another day. As always, I knew I'd drive away empty-handed.

As Jen's blue car was pulling in, I bent my head down as if I were entering some very important appointments into my planner. I looked up when a car stopped parallel to mine and saw her eyes boring into me. She knew. She knew I was following her. Her car sat motionless a couple feet from me, stopping all the cars in a line behind her. Her door opened and she jumped out. I inhaled and rolled down my own window and met her eyes. I wasn't a confrontational sort of person. In fact, I normally avoided confrontation whenever possible. But I wasn't afraid of Jen.

"What are you doing here?" Her voice was hard and accusatory. She was bent over toward the window, her long blond hair settling over her shoulder. Jen was still pretty, always had been, but her brown eyes were filled with hate.

"I don't have to explain anything to you." A horn honked behind Jen, and I began to roll up the window.

"I've seen you before. I know what you're doing. Stop this now!" She raised her voice to a higher pitch as my window was closing, "I'm warning you, don't try to talk to her."

I shrugged to say, you're nothing, I don't have to listen to you, and looked away. I was shaking and closed my eyes, breathing deeply to calm myself. When I looked over again, the Toyota was stopped in front of the school and Lizzie skipping toward the opened door. I got to see no more than the tail end of her ponytail swooping inside the car and back lights on the car as they drove away.

The next evening, the entrance of the Red River Elementary School swarmed with parents, grandparents, siblings, aunts, uncles, friends. I filed in among them and claimed an uncomfortable metal folding chair next to the aisle and waited. I tried to keep my eyes focused ahead, on the stage. The outdated brown curtains rippled every now and again from children setting up props behind it. The mix of stale French fries and ammonia assaulted my nose, while the hum of chatter filled my ears. I didn't want to look around and see Brett and Jen together as Lizzie's parents. But I recognized the back of Brett's head several rows from the stage. Jen rested her arm on the back of Brett's chair and stroked the back of his neck. I felt my chest tighten and tried to turn away, focus on the stage, but my eyes reverted back to their insidious display of affection.

Opening the program, I read through the characters and names to distract myself. Three third-grade classes were performing fairy tales. Lizzie's class was last. I scanned through the program and was surprised to see Lizzie Porter listed as Elizabeth, Little Red Riding Hood. I couldn't hide my smile and could hardly wait to see her skip onto the stage with her basket of butter and bread.

I waded through two mediocre performances—The Little Mermaid and Snow White—by the other third-grade classes. The children were obviously in charge of creating their own props, as awkward trees and disproportionate flowers, painted in bright yellows and reds and purples, crowded the stage with their ugly heads and mismatched leaves.

Finally, Lizzie's class emerged from behind the curtain. Lizzie burst out in the moving spotlight, wearing a red-hooded cloak with a blue gingham dress underneath, white tights, brown boots, and her hair tied into two braids. I could see red circles painted on her cheeks and bright red lipstick on her lips. She recited her lines confidently and loudly, not in the least bit afraid of the stage or what was beyond it. She swung her basket and skipped along the front of the stage. This was the closest I'd been to Lizzie. I leaned forward in my seat but couldn't see her face through the heavy make-up and ached to get a closer look.

When the performance ended, Brett and Jen bounced up in unison and clapped heartily, as the perfect proud parents.

I lingered while parents and teachers folded and stashed away the chairs. I leaned against the cinder block wall and waited. I knew Brett wanted me to leave, but I couldn't. I needed a better look. When she walked through the side-entrance door, Brett and Jen hugged her. While one was hugging, the other was squeezing her shoulder or patting her head as I stood and watched. As they were readying to leave, I heard Lizzie say, "Dad, I've gotta say goodbye to Ruth before she leaves," and then Lizzie ran in front of me. I watched her talk to her friend as Brett's eyes bore into me, repeating to me what I knew: I'd overstepped my boundaries just by loitering afterwards. When Lizzie and her friend broke their tête-à-tête, Lizzie ran back in front of me. I hadn't planned to do it. It wasn't premeditated, but I swallowed hard and blurted, "You did a great job, Lizzie."

She stopped mid-step and looked at me, then tilted her head and squinted her eyes, trying to place my face. "Thanks," she said, holding the "s" as if she were going to put a name at the end.

Brett came up behind her, "It's time to go home, Lizzie" and ushered her off. Jen put her hand onto Brett's back as they walked away. At the door, Lizzie's head turned back to me again. Her eyes widened as she realized who I was.

Betraying Brett wasn't my intention. It made me feel sick and hollow, like I hadn't eaten in days. I knew it was wrong, but I'd had to do it. I had just one day left. When I returned to the hotel, I threw on a t-shirt and a pair of pajama bottoms and flicked on the television. I lay in bed flipping between a rerun of Seinfeld and the nine o'clock news when a knock came at the door. I knew straight away it was Lizzie. Only 45 minutes had lapsed since I'd seen her at the school. I hopped to the door and swung it open to see Brett with his arm wrapped around Lizzie's shoulder. His hostile glare bore into me. Lizzie's eyes were red and swollen and her face was wiped clean of the bright make-up she'd worn earlier, but her hair was still fastened in two loose braids with stray hairs splintering from them.

"Come in." I smiled at Lizzie and stood back, holding the door open. Glancing up at Brett, I said, "I didn't know you knew where I was staying."

"There are only two hotels in town," he said in a flat voice. They walked in—Brett pushing Lizzie forward, guiding her with his hand on the small of her back.

"You want to sit?" I gestured to the chairs by the window. Brett sat down but Lizzie just leaned into him; she wouldn't sit. I sat on my bed. "It's good to see you again, Lizzie." She shied away and nestled in closer to Brett.

"Lizzie," Brett said pulling her out, "you wanted to come here."

"You were a wonderful Little Red Riding Hood tonight. Did you have to practice a lot?"

"Yeah, we've had rehearsals for a couple of weeks," she said looking up, her eyes as round and sweet as I remembered.

"Did you know that you were Little Red Riding Hood for Halloween when you were two? Grandma made your costume."

"Yeah, I have some pictures." She held my gaze and asked, "Are you coming home?"

I looked at Brett, and he gave me an I-told-you-this-is-how-it-would-be look, then looked back toward Lizzie and swallowed. "Lizzie, I live far away now. My home is in St. Louis. Do you know where that is?"

"Yes." She nodded, her eyes squinting as if she was trying to locate it on a map in her head.

"I have a job there and a cat," I said. I didn't get the response I expected from her. When Lizzie was three, she would have warmed at the mention of a cat or any other soft, furry animal, but this child had grown up. She stared back at me with an even, unamused gaze. Then I said, "I won't be coming home, Lizzie, but I miss you and wanted to see you."

She shrugged and said matter-of-factly, "I have a new mom now." I felt tears welling but blinked them away. I looked toward the silent television, avoiding her and Brett's eyes, and watched a news reporter mouthing words in front of a restaurant parking lot. Why did Lizzie's reaction surprise me? She's shielding herself from me. Although it hurt to hear her say it, I knew she needed to do it.

"I hear you're good at ballet." I turned back to her, trying to resuscitate my chance—probably my only chance—to talk with her.

"I love dancing," she said. "My friend Bridgette and I take ballet lessons together. Our class is doing a spring recital. Miss Tanya said I get to have a solo in the ballet part."

"I'd love to see you dance sometime," I said, offering something I knew I couldn't follow through with. I supposed my main goal at this point was to establish some sort of relationship with my child. What exactly did I want? A pen pal? Did I just want her to know that I existed? I wasn't sure why I'd come here.

Being here was a mistake.

I knew I didn't have anything to offer her. I just assumed she'd accept me, the way she had when she was three. When I had yelled at her, then apologized. I'd tell her I was wrong and was working on being a better mommy, and she had put her arms around me and said, "You're the best mommy." Always blindly forgiving and accepting, the way small children always did. More love to give than they received, not measuring or counting.

"You can come for the recital if you want." She leaned into the crook of Brett's elbow, nestling in even closer to him. Her eyes shut and she batted them open, she wanted to stay awake no matter how much her body wanted to sleep. Brett realized too.

"It's been a long day, Lizzie," I said. "I'm so glad you came by." After all I'd done to see Lizzie, I was eager for her to leave. Seeing her face stung me with reality, that there was no way to make this all better. There could be no such thing now. I couldn't keep searching her face for something I needed; I'd only end up disappointed and disappointing her.

Brett helped her stand up and held on to her hand. I wanted to touch her. Hug her, feel her skin next to mine, hold her as before—and make the pain and the last five years melt away. I wanted to take in her smell as a token to remember on the plane back home. I was afraid to ask if she'd let me, afraid she would feel uncomfortable and shy away. I stood against the wall and opened the door. As they walked through the door, Lizzie stopped. I leaned over, waiting to hear what she was going to say. She let go of Brett's hand, then looked up at me with tears brimming her red-rimmed eyes. "Why did you go away?"

How could I answer this question? There was no answer. Every excuse I'd used before to explain my convoluted reason for leaving to Brett or Anna or my mother or Quentin. Nothing rang true as I looked down into Lizzie's eyes, clear and shiny with tears I'd caused. All my excuses were laced with self-denial and lies.

I clutched her shoulders and said, "I'm sorry. I made the wrong decision."

She shrugged me away and walked to Brett who was waiting for her with his arms open. He lifted her against him and lofted her up, holding her like he had when she was a toddler. She closed her eyes and laid her head on his shoulder and didn't look back at me again, like she had fallen asleep the instant her head lay on his shoulder.

"I've got those papers for you to sign. I'll bring them by tomorrow morning before you leave," Brett whispered. I nodded yes and shut the door to silence the sound of his retreating footsteps.

Chapter Fifteen

As I packed that night, balling up my dirty clothes and crowding them into my suitcase, I resolved that as soon as I put my signature on those papers, I'd head away from Red River and never return. I still had one day more before my flight, but I would get a room in Portland to sleep.

I flipped on the television and stared at the movements on the screen. Then switching off the television and the lights, I tried to sleep but sleep was as willing to come to me as Brett. I rolled from side to side, stomach to back, back to stomach, back to side, for what seemed like hours. Frustrated, I turned on the lights and sat up, squishing my pillow into the cheap headboard. My legs were shaking and I was jittery; I needed to get out this room. Walking and running, movement, helped me through the last five years, and tonight I needed it most. I pulled a gray hoodie out of my stuffed bag and zipped it over my t-shirt, slid on my tennis shoes, and stepped outside.

The dark sky dripped a light, steady rain. I stayed on the sidewalk, not looking up at cars driving past, their headlights a moving spotlight on me and wheels splashing water toward me. I stomped through the puddles in my path. My ankles were cold and wet, and my clothes splattered with rain. At this rate, I wouldn't have any wearable clothes left. All I had left now was my lonely pride. I wanted to be away from this place. There was nothing left here.

A nest of lights and shouting came from the direction of a bar, The Rim, up ahead. A rowdy group of guys pummeled out the door. I slowed my pace to avoid walking past them. A

BMW was parked along the street out front, looked like Brett's. I walked past the lit doors, not looking back. No, I shook my head. There's nothing left to do here and nothing left to say to him.

But I didn't keep walking away. I stopped and turned around and marched back to the Rim and through the door. After my eyes adjusted to the smoke and lights, I scanned the tables and found Brett sitting alone in a corner. His only friend was a half-filled pitcher of beer sweating in the center of the table. He sat slumped in his chair, still, a hand resting in the crook of a mug's handle. His head was turned to the television screen mounted on the wall, and he didn't look away. I stepped forward and slid out a chair from his table and sat. He turned at the movement, his eyes glazed over, and turned back to the television, clearly unruffled by my appearance.

"How long have you been here?" I asked.

"I don't know. An hour."

"I won't come back here again. You were right."

He nodded, eyes on the television screen. As if he'd already heard me say it so many times and it was so clearly true that it didn't warrant a response.

"Okay." So, I was unwanted here—in this town, at this table. Maybe now was a good time to slip away.

Brett finally looked to me. "I told you not to talk to her."

"Come on, Brett. I didn't have any effect on her. You heard her yourself. She has a new mom. She doesn't care about me."

"Yeah? She doesn't care?" He nodded slowly in mock agreement. "Is that why she cried for the last half hour until I said I'd to take her to you? Jen has been wonderful for her. Lizzie knows how much Jen cares about her, but Jen isn't her mother. What do you expect Lizzie to say? She was offering you a place in her life again and you rejected her—again."

"What are you talking about? She asked if I was coming home, and there is no room in your home for me. You know that."

"I know that, but Lizzie just hears you live far away and you're not coming back to be her mom. Still. Your coming here for a week doesn't change her life; her life will continue on the way it has always been."

Just then, a man with a goatee and a Seattle Marlins baseball cap, approached and asked if I wanted anything to drink "Yeah. A rum and Coke." He walked away, leaving us in silence, amidst the random chattering and bursts of cheers from those around us watching the basketball game.

"Before I leave, I want you to know something," I said and waited for him to look to me and he did, with vacant eyes. "I was happy before. If I could have just kept that life, I would have never left."

He spoke, "Why did you really leave? And don't give me this sacrificing-for-the-good-of-your-family bullshit."

After Brett had seen me blank out when Lizzie had asked the same question earlier tonight, I knew he'd cut right through the shit, all the excuses I'd let myself believe: that Lizzie was better off not being emotionally abused by me; that he had the freedom to find a woman who would love him better than I could; that everyone forced me to leave from their antagonizing looks and pity. All these excuses reeled through my head, but I didn't dare fall back on them. I swallowed and released a combination of words I didn't wholly understand, "I couldn't stand the guilt."

"Alex, that's no reason to leave. Any grieving person has guilt."

"Really, Brett? You thought I was responsible for Claire's death. You said it to me that night Lizzie swallowed the earring. How could I stay there, knowing that you blamed me?"

"You know I didn't mean that."

"Brett, look me in the eye and tell me it's not my fault Claire's dead."

His eyes met mine. He stared for a moment with no words. The man with the goatee placed my drink in front of me. I didn't break the stare, and the man turned and departed with no words. Finally, Brett said, hushed, "I don't think you meant to kill her, Alex. It was an accident."

I froze. "This is why I left, and this is why I could never come back." I stood to leave. He didn't understand what he had done, I could tell from the question in his eyes. I hadn't taken a drink, but the room was spinning circles. If I turned away or took a step, I'd fall.

Brett grabbed my wrist, "Please, at least finish your drink." He tugged me down, and I fell back into my chair. Not because I wanted to stay here with him. Closing my eyes, I breathed—in and out, in and out, several times.

"I never stopped loving you," Brett said, in a hoarse whisper.

"And I didn't leave because I didn't love you."

He reached over and took my hand. I closed my eyes. When I opened them, he was the man I'd fallen in love with again. Years had slipped away.

"How could you say that?" I asked. "That I didn't mean to kill her? Don't you know that crushes me?"

"I *didn't* mean it that way," he said. "I meant that it was a car accident. Even though the police report said you were responsible, I know you would have never willingly harmed Claire. I know you loved her."

I yanked my hand away from his. Why couldn't he just say it wasn't my fault—period? He kept carving some loophole into his statements, whittling them with each sentence. He might as well carve my heart out with that whittling knife. He still blamed me. That was clear. And I couldn't touch him, not now. "I have so much guilt already—the fact that I let her cry herself back to sleep in the middle of the night instead of going to her, picking her up, whispering a lullaby into her ear, rocking her to sleep; that when she said 'cookie' for the first time, I didn't give her a cookie because she needed to finish her carrots first and never got her cookie; that she had to die because I signed Lizzie up for a ballet class." I picked up my full glass and drank half of it in one gulp, then clinked the glass back down to the table.

Was this why I was here? If he took the blame from me, then it wouldn't be my fault. But he still blamed me. I had hoped time would have melted away the blame he put on me, but here it was, as icy and cold as it was when I'd left. Time hadn't changed anything. Why had I expected otherwise? He hadn't asked me to come back. He had allowed me to stay lost. I came on my own, hoping. I had shown up here, begging him to say the right things so I could move on with my life. Maybe this seemed selfish to him, but he held my life in his hands. I needed him to forgive me, to absolve me of this gnawing guilt.

"Yes, I'm at fault. I could have driven the back roads instead of the main road. But I didn't. Don't you think this haunts me already?" My voice rose but not enough to draw anyone's attention in the noisy bar.

"I know it was hard for you. It was hard for me. And Lizzie. No one should have to go through something like that."

"I just want to know why—why me? Why us? Why our family?"

"Alex. I have asked myself those questions over and over again. You can't get stuck on the why. You'll never be happy with the answers because there aren't any. I tried to work through these questions years ago. You want to hear something ironic?"

"Yes," I answered, gripping my glass and taking another sip.

"After I said you needed therapy, I'm the one who spent hours in sessions. For years after you left. Every Thursday morning at ten. I needed it. Probably still do. I guess I haven't dealt with blaming this on you too." He stopped and took a drink of his beer. "Alex, I'm sorry that this is still tormenting you. I wish I could give you some peace."

I choked out a laugh. "I will never know peace."

From the top of the mountain, where I was still trapped on a rock of agitation, I could see Brett, waving a white flag below. I wanted to climb down to him, take this hike alongside him now. Take a sip from his thermos, his reservoir of water. But I was stranded.

An offered hand, Brett said, "Maybe we could move the furniture around in your hotel room, that seemed to bring you some sort of peace once. Or so you said then. Do you remember all the furniture moving you did right after Claire died?"

"I had to do something to get through those days," I said, picturing myself lugging the sofas and chairs around each room while Brett was at work. He never really spoke of it then, as if he didn't even notice the rooms had changed. "You know, now that I think about it, the hotel room could use a makeover. The bed would be great up against the window and those chairs could face toward the couch by the television to create a great conversation area. That's what I should have done tonight, instead of walking."

"Whatever works," Brett said.

"How about it? You want to come help me with the heavy lifting?"

Brett didn't answer. He filled his mug halfway and drank it in one slow swallow. The basketball game had ended and most everyone had staggered out. I looked around and noticed the servers watching us, waiting for us to leave so they could lock up for the night. "Okay," he said somberly and raised his eyebrows, "I do charge by the minute, though."

He stood up and pushed back his chair, screeching on the floor. I was beginning to feel lightheaded as I didn't drink often. Brett was drunk, which was obvious by the way he held on to me as we made our way to the door, leaning against my shoulder. He smiled and I was reminded of that far-away time when he was a handsome, mysterious stranger sitting in a film class discussing cinematography and symbolism. I remembered how I'd yearned to touch him—no, even just to talk to him with more than a monosyllable and to keep from dripping sweat from my palms.

The rain had picked up and was falling in diagonal torrents, slapping the pavement outside.

"Where's your car?" Brett asked.

"I walked here."

"I can drive."

"No, you can't. You just drank two pitchers in front of me. I don't know how much you had before I came. We can walk. It's not far," I said and spread my arms, like a playful child, and looked straight up into the falling rain. He yanked on my wrist and we ran like children run through the sprinklers on a summer day, bumped into and caught each other, holding on, steadying each other. The world was just Brett, me, and the rain. I didn't notice cars driving by—if there were any—or anything around us. We laughed and ran and jumped through puddles until we reached my hotel room.

Brett followed inside. No words. Our clothes were dripping from the rain. As I shut the door, he pressed me against the wall and kissed me violently, biting my lip, crashing teeth. He could probably taste the metallic flavor of the blood in our kiss, as he slowed, licked the rain from my face and neck. We slid down to the floor.

I ran my hands through his soaked hair and tasted him again, through the rainwater, his familiar taste mixed with beer. He peeled my suctioning top off me and kissed the hollow between my breasts and kissed down to my stomach. I fumbled with the buttons on his shirt, then peeled it off his skin, like the rind off an orange. He laid back and let me kiss his chest. He went still.

I moved up and tried to kiss his mouth again, but he turned away. "I can't do this," he mumbled, grabbed his shirt and stood up and walked into the bathroom, shutting the door. Grappling on the floor for my shirt, I found it in a wet pile and slid it on, cold and dripping. I closed my eyes and rested my head against the wall and waited. Shivering, I wrapped my arms around my torso and held myself.

When Brett opened the bathroom door, he was dressed. I waved from where I sat on the floor. He stood above me and said soberly, "I've got to get home."

"Do you want me to drive you to your car?" I asked.

"I'll walk." He turned to leave.

"Brett, wait." I stood up too, grabbing for his arm. I edged closer to him, but he stood miles away in his resolve. "I just—" then I hesitated, not sure what I should say. I hated to bring up the divorce now, of all times, but it was the only uncut thread we had holding us together. I began again, "Can I see you again? Could we meet for breakfast and I'll sign your papers, and maybe Lizzie—" I gulped, feeling vulnerable.

"Alex. I'm sick already about what I've done," he stepped away, anxious to leave. "I can't think ahead to tomorrow, but don't count on it." I nodded that I understood. He walked out, pulling the door behind him.

I grabbed the knob and followed him outside, the rain dripping down on my face where it mixed into my falling tears. Brett turned back as he walked down the stairs. He didn't wave, just looked and continued on. I whispered, "I'll come back. Just tell me it's what you want." I shook my head with regret for what my life had become and all the steps that had led to my being here as I watched the man I loved walk away, leaving me alone and cold.

Back in the hotel room, I shed my wet clothes, showered, and changed into dry sweats, then slept for several fitful hours. Lizzie came back to me in my dreams, small again, too little to get up onto the swing by herself. I plucked her from the ground and set her on the swing-ride seat, still blue chipping paint. Back at the carnival. The music-box melodies fought harder tonight, shouting out harsh songs, shouting at the spent parents and crying children. The chain I was latching around Lizzie's waist wouldn't budge, the metal clinging together despite the latch. I tucked the chain under her leg and walked back to the periphery to watch. The ride began cranking its circles, Lizzie kicking her legs back and forth, unrhythmically to the discordant beats of songs still fighting it out. She smiled and waved to me on the first slow circle; on the second, she squealed; on the next circle, her smile was gone; the next went faster and her eyes were closed, her hands clutching at the chains on each side and her head leaning still feeling the wind on her face. I lost her again, with the swing spinning at full velocity. As I searched the circling ride— child after child—I saw the back of my golden-haired child as she walked away into the hordes of people, two stick legs walking under striped blue and green dress, her white sandals plodding through grass. Walking away, hand in hand, with a man. I wove through people and children to get to them. But I was invisible. Invisible in my own dream. They were walking together and when I shouted to them, when I stopped before them, they couldn't see me or hear me and I was nothing. I tried to grab for Lizzie's other hand, vacant and dangling, but my invisible hand swept right through hers. Shouting more, and crying for them to see me there, they kept on walking, kept on walking until I was left standing and they disappeared into the forest at the edge of the carnival. The dizzying songs crashing at my ears, laughing at my loneliness.

In the morning, I woke and lay in the bed, replaying the odd ending to my familiar dream. Lizzie was gone, I was gone to her, invisible as I'd been in the dream. I realized with a cold dread that Brett wasn't going to be looking for me today. I'd wait here and sign right on the dotted line just as he wanted me to.

Climbing out of bed, I pulled out a wrinkly pair of jeans I'd already packed away and unrolled a green shirt and put them on. Then I found some hotel stationery from the nightstand and wrote a letter to Lizzie. I'd ask him to give it to her after I signed the papers. I filled three unlined pages with my slanting scribble about how much I had loved her, how I wished I hadn't left, how she had never done anything wrong. I told her I would always love her, whether she wanted me to or not. And if she ever wanted to call me or see me, I would try to do everything I could to make it happen. I realized what I was offering her wasn't much. I didn't know how to offer her anything more. This was all I had. It probably wouldn't matter, but at least she'd know that I loved her. Hopefully she'd believe me.

Folding the letter, I set it on the table near the door and waited. I didn't eat and flipped on the television instead, but the noise just annoyed me, so I turned it off again and paced the room.

It was nearly noon as I sat with my suitcase packed and waiting when the knock came to my door. I hesitated a moment, covered my face with my hands, exhaled, then opened the door. He held the papers by his side and said, "Let's get this over with." His words were hurried, tossed away haphazardly like our marriage was about to be, officially. I held the door open, for him to come in. He walked in and set the pages onto the desk. They were fastened together with a black office clip. I sat down, like a good little girl, without speaking, and pulled a pen from the drawer, took off the lid, fixed it onto the other end of the pen, and looked at the pages.

There was an X next to the blank lines and I dutifully wrote my name by each of them. Alexandria Porter. Alexandria Porter. Alexandria Porter. I didn't read the words. I just signed. I didn't want to see the reasons why we were divorcing. Too many fingers pointing at me. So I glazed over the black print and looked for those blue-inked Xs. After I went through all the pages, he picked them up and went through them. Making sure I'd signed him free. No more complications. Now he was free to marry. He had legally edged me out of his family. But what did it matter—I had edged myself out already. I looked at him, hoping he would understand that my eyes were asking him to take me back. Asking him to love me. But he wouldn't look directly at me.

"Thanks." He turned to leave, and I remained seated at the desk, staring down at the cheap oak-veneer surface. His muted footsteps crossed the carpet. I could have said something, goodbye at least. But there was nothing left we hadn't exhausted. He didn't want me near Lizzie. He didn't want me near him. He still blamed me for Claire's death. What more could we say to each other?

He paused at the door, then I heard the door squeal open and click shut.

When the latch caught, I remembered the letter. I jumped up and grabbed it from the nightstand and darted after him. He was standing outside my door, as still as a statue.

Maybe it hadn't been as easy as he'd led me to believe. Of course he wanted the divorce—how could I hold that against him? Yet, I still felt like he owed me something, like he needed to feel something or care that I was leaving today. It wasn't fair, I knew, but I still felt it. And I felt relieved to find him still standing outside my door.

"Brett, here, this is for Lizzie." I held out the letter and he took it, looked at it and tucked it in among the divorce pages. "If you want to read it, that's fine. But I hope you'll give it to her."

"Alex," he said and locked his eyes onto mine. There was something in them so reminiscent from before, from when we'd fallen in love with each other before life screwed everything up for us. When we still naively thought we could make our world turn just by loving each other.

"I'm sorry, Brett, about this—coming back." I swept my hand toward the hotel door. "I hope I haven't caused you too many problems. And I'm sorry that I walked away." The last part I said carefully, hoping he realized that I meant it.

He didn't speak.

"You know how after a while, it became easier to think about Claire's life, instead of her death? Maybe you can do that with me too? Instead of thinking about how I left, you can remember how great we had it for a while. Before. I know that's how I want to remember it."

His eyes were still deep in mine, like there couldn't possibly be anyone else around or car doors slamming in the parking lot or the barking dogs. Nothing outside the tunnel from his eyes to mine could enter. In my mind, I begged him to kiss me. I wanted him to put me in his arms and hold me and tell me it was okay, that it wasn't—nor had it ever been—my fault that Claire died. If only he could have done that.

Finally, he spoke. "I'm sorry too." And that was it. He didn't say why he was sorry. He didn't touch me. He simply walked around me and stepped down the stairs to his car that was still running and parked along the sidewalk, not even in a parking spot.

I went back into my room, yanked my suitcase from its resting spot, and headed down to the lobby to check out. I returned my plastic card key and signed the receipt from my credit card for the room.

Lobbing my suitcase into the trunk, I decided I needed to stop by the cemetery to say goodbye to Claire one last time. I sat on the wet grass, close to the headstone, and once again smoothed my hand over the rough letters. Fixing my eyes on an old farmhouse several miles off, I stared, unwilling to take in the mountains in the distance and the clouds billowing around them, clinging to them, like a hug.

I drove past Sammy's house on the way out of town. I thought about stopping, knocking at the door, telling her goodbye, but drove past instead. She probably wouldn't be home anyway.

Driving back to Portland through the plump pine trees—which seemed so green and alive compared to the dead, gnarled branches I was used to seeing in Hanover in winter—I knew I'd never drive this stretch again. I felt an aching relief at the thought.

My eyes focused on the dashed line on the road ahead. As I drove, I wondered why Brett had apologized. What was he sorry for? For not wanting me back? For not letting me see Lizzie? Not forgiving me? It didn't matter. I'd never know. I tried to shoo away recurring thoughts of Brett and Lizzie, like bees buzzing around my plate, and felt the sting of my solitary existence.

I had the divorce. Wasn't that why I'd come? When I tried to think about Quentin, it offered no relief. What's worse was that when I tried to think about him, I couldn't get Brett out of my head. And Brett's eyes, the way they penetrated me.

In an attempt to remove Brett from my thoughts, I chose to focus instead on the imminent deadline at work next week, which I knew would keep me up late. After all, I had gotten pretty good at distracting myself from what really mattered.

When I arrived in Portland, I checked in to a room at one of the hotels near the airport, the Ramada, then locked myself inside the room with my research book and laptop and spent the rest of the day working. Like the last time I walked away from this place, I felt comforted at the idea of putting all my energy into something that couldn't love me back, this time it was just another project at work. The last day was filled with writing feeling-less copy, eating a stale room-service Cobb salad, and pulling the blinds at the window. I didn't look outside until a couple hours before my flight the next morning. I called Quentin as I waited for the plane to load and left a message on his answering machine specifying the time my plane was scheduled to land.

Chapter Sixteen

Quentin was pressing numbers into his cell phone as I shuffled down the corridor toward the baggage claim, rolling my suitcase behind. He looked small and inconsequential standing amongst the loud, anxious people yanking bags from the conveyor belt. He seemed oblivious to the chaos around him. People were hugging each other, kissing, smiling so wide that I wanted to rip the smiles from their faces.

Walking toward him, my body stiffened. I resented Quentin for being here now, for being part of the reason I went back. It was because of him that I needed to get the divorce and get my closure. I'd done it for him, for our possible future. I didn't want him to see me, didn't want to explain what had happened in Oregon. I considered hiding, crouching down behind an information booth, or in the bathroom, until he gave up and went away. But sensible Quentin would ask at the information desk before leaving. I could already hear my name booming over the loudspeaker—permeating the airport, invading every nook. As I walked toward him, I tried to disguise my irritation by smiling weakly but not directly at him. "I don't have any bags to pick up," I said, gesturing toward my suitcase as I walked toward the neon-green exit signs. I didn't want to stop, didn't want to have to hug him. I didn't want to explain it now, that I'd morphed into something that wasn't quite the right size to fit back into the place here I'd left.

He walked alongside me and said, "It's good to see you."
"Thanks." I offered no reciprocal endearment.
"Is everything okay?" he asked, falling into my step.

"Yes," I lied, staring ahead. "I've got a lot of work to do this week. We've got a huge deadline and I'm not ready. I might go into the office today."

"I was thinking that we could stop for a bite on our way home. I know this great little Greek restaurant nearby."

"Not today," I said. "I can't waste any time." It came out a little harsher than I expected it to.

"Okay, what's really going on here?"

I shook my head and stopped walking, two steps after he had, and looked back at him squarely in the eyes. "I don't want to talk about what happened. I don't want to think about it. I just want to drown myself in work right now." I looked at him, pleading for him to understand.

His face fell, and he looked toward the door leading out toward the parking garage. "Got it," he said. "I won't bother you with any more questions." People darted past us toward the exit with loaded arms and urgent footsteps.

Regretting the way I'd spoken, I considered trying to apologize, to soften the words, but I couldn't. I didn't have the energy. Not for that. Not for him. I shrugged it off. "Thanks," I said. I continued walking toward the parking garage. When we reached his car, I brushed off his offer to help with my suitcase and stuffed it under my feet.

I fixed my gaze on the brake lights of the cars ahead of us on the road and focused my attention on the music playing on the radio. *Carry on, Wayward Son* by Kansas. Hearing the same line over and over. *There'll be peace when you are done.*

Finally, I looked at Quentin. Now that he was driving and we were moving, I felt more relaxed. "Quentin, I'm sorry about what I said back there. It's just—things didn't go as I'd hoped."

"Andria, if you don't want to talk about it, I understand. But if you do, I might be able to help. Or if you just want me to listen, I can do that too." Quentin irritated me with his constant complacency and understanding and willingness to let me be irrational. I wanted him to throw up his hands and walk away, give up on me. Leave me alone. Stop being so damned nice.

"I'm not sure what I want," I said. I rolled this morsel of truth round and round—like sucking on a piece of hard candy, pulling its flavor, swallowing, feeling it grow smaller and smaller, until it was a tiny sliver that chaffed my tongue. This bitter candy had lasted five years.

"Well, you're home now," he said. "You can get back to your work." I nodded while he drove. Then he continued, "Hero misses you. I stopped by and talked to Debbie. She told me Hero's been begging for attention." I imagined Hero sitting at my window, hour after hour, peering out and watching people pass on the sidewalk and cars driving by below. She'd be watching for me to come home, as she did every day when I returned from work.

When Quentin parked along the street in front of my apartment, I said a quick thanks and rested my hand on the door handle, looking toward the house and up into the third-story window where Hero was waiting. "I just need a little time to get settled back in. Can I call you tomorrow?"

"Sure." He stepped out of the car—probably to open my door—but I swung it open and jumped out, lugging my suitcase behind me. He waved goodbye from halfway around the car and climbed back in. He waited in his car while I trailed my suitcase behind me on the sidewalk until I turned the corner.

I heaved my suitcase up the familiar steps to my apartment and unlocked the door. Hero was at the door. I dropped my bag and fell onto the bed and spent the next ten minutes petting her, scratching behind her ears, under her chin, across her body and ending at the arrow of white at the tip of her tail. Hero curled up in the crook of my arm, slapping my hip with her tail—and we both slept. Through dinnertime and on through the night until the next morning. I was wearing the same clothes I had worn for the past two days. Even though I had showered at the hotel room in Portland, my clothes were dirty and I'd had nothing clean to change into. I stripped the green shirt and jeans off and stepped into the shower.

Hot water drummed on my head and a river ran down my body, the tinny sound of the water hitting the edge of the tub. I closed my eyes and remembered how the rain pummeled Brett and me as we ran through the streets of Red River, thought about the way he'd kissed me that night. He hadn't hidden. I saw him, his emotions raw and lingering at the surface. I shook this memory from my mind and let the water run down and wished it could wash the past week off me. When I stepped dripping into the towel, the memory still loomed, fresh and insidious.

I wouldn't be able to step back into the world I'd created here. It wasn't a movie seat saved for me while I went to get popcorn. Now that I'd gone back there, I wasn't going to find blissful, ignorant happiness with Quentin. Before I left, I thought I had found some meaning, some reason to live beyond working, eating, sleeping, but I'd just latched on to the first possibility of happiness and ran with it. I thought I'd found happiness. I laughed at my foolishness. I'd been a grade-school student ready to marry my first crush. The thought of hearing Quentin's voice on the other end of the telephone—always so cheerful, upbeat, optimistic—repulsed me. I was not going to call him. I could already hear him counting off the ways I could solve my problems. But that wasn't what I wanted. I wanted to wallow in self-pity and rebuild the wall I had mortared around me, the one Quentin had chiseled down, stone by stone. I yearned for its security and isolation. It was my barricade, and I needed it to keep *him* away.

I went into work on Sunday, played catch-up, and turned in the project on Tuesday, working until early morning Monday night.

Avoiding Quentin's phone calls had been easy. I left hurried messages on his voicemail to cancel our walks, which would never resume. My plan was to stay hidden for weeks and then venture out alone again, as I had done before. But Hanover was a small town, and it wouldn't be easy to avoid him forever. Our paths were bound to cross. But for now, I needed time.

Thursday evening, with no pressing work to occupy my mind, I paced my apartment half the night and then sat propped up by my tower window with a book, open and ready, while my eyes focused on the street below. A cluster of clouds hid the moon but not its glow; and the edges were illuminated, scalloped, the way children draw clouds. The clouds carried on their way, leaving the round lonely moon gazing back at me. I broke my stare at the moon and followed two cars pass down on the street below, whooshing as they passed.

That's when I noticed him, the familiar figure of Quentin leaning his back against the lamppost below, his shadow from the lamp light extending deep down the sidewalk to the next house. What was he doing here? I'd called earlier and cancelled. He wasn't looking up into my window, but just waiting, looking out. Maybe he found solace in the moon tonight too.

After five minutes, I slipped on my shoes and coat and headed down the stairs. As I came around the corner, I tried to come up with some playful thing I could say to him. But I had nothing left, definitely nothing as lighthearted as the things that used to spill from my mouth when I was with him. That was one of the reasons I'd craved his presence, he'd pulled something from deep inside me when no one else could and brought to light parts that had been dusty and idle. I'd laughed, had a sense of humor with him. We'd talked about things so intimately, so openly, that I felt I never wanted to stop. And each night had seemed better than the last.

He must have heard my footsteps, for he slowly turned toward me. There was a shadow over his face, so I couldn't see any emotion. He was holding a Styrofoam cup in each hand. He handed me one of the cups and said, "I saw the light of your tower on. After my long swim, I thought I'd swing by and get us each a café mocha. I know it's your favorite." He was speaking so fast he didn't breathe. I could feel his anxiety; maybe he'd already had a cup of coffee or two? I was ashamed, however, knowing that I was responsible for reducing him to the timid little boy standing before me. I wrapped my cold, bare hands around the warm cup and smiled at his Hero and Leander reference.

I brought the cup to my lips, taking a long drink of the warm, sweet coffee. "How long have you been here?"

"Maybe ten minutes." He shrugged and took a sip of his own.

I needed to explain, but I clung to my pretense. "Sorry I've been so busy. We just finished our project." After all, I had really had a deadline. I wasn't lying; it had just been convenient timing.

He looked into my eyes and said, "Andria, you know as well as I do that project isn't the reason for your distance."

Yes, I'm guilty. You got me. The nervous energy I'd felt lifted and left me feeling bold. This was Quentin. The guy who was so easy to talk to, the understanding listener. He would understand. He sure as hell would try if he didn't. He was the reason I'd gotten myself into this trouble. Spilling everything to him. He hadn't asked for my confession; I'd openly offered it to him, an unwanted gift, shoved on him. I admitted humble defeat. "I'm just angry, angry at the world, angry that this is my life. I'm even angry at you," I said and laughed at this irrational truth.

"At me?" he asked patiently. Always patiently. Quentin looked toward the house, and I followed his gaze to where I saw Debbie peering out between the curtains from her lighted front window, reminding me of the first time I'd sat on the front porch with Quentin throwing around fresh fruit prices by the pound.

"Want to walk?" I asked, ready for a truce.

Our steps slow, we sipped our coffee as we walked along Main Street, slower tonight.

Knowing my words were going to come out wrong, I spoke anyway, "I know what I'm feeling isn't fair to you. But if I'd never met you, I wouldn't have opened the dam. I never would have gone to deal with it. It got me absolutely nowhere. In fact, if anything, it put me a step behind. Yes, I have the divorce now. I'm free. But I'm still here alone, and now I have to sort through all these newly awakened feelings. And Lizzie wants nothing to do with me. Nobody does. I'm more alone now than ever."

Quentin didn't speak. He looked straight ahead, then took another sip of his coffee, probably not wanting to speak.

"And there's more," I said, glancing toward him, then down to my feet.

But before I could continue, he cut in, "You're still in love with him." He said it so straight and simply and when I heard him say it, I knew it was true.

From the lamppost's glow in the distance, several snowflakes began to fall in dizzying spirals. I looked into the sky and saw a whole army of snowflakes following behind. He was waiting for my response.

"I didn't know how I was going to feel when I saw him. I don't know what it is I feel even now. But it's so much more complicated than I thought. It doesn't matter though. He doesn't love me."

It was at that moment, when I thought he would see me how I saw myself—as undeniably unloveable—he surprised me. "But I do. And you're not alone. And I'm not going away so stop pushing me. It doesn't matter how much time you need." Maybe he was what I needed after all. Unconditional love, like a parent would give. It seemed so sensible. There was no hurry. And there was no reason to have to make any type of decision tonight. When our walk ended back at my apartment, he drove home and I climbed the stairs and began readying for bed.

In the bathroom, I smoothed a headband into my hair, to keep my bangs from falling into my face and began splashing water onto my face at the sink. After patting it dry with a hand towel, I flicked my head up and caught my reflection in the mirror. I brought my face closer, studying the barely visible scar. Normally, my bangs hid it. I turned my head a bit, to see if from a different angle, and realized for the first time that there was a slight indent where my skin had been pulled back together—just barely there. Flustered, I grabbed my headband and let my bangs flop to their natural position, swept over to the left, completely hiding the scar.

I continued looking into the mirror, much more comfortable now that the scar was hidden, and thought about what Quentin had said. He loved me. We had taken some steps back—I hadn't even touched him tonight. I couldn't. Not yet. It was more like we had returned back to our "friend" status from before. I felt oddly comforted at the amount of room he had given me, I could flail my arms about and turn circles if I needed to. I felt such relief at this thought and even though my lips weren't smiling back from the mirror, my eyes were.

I turned out the light in the bathroom and was padding across the wood floor, when I heard the soft tap of footsteps on the staircase outside my apartment and froze, not wanting the sound of my steps to travel through the door. I checked the clock. It was 10:45. I listened and heard a shuffling outside but no knock. I stared anxiously at the door, waiting for the inevitable knock. No one but Debbie and Quentin knocked on this door, and Debbie would never be up so late. I walked to the door, and the wooden planks creaked beneath my feet, giving me away. When the soft knock finally sounded, I swung the door open and was looking straight into the stormy eyes of Brett.

Silent and unmoving, I stared into his face, wondering if I could possibly be asleep and this a dream. I wouldn't have been as shocked had he been standing here anytime within the last four and a half years, but right now, after last week, why would he be here? "Brett? What are you doing—?"

He didn't speak, just stood there motionless, his eyes wild, troubled, as if he didn't know how he had gotten here. He was wearing a tan sweater with a plaid-shirt collar and tails hanging out of the sweater, but no coat. A single white calla lily hung from his hand. Snowflakes landed on his hair and shoulders. Opening the door wider, I gestured for him to come in. He stood. The cold air and some falling snow made its way inside, and I wrapped my arms around myself. I'd never seen Brett like this and was suddenly frightened. "What happened? Is Lizzie okay?"

His eyes flashed recognition and he shook his head, coming to. "Lizzie? No, she's fine." He stepped into my apartment, and I reached around him, shutting the door.

We both stood near the door for an awkward moment. I wished he'd had a coat because then I could at least ask him if I could take it, lay it on the couch and that would give me something to do with my hands, which were shaking. "Do you want to sit?" I motioned toward my Queen Anne chairs, but he shook his head no.

"I'm not ready," he finally said. And I sighed a bit of relief just hearing words leaving his mouth, although I didn't know what he meant by them.

"It's okay," I said. My words were nothing and meant nothing, just fillers.

"I'm not ready," he started again, "to let you leave again."

"But you said you didn't—" but I didn't finish my sentence. It was strange to see him standing here in my apartment where I'd spent so many years trying to squash thoughts of him and our life together. Every chair or dish or towel here represented my life without Brett Porter. And with him standing among these things, the world seemed wrong. He didn't belong here; he was too much for this little apartment and the many emotions that followed along.

I didn't come nearer to him and he didn't to me. We both stood still, our feet impossibly heavy, molded into the floor.

"We're not over."

"What about Jen?" I asked.

"I never loved her as I loved even the memory of you."

I couldn't respond. I wanted to say, yes, I love you too. I know that now. We can be together again. It can be like before.

But it couldn't. It could never be like before. It could be close. And I could have Lizzie and Brett and be part of my family again, where I'd always be loved and never be sitting on the outside, hiding from the smallest affection. Beads of sweat were forming on my forehead, and I walked to the window and opened it. Snowflakes spiraled down onto the windowsill and melted into little pools.

Walking back, I planted myself closer to him and said, "Brett, are you sure this is what you want? Can you forgive me for leaving? And can you forgive me for Claire?"

Most importantly, could he forgive me for Claire?

He didn't speak, just nodded yes to both, his eyes narrowed in slits.

"Where are you staying?"

"I got a room, the motel across the street."

"Brett," I said, my voice as soft and smooth as I could make it, then I stepped in slow motion toward him and put my hand on his arm. "Go back to your room and sleep tonight. Make sure you're ready to accept me, all of me, and I will come back with you if you are." My hand was still resting on his arm and I couldn't quite pull it off; I didn't want him to leave.

He nodded and turned back toward the door and walked out, leaving my hand swinging down. He turned back and handed me the calla lily with no explanation, then walked outside. I listened as his footsteps slapped against steps, then watched him from the window as he went across the street, a trail of footprints following in the snow, toward the old Motel 7.

I turned back toward my apartment, taking in my home for so long, and realized just how alone I'd been. Going back home to Brett would be so easy. And Lizzie would be mine again.

But Brett. This never was about not loving him. I had still loved him when I left. But even tonight, he didn't seem sure about anything. Would he ever—amidst the worst fights—say that I was responsible for Claire's death? Had he truly absolved me? Would he help me shed that heavy cloak of guilt I wore? I looked at the flower he'd left in my hand, with its curved pointed head and simple elegance. It had been my favorite flower, back in the days when I had one. Before flowers had represented something so dark and black as death, as the death of my daughter and my family. Back when I walked down the aisle of a church in a satin bustled wedding gown, my hair swept up, my smile of optimism about what a marriage meant and how I loved that man who waited with a nervous smile at the other end of the aisle. Back when flowers represented love. I held the satin velvet flower up to my cheek for a moment, then flung it onto the floor.

Here it was—what I'd wanted, but I couldn't do it. I couldn't go back. I collapsed onto the floor and buried my face into shaking hands, pulled my knees up toward my body, like a child willing life away by closing my eyes so tightly. I curled myself into fetal position and wept for my baby girl who died and left me with unanswered hopes and dreams, for my Lizzie who would make me climb a mountain before she'd accept me, for Brett who I loved but the damage done seemed insurmountable, even for Quentin who I knew I would never see again. My time here was unraveling before me. I heard the clock's rhythmic beating, when the sobs hushed, like the ticking of a bomb, just waiting, waiting, waiting for the imminent explosion.

I wouldn't wait any longer. I knew what I had to do, and I would do it fast. Before Brett could find me at this door again. He could knock, but I wouldn't be here. I had to leave tonight with night's shade to conceal me.

I shoved some things into a couple boxes—mainly clothes, my books and photos, but left everything else. I made several trips down to my car, careful to not let the pop of my car door wake anyone or bring Brett to his motel window. I would call Carol from wherever I ended up tomorrow, tell her I had to quit my job. I'd leave my key in my mailbox slot for Debbie to find in the morning.

The thought of leaving Debbie filled me with sadness. The smell of her cheap flowery perfume that I'd breathed through my mouth to avoid in her presence had become a comfort when I thought of it tonight. I'd miss her. That smell always made my eyes water and seemed to travel through my consciousness, and I wiped a stray tear from my cheek.

Hurriedly stuffing Hero into her plastic carrying case, I turned out the lights and stepped down the circular steps, padded with a thin layer of snow, one last time. My feet and body ached. Each step was a little more difficult to take. My guilt weighed me down. Hero meowed to be let out of her plastic jail. Ignoring her pleas, I set her into the passenger seat. The dark clouds were plump with the idea of snow. I looked into the sky before slipping into my car, only the heavy fog hovering, blank without the moon, blank as if the sky had erased the last ten years of my life. This was a good omen for starting a new journey.

I left my key in the mail slot on the front porch. As it clanked against the bottom of the metal container, my hands were empty. It was done. I climbed into my car and settled in, readying for a long drive, while Hero continued meowing her disapproval. I turned up the radio to some fast-beat oldies to fade her out and distract myself.

Chapter Seventeen

So here I was. Running, again. Just heading somewhere—somewhere away.

Leaning into the glove compartment, I pulled out the same bent and curled atlas that had brought me to Hanover. I opened it and pressed it down on top of Hero's carrying case. Keeping my eyes on the road, I lifted my finger to dab at my next blind destination. The atlas coiled shut and fell onto the floor. The road was slick, covered in an icing layer of snow, and the plows hadn't been through yet.

As my car hooked onto the highway, the snow began to fall from the sky, snowflakes rushing past each other in some kind of hurry, white winter falling stars showering the windshield. I watched the snow land, so quiet and peaceful. The snowfall picked up then, obscuring my view until I couldn't drive over 15 miles per hour, and my tires slipping and gripping onto the black asphalt. Red brake lights were ablaze on the one car ahead of me. I stepped on the brakes, and my car swerved to the left.

My heart was beating in my chest, pounding through me, causing my hands to tremble. I yanked the steering wheel to veer away from the stopped car. My car slid over the shoulder into the grassy ditch, where it came to an abrupt stop. My knuckles were white from gripping the steering wheel. I stared at my hands and remembered them in this exact position five years ago—waiting at the intersection to turn left. I turned off the radio and placed my hand back on the wheel, inviting the memory to take me.

Music reeled through my mind and carried me there, that Peter Pan song. We were singing about never growing up. Lizzie pelting out the words. "I won't grow up. I won't grow up." The baby rattle was pinging from where Claire sat shaking it. The light was green, the blinker singing its dull, monotonous tune beneath the singing, and I was waiting to turn. Lizzie's first day of dance lessons. When there was a pause in the traffic, I pressed my foot on the gas pedal. My car lurched into the intersection, but my foot slipped and left us rolling. I gripped the steering wheel. If gripping could have willed us out of the intersection, we would have driven through easily, but it couldn't and didn't. And I saw it—two trucks driving toward us, not slowing, no squealing of breaks. My foot finally found the gas pedal, but it was too late. The car lurched again as the metal crashed against metal.

I cried into my cold hands. That day, the one day that darkened my life forever. At one time, I had wished for these black minutes and had thought that this would make everything right. But what did it matter now? Claire was gone. No memory or blame would bring her back. Lizzie and Brett would never love me, no matter what Brett said. The thought of going back felt like a trap. But here I was, too much a wreck to stay in one place, too emotionally fragmented to live a normal life.

And how many more times would I run? I thought about all the places I could go. How many more cities would follow this one? There's a whole world out there. What exactly was I running from, and what exactly was I looking for? Leaving had secured me from falling back into the life I couldn't live five years ago. But next time, I wouldn't open up as I'd done in Hanover. Not to anyone. It wasn't Quentin who'd forced me to open up. I had done it, willingly and hopefully. I blamed this all on Quentin and Brett and Jen and whoever came along I could point my finger at. But no matter where I hid, I would be found. And the one thing that could keep me down, just like being buried myself—regardless of what I was doing or where I was living—was my guilt.

The guilt would follow wherever I went. I would never be happy because it crouched over me, waiting to pounce. Never leaving. As long as I kept it around, like a blood-sucking parasite feeding off my misery. Telling me that I didn't deserve happiness. Repeating, in the stillest hours of night, that I killed my daughter. That I was responsible for the demise of my family. And I'd chosen to keep the guilt around; I'd let it keep its grasp on me. I chose it as my constant companion, deserting everyone else. Tennessee, New York, Europe, the remotest island, I could not escape the guilt. Like my right arm, it would go where I did.

Several cars had passed since I had slid off the road. When they did, they were cautious and slow and probably only glanced my way for a moment before gripping back onto their own steering wheels, glad they still had control of their car. I looked up through the windshield and watched the snow still falling and hushed, quietly wreaking its havoc.

Minutes later, I saw the twirling blue and red lights reflecting in the snow before I heard the police car come to a stop on the shoulder of the highway. A police officer got out of his car and took long lunging steps down into the wide ditch where my car sat humming.

When he came to the window, he looked in and tapped on the frosted-over window with one knuckle. "Everyone okay in here?" He was wearing a snow-glistened hat and had snowflakes lodged in his handlebar mustache.

I rolled down the window, said yes, and nodded slowly. "My car slid off."

"Yeah, you're not the first car that's slipped on the ice tonight. Are you stuck?"

"I don't know. I haven't tried to get out yet."

"Slip it in drive and see if we can't get you out of this ditch on your own." He moved back several large steps.

At first, my wheels spun, turning in the muddy snow. I tried for a good while, listening to my car's engine whir with effort but going nowhere. I looked over to the police officer, shrugged my shoulders that I didn't know what else to do. He walked back to me, and I rolled the window down again.

"Put the car in neutral, just slide back a bit, then try it again, from a different spot," he said, then backed up again. The car rolled back a foot or two, then I put the car in drive again. After a moment of tires spinning again, they caught on something, a pocket of snow with a little more substance, and my car pulled me up onto the shoulder, heading back from the direction I came. Before getting onto the highway, I waved and said thank you before I pulled onto the highway heading back.

I'd have to take the Hanover exit—the undemanding exit that had lured me to this little town the day I'd arrived—then turn back again. The night ahead would be a challenge. Maybe I shouldn't drive through this storm. Maybe I should head back home and wait until morning or until the storm passes and then head out. Or maybe this was my omen.

My mind detoured to that pivotal moment when I'd driven away from my home in Addison. I'd thought I was freeing myself by leaving my family, getting away from Brett who had blamed me, who I'd blamed for spreading guilt over me and around me, like a scratchy woolen blanket and the rashes it left where my skin was never free to breathe. And it had never been removed, always there, as sure as my grandmother's warm quilt was piled in my back seat now, on top of a box cradling my books.

I felt nauseous with the realization that I didn't go back to Oregon just to sign some divorce papers or to see Lizzie. I went there seeking approval. If Brett forgave me, I could release myself from my guilt and forgive myself. But he didn't. That's why I'd returned here disheveled and tormented, back to a life that I hadn't known was unliveable. And now he said he had forgiven me. But it wasn't *his* forgiveness I needed; it was my own. As I realized this, a heaviness lifted off me, the scratchy woolen blanket removed.

Keeping my eyes glued to the road ahead, I drove. If it weren't for me, Claire would be alive. I'd been driving the car. My foot slipped. One simple slip gutted my life, tore my marriage like a simple rip through a sheet of paper, sent me out lonely and lost—searching, hiding, wrapping myself into a ball and waiting. "Yes, I did it," I said aloud, startling Hero from her sleep. I'd carried this long enough, and I had to free myself. I repeated it over and over and over. "I did it. I did it." I yelled it like a crazy person, with a torrent of tears streaming down my face. I coughed each of the words out, to separate and disintegrate, shattering each particle, falling to the earth, like glass snowflakes, on the road as I passed by. Then they dissolved into nothing.

I pictured in my mind Brett, Lizzie, Claire, and me—a happy family, jetting through the house getting the girls bathed and ready for bed. And us outside raking leaves in the autumn, laughing and running and leaping into a cushy pile of sun-baked leaves. I wept for them and for not having them, for never being able to be the person I was then. I wanted to feel peace with the memories and let myself play them in my head, and rewind them, when I needed to. As I drove through the dark highway of memories I'd abandoned for years, I came upon the exit to Hanover. Perhaps I could live, maybe not the happy fairytale life, but a life in which I wasn't always afraid and from which I didn't have to keep running.

This wasn't over. I'd need to forgive myself, a continual pattern, then release myself, and maybe I could find a place—a place where I could fit and perhaps I could find that with Brett and Lizzie. We could talk about Claire and remember her and compare memories. And we could all cry over her when we missed her, and they would understand me, why I had done what I did. And forgive me. And I would forgive me.

I took the exit back through Hanover and parked my car in front of the old Victorian house I'd called home. I pulled Hero's carrying case from the car, fished my apartment key from the mailbox, crept back up the stairs to my apartment, and freed Hero. As I stepped into the apartment, I saw the abandoned calla lily where I'd left it. Plucking it off the floor by its sturdy round stem, I brought it up to my face and looked it in the eye. Inside its center, the timid yellow spadix was peeking up, shy and waiting to see if I would care for it. I fingered its velvet white flesh, soft as a baby's skin, and decided to take a chance on it. I knew it would die as all flowers do, but I could watch it take its last living breaths beside me, perched on my counter. I finally found the beauty in this heart-shaped flower because it held the hope that I could be loved and love again. I filled a glass pitcher with water and let the flower stand overlooking me as I collapsed onto my bed where I spent the rest of the night, in restless sleep, waiting for a knock on the door.

Acknowledgements

Many people have helped me during the time I spent writing this novel, from my amazing writing group to my wonderful book club friends to family members and neighbors. I appreciate all the support and encouragement you've given me along the way.

But most important is my family. My husband Eric was with me every step of the way—through the ups and the downs, encouraging me and brainstorming with me—to finally seeing this novel materialize. And finally, I give a special thanks to my three darling girls Bianca, Miranda, and Portia who are my world.